# THE
# MUTINY
# BRIDES

THEIR JOURNEY FROM FRANCE TO AMERICA
WAS JUST THE BEGINNING...

## BARBARA
## SONTHEIMER

# Also by Barbara Sontheimer: Victor's Blessing

Victor Gant's life is abundant with blessings. Although his mother was an Osage Indian slave, he is a valuable member of the French community of Ste. Genevieve, Missouri. As the town blacksmith, he makes a proper living for himself. He is further blessed when he marries the only woman that ever caught his eye.

But blessings can be fleeting. When the Civil War erupts, Victor will have to make choices. Torn between doing what's best for his family or following his conscience, between keeping promises or following his heart...to finally bestowing an *agonizing* blessing of his own.

*Victor's Blessing* takes the reader on a journey from the patent offices of Washington, D.C., the battle of Wilderness and finally to the infamous Andersonville prison, where in order for Victor to keep one promise, another must be broken.

*For Aubree, who suggested a trip to Biloxi...*

# *Introduction*

In January of 1719, *La Mutine* left France with ninety-six women on board. They came against their will and were shackled together in the ship's hold. By the time, the ten-week voyage was over, nearly half the women had died. The survivors were then dropped on what was then called *Ilé de Massacre*, today's Dauphin Island, off the coast of Louisiana. Unlike the women who came on the Mayflower, the stories of the women of *La Mutine* have been forgotten for over three hundred years.

Despite insurmountable odds, these women not only survived but *flourished* in the new world, becoming the founding mothers of French society in Louisiana, establishing large families, amassing fortunes, and shaping the distinctive *La Nouvélle Orleans* culture we know today.

Although Héléne, Suzanne, Maélle, and Josianne are products of my imagination, the hardships these women endured are well documented.

Here is the story of four women, who, unjustly

banished from France, left their unique mark on American history.

# One

∽

December 12, 1719,
Le Havre dock, France

The mule-drawn cart stopped with a sudden lurch, forcefully pitching Hélène Francois to the opposite side. She landed in a heap against the rough slats of the cart and felt a splinter stab into her cheek. It was bad enough having a saucer-sized port wine birthmark on her right cheek, but now it had a long splinter embedded in it. Her cheek stung, and reaching up to touch it, saw blood on her fingertips. She struggled to her feet amidst the squawking and complaints of the other women.

There were eighteen women in the cart, chained together at the waist in groups of three. This was the first of several carts full of women whom France had decided were "undesirable" and rounded up indiscriminately from the streets. They were guilty of the gravest sin in Paris in 1719: being *poor*. Charges were often fictional,

1

and paid "witnesses" showed up at hurried, mock trials where defendants were unceremoniously imprisoned at *La Salpêtrìere*, which was originally designed as a convent/hospital, but was used mostly as a prison.

A woman could be sent there for any number of reasons, most of which were fabricated by the corrupt police of Louis XIV's France. Even though Louis XIV died in 1715, the mess in which he left his country continued to worsen. The regent *Philippe d'Orleans* continued the practice of transporting the 'undesirables' of Paris to the colony of *Louisiane*.

Louis XIV's Paris was on the verge of financial collapse. There was a myriad of reasons for Paris' failures', only one of which was the wars the country participated in. And the unfortunate result of all wars, is cost, which was unfortunately paid for by the poor of Paris. As a result, Hélène and hundreds of other women were unjustly imprisoned at *La Salpêtrìere*.

"You're bleeding, Hélène," Maélle said, resisting the urge to touch her friend's cheek, wincing at the nasty two-inch splinter embedded in the skin. She wanted to squeeze the flesh, force the foreign object out, but knew how self-conscious Héléne was about the birthmark, and resisted the desire.

"Your face!" Suzanne, one of the girls in the cart, cried.

"It's nothing," Hélène said, wiping her face with the back of her hand, feeling the wound pulse with each beat of her heart.

The spring of that year in Paris had been totally dry, and by summer, Parisians were complaining about the heat. The farmers' crops were decimated, there was no fodder for animals, wells were dry, and the river was polluted. These dire circumstances also brought with them smallpox, dysentery, and other diseases referred to as 'fevers.' The summer at *La Salpetriere* had made the normally squalid conditions of the prison even *worse*.

But it was winter now and made the fetid conditions of the prison, the biting cold and hunger unbearable. As Héléne watched the gloomy countryside roll by, she wondered how things could get any worse.

"Is that our boat?" Suzanne asked and instinctively clung to Maélle's hand.

It was a frigate, and since none of them had ever seen a sea-faring vessel, it looked large and other-worldly to them. But what none of them knew was that it was too small for such a treacherous crossing. The average size vessel for such a journey was 350 tons, and *La Mutine* was a mere 180 tons: minute by compari-son. In addition, it had been hastily built, and even its captain worried it was not worthy of such an arduous trip.

Usually, a ship being sent on such a voyage was outfitted with a new "lining" to make it not only water-proof but also stabilize it, thus reducing the pitching of the ocean, especially in storms. *La Mutine,* moored at the shore at the port of *Le Havre,* had been built in 1704. But it was a hastily retro-fitted *negriere* ship and had an ominous reputation. When *La Mutine* left an island on the Gambia River in Africa in 1704, the captain at the time picked up 196 slaves. Within two days of the voyage, the first death was reported. The following day, three more deaths. In eight weeks, forty-six of the enslaved Africans aboard had perished.

If the ship being too small for such a crossing, not well-built, with a reputation, was *not* ominous enough, it was also insufficiently stocked with provisions for the voyage.

"I have no idea," Maélle said, looking up, feeling the thin soup she had eaten being chased around by hunger. "I have never seen the sea or *any* ships before." But trying to dispel the gloom in the air, touched Suzanne's cap. Marveling that Suzanne managed to stuff her glorious golden mane into the cap.

"What color dress do you want me to make you in Louisiana, eh?" Maélle had managed to smuggle out her needles and small scissors without *Madame* Pacletain's knowledge and wanted to take Suzanne's mind off the fear that was engulfing them all. "Something blue to match those eyes?" Maélle gently touched the perfect face.

It had been a horrible three years at *La Salpêtrière* for Maélle, and yet poor Suzanne had been there her entire life. Maélle calmed her breathing, knowing it was absurd to talk of frivolous things but afraid to think of what might become of them.

The thirty-foot walls of *La Salpêtrière* were old, and notoriously damp. The few times Maélle had ever been able to wash a garment, it had taken three days for it to dry. Each five by four foot cell housed five occupants, so small they had to take turns sleeping.

There was one window near the ceiling, and Maélle remembered when Suzanne had first become one of her cellmates and how she had whispered to Suzanne one morning to look up at the clouds and describe them to her.

"A *dress*, Maélle?" Suzanne cried, her sapphire eyes brimming with tears. "How can you think of something so silly right now?" She wiped fat tears from her cheeks. She was thirteen, and it broke what was left of Maélle's heart to see Suzanne in such a state.

"Which boat are we getting on?" Josianne, another of the women from the cart, asked. The pupils in her hazel eyes dilated. "I've never been outside of Paris." She turned frightened eyes to Maélle and clasped her hands. "I've never been on a boat." Josianne's nails were somehow still rounded and pretty, although there were lines of dirt underneath them.

"Neither have I," admitted Maélle.

The harbor was frantic, with men calling to one another and loading and unloading ships. But instead of watching them, the women who had been inside the stifling walls of *La Salpêtrière* for years were mesmerized by the birds. None of them had ever seen seagulls that dominated the sky above the ship. The ship would be their home as they made the journey across the Atlantic Ocean to a territory that was being hailed as the land of "opportunity and abundance." Hélène laughed when she heard this, saying, "If this land is so rich and ripe for the taking, do you honestly think they would be sending the likes of *us* there?"

"What a curious bird," Suzanne whispered, watching a pelican land on a post, folding its enormous wings next to its body. She glanced at the water resting calmly at the shore and wondered why it did not look foamy at the shore like she had heard in a song about the sea. But it was the mouth of the Seine she was looking at, and the beginning of the English Channel. Although she had been taught to sew, knit, and embroider at the hospital, geography, as well as other studies, had been neglected. But in truth, Suzanne had been one of the lucky ones at *La Salpêtrière,* because she had been taught to read.

"Come on, get out," one of the guards barked as he dropped the cart's gate with a thud. "Eighteen days of the likes of all of you is long enough."

"You were paid to feed and transport us," Héléne argued. She had seen the money he was given for their upkeep and knew he had pocketed most of it instead of feeding them.

"Shut up! You're nothing but whores, and besides, I need to make a little more along the way since transporting you pays less than when I move the *galeriens.* You all are just *bons por el iles.*"

It was a term Héléne, and all the women took exception to, because they were labeled as despicable women 'fit only for the islands.'

It was difficult to get out of the cart chained together as they were by the waist. When Maélle stepped down it pulled Suzanne down on her hands and knees. Enraging the guard because when one stumbled, they all stumbled, like a set of broken dominoes.

"Get up!" The guard hissed, jerking Suzanne up by her neck.

"Don't touch her!" Hélène yelled, but the guard's jerk on the chain sent Hélène tumbling out of the cart, bringing Suzanne and Louise to both land painfully on her.

"Shut up and get out *pour l'amour de Dieu*!" He was tired of these women, tired of their whimpering and crying. He realized they were even thinner than when he had picked them up and wanted to be rid of them before one of them died on his watch. It would mean additional paperwork and less money.

Hélène got up, glaring at the guard. In her twenty-seven years, she had never met a man she did *not* despise, from her brothers who had cared nothing for her to her father who hit her, to the man who had raped her in the alley. Men were hideous and horrible. All of them.

Struggling to stand up, Louise looked at the huge cathedral in front of her. Tears blurred her vision, and being a Catholic, instinctively she made the sign of the cross.

The smooth brown stones that made up the walls fit snugly together, and above that was a black tiled roof with arched windows under it. Louise was from *Auvergne* and spoke a rural dialect that was not well understood by the other women. It was a lonely, horrible existence, and she wondered sometimes in the months she had been imprisoned at *La Salpêtrière* why she had yet to run out of tears.

The heavy chains rattled as they walked. Maélle was in the middle, Suzanne ahead and Louise behind. Maélle could hear Louise sniffing back her tears and reached a hand behind her to comfort her. She smiled when she felt Louise's small hand grip hers.

Maélle still wondered how she had ended up where

she was now, and to this day, had trouble understanding how it all happened. She had always wanted to make pretty things, and only three years ago she had been apprenticed to a well-known seamstress, *Madame* Oudart. The shop was in the fashionable district of *Saint-Germain-des-pres.* Overnight, the once respectable area became a target for random gangs that came barreling into the shops and looting. She had no idea the man responsible for the chaos Paris was experiencing was the Scottish financier, John Law. It was this turmoil and financial ruin that prompted her father and brothers to send her to *La Salpêtrière.*

Standing in line to board, Maélle looked up again at the huge frigate. It had enormous sails and a center mast that jutted up so high into the sky that she feared it was too flimsy to support the weight. It was crammed with barrels, crates, casks, and more rope than she had ever seen.

*La Mutine* had a raised second deck with small windows and another raised deck on the opposite end. She could see a tall, uniformed man standing with his hands pressed against his back. Realizing he was the captain, she swallowed hard, hoping he was a good man since he would be in charge.

# Two

Freezing, Hélène woke up with a sharp pain. Her teeth were chattering so violently that she bit her lip hard enough to draw blood. Swallowing the bitter, metallic taste, she blinked awake in the murky darkness. She could feel the endless rolling of the ship and tried to quell the grumbling of her empty stomach. Hunger had been a part of life at *La Salpêtrière,* but the intense hunger she was experiencing on the ship was new even to her.

She had never before been so hungry that she was nauseated, and her body rejected even sips of water she took, trying to settle it. The only remotely good thing was that since she had eaten so little, she'd not been as susceptible to the dry heaves that plagued little Manon, one of the younger girls who had also come from *La Salpêtrìere.*

They had been at sea for two weeks and so far, the

biting cold of the January winds and the endless listing of the ship made most of the women green with seasickness. At first they had been ashamed to vomit and tried to clean it up by pushing the wet straw that covered the floor to the corners. But so many of them had been sick so often, no one bothered to do anything about it anymore.

Looking up at the dark ceiling, Hélène rolled over to her side. The vomited-upon straw was clumped together and damp beneath her. She ignored the smell and tried desperately to go back to sleep. Sleep was the only reprieve from the nightmare they were experiencing.

There were ninety-six women down in the stinking bowels of the ship. When they had first been chained together upon leaving the hospital, Hélène thought it was to prevent them from escaping. Never in her wildest nightmares had she thought they would be chained together for the entire voyage. The heavy weight around her waist wore a hole through her dress, and the metal now rubbed her skin. Reaching down, she felt a bumpy scab where the chain rubbed her hip raw. She also felt the sharp outline of her hip bone protruding from her skin.

Sitting up in the darkness, Héléne waited for her eyes to focus and felt the familiar scurrying of lice underneath her cap. Tugging it off, she shook her hair, trying to rid herself of the pestilence. Her long brown hair straggled down to her waist, and she fingered it quietly in the darkness. Because of the birthmark, she had never been vain but had at least been fond of her hair-the hair that she now found in clumps on the matted straw where they all slept on the floor.

The ship creaked loudly, and she looked up again at the rough ceiling. Down below where the women were kept, there were no candles, no fresh air, no windows. She looked forward to daytime when the crew was awake, and she could watch the silt drift through the boards above them from their footsteps. She looked forward to the banter of the crew. It was at least some distraction from the never-ending listing of the ship, the hunger, and the boredom.

"Why are you awake?" It was Maélle, sitting up in the darkness as well.

The splinter that had lodged into Hélène's cheek was infected, and it painfully pulsed with each beat of her heart, but she did not want to distress her friend. "I am listening to the ship," Hélène lied, "and I felt lice in my hair."

"We've got fleas too. We are animals for sure now." Maélle's legs were covered with flea bites. "How long have we been on the ship?"

"Fourteen days. We are almost halfway."

Maélle knew what her friend was trying to do. Although she appreciated the optimism, it did little to raise her spirits. "Four more weeks of this endless, dark penance."

"Penance?" Hélène questioned, "I don't think God has anything to do with this. But it will be a new world. We will make it through."

"I am sure that it was what Marie Terese thought as well." Maélle shuddered, remembering the small woman who had died two days ago. The Midshipman was surly as he unchained the poor creature, then carried her dead body up the stairs. But what surprised Maélle was the shock on the man's face. The smell of the unwashed women existing in squalor below his feet, and the piss bucket, made him throw his hand over his nose, and as he walked through the seasick vomit all over the floor. The dampness made the flea-infested straw stick to his boots. "At least she is at peace," Maélle added.

Hélène shuddered in the darkness. Although she had not heard Marie Terese's body, which had been strapped onto a board and weighted down with stones, hit the water, it was still a horror in her mind's eye.

The ache in Hélène's cheek returned. She moved her tongue inside her cheek and felt a stab of pain. It was hard to have such a birthmark, and now it would be even more unsightly with a scar.

"Remember what *La Salpêtrìere* was like? We had no future at the prison. None. At least now we can start a new life away from France. Away from the ridiculous nobles and kings who make rules, they themselves do *not* have to follow. How I hated waking at 5 A.M. for prayers, then the ridiculous mass at 6:00. Then for the rest of the day, there was work, until prayers again," Héléne scoffed. She fervently hated *Madame Pacletain*, the woman who had been their warden at *La Salpêtrìere*, a woman who had ruled for five decades over inmates who had no recourse.

"It's odd, isn't it? They tried to force us to love God, but by making us pray so much, that I came to *resent* him, then I felt guilty for that," Maélle said.

"How could we *not* grow to resent God when *Madame Pacletain* was so *evil!* All that sewing and lace making you did at *La Salpêtrière*, and she took it and sold it for herself after saying she would share it with you."

Maélle knew Héléne was rumored to be involved in some sort of insurrection at *La Salpêtrière*. And *Madame Pacletain's* taking the lace that had painstakingly taken Maélle *months* to make had been the last straw. *Madame Pacletain* was in the habit of referring to it as a "revolt" where four hideous "creatures" had risen up and slashed guards with makeshift knives. *Madame* Pacletain would rigorously repeat the tale that the women involved had been screaming blasphemies against the Lord that would make any God-fearing person quake. Maélle remembered the night. It had been a minor infraction quickly squelched when armed soldiers arrived; it was nothing at all like the warden reported. And the same warden used the so-called uprising to add more names to her list of those who were bound for the islands. Maélle never knew how deep Héléne's involvement went, but in truth, did not want to know.

"I know, but she cannot hurt us now." Maélle's stomach rumbled. The rations they had been fed at the hospital were just enough for them to slowly starve: a bit of bread, a soup so thin it was almost clear, and a few sips of wine. Maélle, who had always had a husky build, found she had to keep moving the button on her skirt as her weight quickly dropped.

"But I hate that she labeled us as prostitutes, thieves, and beggars; what if no one respectable will marry us?" Maélle countered.

Héléne snorted, "what makes you think there is anyone respectable in *La Louisiane* or the Islands or

Mississippi or whatever *else* they choose to call it? Besides, with the records our lovely Captain de Martonne is keeping, no one will *really* know who we are. And although no one may believe us, we were *not* prostitutes. You were a dressmaker on the left bank of Paris. You can make pretty things. You will be able to make a good living without a man."

Maélle nodded, knowing it always angered Hélène when any of them mentioned finding husbands. It was as if she saw it as a weakness. It was not that Maélle only wanted a man to take care of her; she was proud of her responsibilities at the shop. Over time, *Madame Oudart* came to trust Maélle with important clients and routinely complimented her on her work. Regardless, when she thought about her future, she imagined a husband, a son, and, if she was lucky, a daughter.

"I do like to make pretty things. I made a dress once out of pale blue silk. I did eight seams on the waist. It was fragile material, and it was hard to keep it from fraying, but I did it. And it fit the girl perfectly." Maélle laid back down in the straw, gazing up at the boards above her. "Then she came back a month later furious because one of the seams burst, saying the workmanship was shoddy. *Madame Oudart* told her there was nothing wrong with the work and refused to refund her. After I repaired the seam, *Madam Oudart* told the girl if she stopped gorging herself at the *boulangeries,* all would be fine."

Hélène laughed, "Can you imagine having enough pastries to pop the seams in your clothes?"

"No, never."

"You will be the most sought-after seamstress in the town," Héléne said proudly.

"And you will work too."

"I will never go back to being a laundress," Hélène said, remembering how poorly she had been treated, how she had been accused, tried, imprisoned, and now banished. "And the clothes they said I stole belonged to a soldier who left the key for me to get the wash. They never even *looked* at the clothes to see they were still filthy and stiff with dirt. I merely picked them up to wash and return. And why would I steal a *man's* set of clothes? I never stole anything. Never." She glanced down in the darkness at her rough hands.

Laundering was not only low paying; it was the most menial of work. If that was not bad enough, it had permanently damaged Héléne's hands. Plunging them repeatedly into hot water aggravated the nerves, but the winter was no better when she had to break the layer of ice in the wash buckets with her hands. There was also the harsh lye soap, the constant scraping of her knuckles on the washboard, the borax that dried her hands, the indigo that left them stained blue, and the strength it took to wring out the clothes. After ten years of being a laundress, her hands began to tingle at night. In the beginning, she could alleviate the pain by rubbing her aching hands, but as time wore on, they would wake her up with their throbbing. The remnants of the damage were still there because whenever it was damp or cold, her hands would ache, and sometimes, she had trouble forming a fist.

"It's no different for Josianne because she is pretty.

When a pretty girl works at the home of the rich, if the master of the house is not after her, his sons are," Maélle said. "Or the wife accuses the girl of putting a 'hex' on her husband."

"And Josianne's story doesn't make sense either. If I stole from the people that I washed for, they would fire me and call the police. It is the same for Josianne. And besides, what in the world would she want with a wrinkly old man? And what chance would a poor girl have of the master of the house divorcing his wife to marry a tart? Why would a girl like Josianne take the *chance* of getting pregnant and fired? In addition to that, who wants to bring another mouth into the world to feed when a girl can barely feed herself?"

"Men are conceited, aren't they, thinking we would risk our livelihoods for a roll on the floor?" Maélle said.

They heard phlegm-filled coughing and realized it was Louise.

"Poor little girl, she's sick again," Hélène said, shaking her head. "And she doesn't understand us when we speak to her. I cannot imagine how alone she feels being from *Auvergne*."

"Hunger, cold, sickness, no place to wash, no room to sleep, lack of sunlight, it will be a *miracle* if any of us survive," Maélle said, then placed a hand over her eyes to hide her emotions.

"You will survive if you want to survive," Hélène answered quietly. "France was not good to me." She glanced at the other haggard women sleeping on the flea-infested straw. "It was not good to any of us. Wherever we are going, we are no one and *anyone* we want to be. I for one, will never again step foot in France. There is only bitterness in my memories. But across the ocean, we have a chance."

"But a chance for what, I wonder?" Maélle whispered.

Suzanne awoke a few days later and realized, to her horror, that Catherine had died during the night, and she was chained to a corpse. Frantically, Suzanne tried to stand up and was hysterical when she could not. The weight of Catherine's body was too heavy, and Suzanne had fallen on top of the corpse, sobbing.

By the time the Lieutenant unchained the body, Suzanne was pale and silent. Even from below the deck, the women could hear the crew scurrying to get rid of the body.

"I wonder how long it will take her to sink?" Hélène asked, relieved the captain would not allow them on deck when the body was disposed of. No one answered, all of them too cold and sad to ponder. "So far, twenty-two women have died. Only seventy-six of us remain."

"Makes you wonder who will be next," Josianne said, wondering if she could do anything to better their situation, knowing that if she did not, more of her friends would die.

# Three

C aptain Philipe de Martonne was annoyed he was tasked with bringing these women to the colony in the dead of winter on a retro-fitted slave ship. He worried they would not make the voyage. As it was, because of bad weather, he feared it would take ten weeks to get there when it should only be eight. But that was not all that was on his mind. Although it was an emotion he was not in the habit of dealing with, the reports from his third lieutenant about the fetid, putrid conditions the women were living in plagued him. It was the pinched, white look on the third lieutenant's face that finally changed the captain's mind.

"Captain, they are starving down there. And I fear they will be covered with lice and fleas by the time we dock. And the *smell*, sir. The piss buckets are overflow-ing." The smell was enough to make him gag when he checked in on the women. He was only seventeen and couldn't help but pity the poor females held at the bottom of the damp ship for days. He wondered how his own sister Gabrielle would survive there. "And they are getting sick, sir, and some of them are too weak to sit up. And there is nary a blanket for any of them, and they are freezing." He wanted to add 'right below our feet' but dared not.

Captain de Martonne stood up straighter, pressing his arms behind his back. He was over six feet tall, well built with a ruddy complexion. A fact that annoyed him ever since his mother had referred to his complexion as perpetually 'blushing.'

Although a good-looking man, his face was weather-beaten, having lived most of his life on the sea. His eyes were a bright blue, which seemed to mirror the sea's changing colors. His hair was startlingly black and pulled back tightly behind his head in a tail. He had gotten a captain's commission by following orders and delivering what was expected of him, and he was not about to jeopardize his career for a cargo in which he had little interest.

"I appreciate your...humanity, but the simple fact is, Lieutenant, that the West Indies company outfitted us with two hundred quarts of flour, which is not even enough for the crew of fifty on board. There were no provisions made in either food or blankets for these women." Turning, he stared at the young man, which caused the Lieutenant to shift nervously from foot to foot. "I cannot turn two hundred quarts of flour into four hundred, and I cannot endanger the lives of my crew." To compound matters, his cook had told him that the flour the West Indies company sent was the cheapest, coarsest flour. Flour not only tended to spoil during the voyage but exacerbated dysentery and other bowel complaints.

In fact, everything about dealing with the West Indies company angered Captain de Martonne. He knew enough about John Law's financial *malignancies* to wish he had never gotten mixed up with him. The West Indies company and the Paris supply chain were corrupt, and greed was rampant. After all, they would send a poorly retro-fitted vessel out into the Atlantic Ocean in the winter, stocked with not only inadequate supplies but *substandard* ones at that, and expect him to deliver the cargo and all souls on board intact.

The Lieutenant nodded and, looking down, noted the saltwater stains on his own boots, which mirrored those on the captain's.

Captain de Martonne sighed silently; a new flush of pink colored his cheeks. His life was commanding a vessel, harnessing the power of the wind, trying to make time when the petulant Atlantic tried to have her way with him. He did not doubt that after he filed his report, *La Mutine* would be removed from service, and he hoped his beloved France would come to her senses and realize that John Law's dreams and visions for a "new France" were, in fact, a nightmare.

"Once a day, bring them up in groups on the deck. Let them stand, empty the buckets." He knew he could not spare to feed them more, but if he could stave off the bloody flux and plague of the seas with the bleeding gums, he would do that. However unscientific it may be, he had been at sea long enough to realize there was some healing power simply in the fresh air and the sun. "How many are chained together?"

"Three to a lot."

"Have the carpenter separate them."

The Lieutenant embarrassedly felt tears clouding his vision; he both sniffed and looked up to prevent them from building. "Thank you, Captain."

# Four

The carpenter on the ship, Henri Genest, was given the unwanted job of modifying the women's chains. He resented that because he had a set of sharp tools, he had been recruited.

He had to duck when he stepped off the last step and realized he could barely stand at the bottom of the hold. It took his eyes a few seconds to adjust to the dimness. Although he could smell them, he was not exactly sure where they were.

"I am here on Captain de Martonne's orders to separate you."

The women glanced around happily. It was hideous to live, sleep, use the piss bucket while chained to another human. It was worse than being at *La Salpêtrière*, Hélène thought.

Henri heard murmurs of excitement and despite the haggard, bedraggled state and smell of the women, eventually he could see the smiles, the light in their eyes and it made him proud to be giving them this gift.

"Can you not take the chains off altogether?" Hélène asked, her voice rising above the happy murmurs. "Where would we go, *monsieur*, jump overboard to drown? It makes no sense to keep the chains."

Henri looked at her. She was thin, and her face was long and gaunt. A nasty, puffed-up wound on her ghastly birthmark was oozing pus.

"I am following orders." Ignoring Hélène, he got out his tools. He saw a little blonde, and when she smiled at him, he could not help but smile back.

"But this is *insane*! Can you not take the chains off altogether?" Hélène's voice cracked with anger. "How can we sleep for weeks, chained to someone else with no room to turn over. We are sharing the fleas and lice. Why, we must *drag* someone with us over to use the slop bucket, and sometimes it splashes up on them." Hélène's dark eyes bored a hole in him.

Henri sighed quietly, not wanting to argue with this haggard woman.

"*Mademoiselle*, I am a carpenter sent by France. I have no authority here." With a brute strength that surprised all of them, he smashed the chains with a mallet and chisel, sending orange sparks flying.

He worked for over an hour, separating them. The sparks entertained the girls, and they talked and whispered amongst themselves. It was the happiest they had been since the old cart had rolled up and loaded them onto the ship. And although it was a more manageable situation, it was still not the freedom the crew above them enjoyed and the injustice continued to annoy Hélène.

"Thank you," Maélle said as he worked separating her from Hélène. She glanced up, watching him as he bent over his work. It was not an easy task down in the bowels of the ship. Not only was it dim, but it took strength to separate the links.

"Is your tool getting dull?" She realized it was becoming harder for him to separate the last of them.

He had not looked up much when the other women talked to him, but he did now. "Yes, the chisel is quite dull. I should have brought the stone with me." He grinned, touched that she had noticed.

He had a slight frame and, because of that, did not look like a man who worked with his hands. He had light brown hair and eyes and an unkempt beard. It was a shame, she thought, that he had covered his face with straggly hair. She would have liked to see more of it.

"What did you do in Paris?"

Maélle had to clear her throat, happy he chose to speak with her. "I was a dressmaker, a seamstress. I hope to be one again in the colony." Nervous perspiration started under her arms. In truth, none of the women knew where they were headed. The words' Mississippi, New France, *Louisiane'* meant nothing to them. Was it a new continent, a river, or an island? Maélle was too ashamed to ask.

"That's a noble pursuit." He stopped then, resting his tired arms against his knees. "I appreciate anyone who can create with their hands. What is your name?" She had a pleasant face, and he was drawn to her.

"Maélle."

"That's a pretty name. I am Henri Genest."

Hers was a terribly common name, and she knew he was just being kind.

"I hope to see you in the territory." He met her eyes. Her eyes were warm and reminded him of oak leaves in the fall.

"Could you get us cloth?" Hélène interrupted, her bony fingers digging into his arm. He turned to her and couldn't help but wonder if he had ever seen a woman as unattractive.

"I don't deal with cloth," he murmured, "The sailmaker and boatswain's mates have access to that. And all the supplies are under lock and key, as I keep my tools."

He noticed the pretty blonde's eyes start to tear. Looking at all of them he asked, "What do you need cloth for?"

"We have no way to wash, no way to—" Hélène paused, wondering how much more demeaning her life could become. "We have nothing to...soak up our monthly."

Embarrassed as well as repulsed, he felt a wave of pity. "Can't you use your underskirt or shift?"

Hélène's rage was barely under control. "We have no cloth, we *have* no underskirts, we have already used *every* shift. "She wrenched his hand and placed it against her bony chest. He felt her pronounced collarbone where her shift should have been. "There is nothing else for us to use except the clothes we have on." She grabbed a filthy piece of tattered shift that was stiff with dried blood, pushing the soiled garment into his hands. "We cannot use it because it won't absorb anymore."

He was unnerved by the glisten in her black eyes and

wondered if she had ever been accused of sorcery. As soon as he was able, he withdrew his hand from her chest, proud that he managed not to shudder. Turning he motioned for the next group of women to come forward.

"Who is the sailmaker?" Josianne asked, smiling prettily.

Despite being fed a near-starvation diet, this one with hazel eyes still managed to have a fullness to her breasts. Her complexion was like ivory, and it was an alluring contrast to the mahogany color of her long hair.

"It will do you no good. It's all under lock and key by the bosun."

Hélène watched in awe the way Josianne pouted, annoyed Josianne was using womanly wiles to get cloth. Hélène thought it was beneath her to stoop to such measures. But at the same time, Hélène had never been able to use womanly wiles, and her "force" had not worked.

"Then who is the bosun?" Josianne asked, tilting her head slightly.

Hélène looked from one to the other, amazed that starving and stinking in the bowels of the ship, the ridiculous game between the sexes could still ensue.

"If you could point him out to me, perhaps I could talk to him?" Josianne smiled.

As Henri gazed at her, she was suddenly not in the filthy bowels of a ship, dressed in rags, brushing away the hopping fleas.

"I will try," Henri answered at last.

"You are wonderful, *monsieur*," Suzanne said with a

smile when he removed her chains. Her face was heart-shaped, her eyes were large, and she was on the brink of womanhood.

"What is your name, little one?"

The shy blush across her cheeks made a part of his anatomy react.

"Suzanne."

"Suzanne, what?"

"Just Suzanne. I was left on the doorstep of *La Maison de St. Louis* as an infant. I didn't know my parents, and I have always been Suzanne."

"How old are you?"

"Thirteen, but nearly fourteen."

Realizing she was way too young, he moved on.

# Five

As Maélle and Hélène made their way up the wooden steps to the deck of the ship to empty the buckets, they felt a gust of fresh cold wind so violent it stole their breath away. They struggled with the heavy bucket but managed to balance it over the rail and empty it overboard. The days of confined quarters and inactivity made their leg muscles atrophy, and at first, they were unable to support their own weight.

Enthralled, Hélène looked down at the waves heaving and hurling in the ocean. As far as she could see in any direction, there was nothing but water. And the sunlight was so bright on the ocean rolling with whitecaps, she had to shield her eyes. Despite the chill in the air, she enjoyed watching the wind hit the tops of the waves and welcomed the fine mist of spray against her face.

Hélène glanced down at the sea three stories below her, marveling at the way the water could look sapphire, gray, green, and even black. She watched the different colors swirling around, contrasting with the white sea foam that moved constantly against the boat.

The sea was always changing. It could be monotonous and boring one day, to spontaneous and lively, the next.

She saw a flash and motioned to Maélle, "Look!"

Small dark shapes appeared out of the water, arcing out of the depths, then disappearing back into the sea, only to repeat their antics.

"I-I think they are fish!" Hélène exclaimed. Delighted, the two of them laughed at the spectacle.

The flying fish, black against the sea chased the boat as they moved along. The fish were deceptively fast, and if they had not seen them with their own eyes, never would have believed they existed.

The crew members watched, transfixed, as the last of the women made it above the ship. They were a haggard lot, but they were still *women*, and it was a treat to see them smiling and to hear their chatter. Some of the men planned to stay in the colony and make new lives for themselves. All of them needed wives.

The air was cold, and watching the women from the other side of the ship, the captain, who was shivering inside his own wool coat, realized the women had to be freezing, insufficiently clad as they were. The fabric on their bodices was so thin he could clearly make out their forms.

He sighed.

It weighed on his conscience that these poor women were not only cold above deck but underneath the ship as well. He sighed quietly with his hands folded behind his back. Providing the women with decent clothing and blankets for the voyage was just another *detail neglige* by the West Indies Company.

He watched as the last of the women came up top to empty the buckets. Even as far away as he was, he could not help but notice one of them. He watched her hair slip from its knot underneath her cap and swirl wildly down her shoulders. It was lustrous brown hair, touched by red. Even filthy and attired in rags, there was a regal air about her. Her shoulders were back, and her head was lifted as if there was no shame in dumping a bucket stinking of waste over the side, and he admired her poise. She reminded him of a countess he knew in Paris once, a woman who had haunted his dreams for years.

Josianne stared at the sea for a few moments, then turned and met the captain's burning gaze and realized he was watching her. She smiled.

Also, above deck, Suzanne approached Henri. But a sudden wave knocked into the side of the frigate, and cold salt water splashed over the rail, drenching her.

"Careful, little one, are you all right? We don't want you to fall overboard and put the mermaids to shame, eh?"

Suzanne blushed, "Have you ever seen one?"

Henri smiled at her naivete. She was so young. "Yes, I see one right here that Poseidon has sent to enchant me." He chucked her on the chin.

She disliked that he was treating her like a child, and said, "I like it better up here."

"Where is your friend Maélle?"

"Somewhere around here." She glanced over to see Maélle, who was frowning at her from across the ship. Suzanne sighed with annoyance.

"Something wrong?" Henri asked.

"It's just that Maélle is always trying to take care of me just because I have the same name as her little sister; I don't need to be watched all the time." Ignoring Maélle, Suzanne turned her gaze back to Henri. "Have you seen the new territory?"

"No, this is my first trip and my last."

"You don't like being the ship's carpenter?"

"I only signed on as carpenter for the voyage. Besides, you do not get rich as a sailor. We make twenty livres per trip," He glanced past her to the captain on the bridge, "He makes two hundred for the same voyage. And besides, the new colony needs someone to build the settlement."

Suzanne swelled with pride, "That will be an important job. I suppose.... you will be looking for a wife." She looked up at him with those eyes, and he wondered suddenly if she was as naïve and inexperienced as she was trying to appear.

"I'll worry about that when I get there," Henri said, wanting to extinguish any hopes Suzanne might be harboring about him. He wanted an adult life partner, *not* a child bride to look after.

He glanced up at Maélle, staring at them from across the ship, and smiled.

# Six

It was twilight when Captain de Martonne heard a knock at the door. It was late in the day for any of the lieutenants to be giving reports, but stranger things had happened.

"Come in."

The door opened, and Josianne stepped in, closing the door quietly behind her.

The captain's brows came together in astonishment. "Can I...help you, *mademoiselle*?" He recognized her as the beauty from earlier on the ship that day. He had just finished his meal and felt guilty when her hungry eyes flicked to the piece of gristle left on the plate.

"I have come for cloth."

Unnerved by a woman suddenly in his cabin, he returned to the table and brought a small glass to his lips, swallowing the red wine. "Cloth, did you say?"

She nodded and breathed deeply. He watched her do this and could not keep his eyes off the fullness of her breasts straining against her bodice.

"*Oui*, we have no clean cloth for washing or...*womanly* things."

Seated now, the captain leaned back in his chair, "I don't have anything extra for you. You see, the West Indies company, in their infinite greed, barely stocked the ship with enough supplies for my crew." He was growing weary of his work with the *Compagnie d' Occidental*. Although it was not his fault, he hated the look in her eyes and repeated his empathy. "I am sorry, *mademoiselle*, but I have nothing extra for any of you in terms of food, water, or clothing." He watched her eyes flick again to his plate. "Would you—" Before he could finish, she sat down and greedily ate the gristle, sopping up what little grease there was with her fingers. He watched with a mixture of horror and compassion. Finishing, she remembered her ladies' maid training, wiped her mouth on the napkin, and folded it neatly next to the plate.

Looking up she noticed the walls paneled in a dark-wood, and that a huge bay window with diamond paned windows faced the sea. She could see the dying colors of the sunset within the panes of glass, and was jealous that the captain could see sunlight whenever he desired. From the ceiling hung a small brass chandelier that held stubs of candles. The chandelier gently swayed from its chain.

She saw a horseshoe-shaped desk in the corner. The desk was littered with maps spread across it, two brass candlesticks holding down the curling edges. She realized he not only ate and slept there but worked there as well.

Although it was nicely appointed, it was not nearly as luxurious as the house she'd lived in in Paris, and it surprised her.

"What is your name?"

"Josianne Daudessont."

He took another sip of the wine from a crystal glass. "How did you end up on my ship?"

Although she was silent, he could tell she sighed because he watched the gentle rise and fall of her breasts again. He noted how the chains still around her waist were low on her hips.

Her eyes met his. "I was a lady's maid."

"And...why are you no longer a lady's maid?"

"The wife got jealous of me and said I did things I did not do. Told the police, and I ended up at *La Salpêtrière.*" She thought about adding how odious the son had been too.

"Were you *trying* to seduce the husband?" Although he had never married, the thought of having this incredibly beautiful creature in his home, he decided, could cause *any* man to stray.

"No."

When he saw the anger in her eyes, he was ashamed for the insinuation. "My apologies, *mademoiselle.*" Awkwardly he got up and getting another small glass filled it with two inches of wine, and handed it to her.

"I do not want wine; I need cloth for my friends." Since the plate was pewter, she wondered how many wine glasses were broken by the unpredictable turbulence of the sea.

Sitting back down, he sighed. "I will talk to the bosun and see what I can do."

"Thank you, captain."

"Truly, if I had...anything *extra* for you women, you see, I have *barely* enough for my crew—"

"I know, I believe you." She didn't know why, but she did. She would not put it past *Madame* Pacletain to make their crossing as difficult as possible.

He felt the color burning his face, hating that his emotions were, as always, displayed on his cheeks. He had been this way since he was a boy and was embarrassed by how his mother and sisters used to tease him about his flushing.

Curious, she picked up a leather-bound book from the desk. "What is this?"

"An instrument of my trade."

"What does this say?" Gently, she felt the embossed name on the front of the book.

Watching her, he realized she could not read. "It says *'La Mutine,'* which was surely a sick joke made by whomever the French Navy endorses to name these ships. I suppose they thought it humorous to name a ship after a rebellious woman." Watching her smile, it occurred to him that she could well be a rebellious woman.

"What do you write in it?"

He sat back comfortably in the chair. "I must keep track of time and make a notation every other hour. Ships' time is different than civil time; for a ship, the day starts at noon rather than midnight. I keep notes on the direction of the wind, our speed."

"Speed?"

He grinned but then remembered she had not grown up on a ship as he had. "There is a line behind the ship, and there are knots in it, and we can determine the speed from it."

She did not seem terribly interested, so he decided to spare her the explanations of leagues and fathoms.

She looked at him and carefully set the important book back on the table.

"How do you know..." She shrugged, thinking that since they had been at sea, there was nothing but empty water, not a landmark to guide them. "How do you know where we are going?"

"I have a compass, sextant, glass, and other tools to help me. I use dead reckoning to plot where I have been. I can figure out the latitude by the stars."

"The stars?"

He grinned, "Yes, the stars. Celestial bodies have guided mariners for centuries."

"I do remember them."

His brows furrowed, "what do you mean remember them?"

"I haven't seen the stars in years. There was only one window in the cell, and it was small."

To hide his horror, he swallowed more of the wine.

She picked up the compass. "What are these little lines for?"

"It's called a rhumb or a point on a compass."

"What is latitude?" She asked.

She was not educated, but it impressed him that she did not want him to feel sorry for her. "The distance north and south of the equator. They are...invisible parallel bands along the earth. And if my calculations are not precise, we could be off our course by hundreds of miles."

"And are we on course to get to our destination?"

She watched the rise and fall of his chest. "Yes, but we are behind time. This should be an eight-week crossing. But the Atlantic in winter is often rougher than I like, and these confounded frigates tend to veer off course. I fear it will be more like ten weeks." He thought about telling her that the great explorer La Salle even had trouble with his calculations but reminded himself that not everyone was consumed with sailing as he was. "You are very beautiful; have you been told this before?" He hoped his hand was steady as he drank.

"*Oui.*"

He was puzzled by her answer. "And this does not...*affect* you, this knowledge?"

She shrugged. "So far, it has done nothing but bring me misery."

Again, he was surprised. "I never thought of it that way before, of beauty being a curse. I am sorry you have had this experience." He stared at her for a few moments. "I hardly recognize France these days; you are lucky to be leaving."

Her eyes met his, "What do you mean?" More at ease, she took the glass of wine and drank. She felt the alcohol sear through her empty stomach.

He laughed, but it was not because of happiness. "They have gone crazy with the schemes from the Scotsman, Law. He has replaced gold and silver with a paper currency, and sensible Parisians stand in line to trade their gold for his worthless paper." He finished the wine. "All anyone in Paris can talk about is their Mississippi stock." He did not want to talk about what happened to the formerly conservative French economy. Ever since the Sun King's death, Law had been given free rein to change the very fabric of the economy. He had even talked the Regent *Philippe d'Orleans into* nationalizing the bank. This may have worked, but it was linked to the French monarchy and controlled *totally* by Law, which only had allegiance to itself.

"I don't know about these things," she admitted, nervous, finished the rest of the wine in one swallow, then got up to leave.

He was on his feet in an instant. He had the oddest sensation he was letting go of a once in a lifetime chance and had bored her with his maritime and political talk.

"Dine with me tomorrow night."

She tried to open the door, but his hand was against it. "How does that help my friends?"

"What does your dining with *me* have to do with your *friends*?"

"I am concerned for my friends as you are for your crew."

He admired her loyalty. "I will talk to the bosun and see what arrangements I can make for the cloth. We will share *one* ration of food."

"In exchange for what?" She asked, matter of factly, as if she was propositioned thusly every day.

She was looking up at him, and he had a terrible time not touching her face. It looked so soft.

"Just the immense pleasure of your company. Tomorrow night at 6:00."

By 3:00 the next day the third lieutenant came down with a bucket with two inches of fresh water in it, and sailcloth, *clean* sailcloth. When the women realized he was leaving this for them they all began to chatter at once.

"Did the captain send this?" Josianne asked.

"Who cares who *sent* it," Héléne marveled.

"All I know is I was told to bring you this bucket of water for bathing, although, for the lot of ya, the last one might have trouble getting clean!" The Lieutenant laughed.

"Oh, *mon Dieu*, this will be wonderful!" Maélle cried, clasping Josianne's hands.

They all began ripping the cloth into smaller sections and got in line to dip it in the bucket, even before Maélle could cut them with her hidden scissors.

Josianne stood at the captain's door. It took her five minutes to gather her courage to knock. It was a dangerous game she was playing, but if she could help her friends, she would do what she had to. It was ironic *that Monsieur* Pelletier, from the house she worked in, had *wanted* her to play such coquettish games. It was as abhorrent to her then as it was now. She shuddered.

When he answered the door, Josianne's mouth watered as she smelled the food on the table.

"Come in, please," he said, getting out of the way,

looking forward to being able to close the door behind them.

The small, rectangular table was set for two. And true to his word, there was precious little on each of the pewter plates. Dry pieces of ham were bordered by a lopsided red potato, a wedge of white cheese, and two small biscuits.

A gentleman, he moved the chair in for her after she sat. The chair was covered in maroon velvet and was lightly padded. It was more comfort than she had felt in weeks.

His blue captain's suitcoat was off, and his white shirt was unbuttoned at the throat. He was attractive and worldly, and Josianne warned herself not to fall under his spell.

He hurried around to the other side and sat across from her. His antics reminded her of a fidgety schoolboy, and she had to suppress a smile.

As she watched him pour wine, she couldn't help but ask, "Am I drinking your ration of wine as well?"

"No, of Bordeaux, I have enough for both of us." Smiling, he took a drink, his eyes flitting appreciatively over her face. He had sampled his fair share of beautiful women, from the Mediterranean women with their dark hair and smoldering eyes to the flaxen-haired Nordic beauties who could melt ice with a glance. But there was something about her that made his pulse quicken, something that intrigued him. "I spoke with the bosun and persuaded him to give me extra cloth. You should receive more tomorrow."

She tilted her head. "Persuaded him? As the captain, are you not in charge of these things?"

He laughed good-naturedly and settled back in the chair. "Yes, I am in charge, but I am also aware that the men underneath me take their positions and rank very seriously. I requested. I did not *demand*. There is a pecking order on the ship from me all the way down to the most menial sailor. And I need their respect. To earn and keep their respect, I must give it as well."

"I thought you would be stuffy and conceited, but you are wise."

He laughed again. He could not stop staring at her, so beautiful in the dim light. Wanting to see more of her, he turned up the lantern a quarter inch. On the ship the other day, her eyes had been murky blue, but tonight, in the dimness of the cabin, they were light green.

They ate the sparse meal, and when they were done, she asked, "Are you a married man?"

"I never had...the inclination. I am away most of the time, and I didn't see a point, really." He grinned and jerked his chin towards the round porthole, "I am married to the sea, and she has her way with me more often than I like." Although suddenly, the thought of Josianne having her 'way with him' was quite appealing.

"You have no family?"

"I have four older sisters."

It amused her that he was the youngest boy in a family of women.

"What made you become a captain?" she asked, the wine warming her skin and making her flush.

He was thoughtful, "the freedom. I was eight when I came aboard as a cabin boy, and I have worked most jobs on the ship. Most ships' officers are gentlemen, but my father was a cooper, and I wanted to make him proud of me."

"How old were you when you became a captain?"

He was delighted she was interested and proud to be able to say, "nineteen."

He realized by the widening of her eyes that he seemed old to her and laughed. "Am I too old for you, *mademoiselle*? I am twenty-eight. How old are you?"

"Seventeen."

"There is little more than a decade between us."

Oddly, this reassured her. "Was your father proud of you?" She was drawn to this powerful, handsome man who, like the rest of them, craved parental approval.

The captain shrugged. "By the time I returned, he had died. So you see, I don't know." He finished his wine, and she watched him pour another glass.

"And you *mademoiselle*?"

"I never knew my father, and my mother died when I was nine. That's when I went into service."

His eyes met hers. "And now you are on my ship in the middle of the Atlantic Ocean." As if on cue, the boat rose on a wave, and Josianne held her breath until the sensation was gone. She wondered if she could get used to always being in motion, as she assumed the captain had.

He moved to her, pulling her up from the table. He touched the thick braid of her hair and gently removed the tattered ribbon. Holding the strands, he ran his fingers slowly down the tresses, unbraiding them. It was the only ribbon she had, and it worried her when he took it from her. She had sponge-bathed along with everyone else but still hoped a louse would not appear.

He cupped her face with his hand, lifting it up, and then his lips met hers.

She felt his hand on her back, pressing her against him, and could feel the pounding of his heart against hers, as well as stiffness at his groin.

"I want you, Josianne."

"I can't," she said, trying and failing to push him away.

"Please, I just...need to *touch* you." The hand that was on her back drifted to her waist. He disliked the feel of the chains around her waist and ignoring it, his hand made its way up.

He met her eyes, whispering, "so beautiful, so *astonishingly* beautiful." Leaning down he kissed her again. A kiss that because of its length and ardor, made her light-headed. The only kissing she had ever seen was when *monsieur* Pelletier kissed his stupid dog, or when the priest kissed the altar before mass.

But the captain had opened his mouth during the kiss, and it was waking up all sorts of things in her. Regardless, she pushed him away, abruptly ending the kiss. He was handsome, experienced, and had an occupation she admired. She was afraid of her feelings for him, afraid it would turn out wretchedly in the end.

"What's wrong?"

"I have to go."

"Why?"

"I just...do." She was at the door in an instant.

He met her there. "Don't go, please. I will behave myself. I promise."

"No, you won't." She tugged on the door, realizing it would not open because he had his foot at the bottom.

"Please, you are my guest. And I behaved...*abominably*. I give you my word as a captain, I won't--" But looking up at him with her hair undone, her lips plump from kissing, he couldn't stop himself and kissed her again.

"Good night, captain." She jerked the door open, but he caught her hand before she could escape.

"Come to me again tomorrow night, please? I promise I shall behave myself."

"What do I get in return?"

This surprised him; he rather hoped to entice her sans bargaining.

"Another.... half ration of food every other day for your friends?" It was the most he could do, and he half worried his crew would threaten mutiny with a reduction in rations.

Josianne nodded, and remembering the ribbon, grabbed it on the way out.

The next night, when she came to the captain's door, he opened it before she made the second knock.

The table was set this time with a linen cloth, and the wineglasses were already filled. On the plates sat white chunks of fish, an even smaller boiled potato with only one biscuit, and no cheese.

"I fear, Captain, you will waste away to nothing if we continue to share rations this way."

Giddy, he laughed. "What a lovely demise that would be. And please, call me Philipe."

"Thank you for having the last of the chains removed." It was luxurious to walk unfettered.

He brought her a glass of wine that was full to the brim. "I don't know why they were put on you women in the first place. My apologies for not having them removed sooner."

Accepting his apology, Josianne smiled.

"To us," he said, his eyes taking in all the lovely curves of her face. Toasting too aggressively, a bit of the red wine splashed on her chest, and like a vampire, he bent and licked it from her breast.

Their eyes met.

He pulled her face and mouth up to his and kissed her. A long, deep kiss that awakened a primal need inside her. Although she warned herself to keep her wits about her, it was difficult when everything about the captain intoxicated her.

Pulling away finally she said, "I think we should eat." She touched the damp place on her chest where he had licked off the wine, and shuddered.

Stepping over the back of the chair like a common sailor, he sat.

Although the fish was dry and flavorless she relished it as she chewed, looking about the room. Covered in dark paneling it was a cozy cave with an exceptional view of the sky and ocean.

"Were your friends happy with the water and cloth?"

His table manners were relaxed, but she had the feeling he could exhibit impeccable cutlery skills when necessary.

"Very much. Thank you so much."

The small meal was finished quickly, and fearing what might happen next, Josianne cleared her throat. "Have you cards? I thought we might...entertain ourselves."

He leisurely leaned back in the chair, like a cat amused by its prey. "Oh, I could be entertained by you all night long, I assure you." His eyes held hers wickedly. "But you would rather play a game?"

"Yes, yes, I would." Truthfully, she would have liked nothing better than to kiss the captain all night long but pushed the sinful thoughts from her mind.

He went to the chest on the other side of the room. One that held a small cloudy mirror in a cheval frame, a lantern and a flat porcelain dish that held cuff links. Yanking on a drawer that tended to stick, he brought a deck back to the table that Josianne had tidied of their plates.

"What," he asked, shuffling the cards, "does the lady wish to play?"

"I only know solitaire."

He stopped shuffling, eyeing her as if he had misheard, "solitaire?"

"Yes, I played double solitaire with the boy in the house where I was a maid." She remembered how many times he tried to kiss her and shivered. It was worlds apart from how she felt when the captain kissed her.

He leaned his chair back on two legs and again forced the sticky drawer open and pulled out an additional deck of cards. Putting the decks together he again shuffled, "And were there.... *wagers* on these games?"

"No."

"Ahh, well, that's because he was a boy, but since you are now playing with a *man*, we will have a wager."

"What are we wagering?"

"If I win, I may have a kiss...anywhere I like." He glanced from her hair to her face to her throat.

"And if *I* win?"

"Philipe," he prodded.

"Philipe," she repeated. "More time on the deck for me and my friends."

He nodded in agreement.

They played furiously until the lantern wick was black and the oil was getting low. They laughed as victory bounced between them, but in the end, the captain prevailed.

"I have won."

"You have."

"I wouldn't do that if I were you." He was staring at her small hand that she had placed atop his.

She glanced at him curiously, "do what?"

He dropped the cards and, lunging over the table, kissed her.

"Captain, please!"

"I am mad for you."

"No, I fear you are simply *mad*."

He lifted her hand until she stood. He stared down at her for so long, Josianne wondered what he could possibly be finding so interesting about her face.

"Have I got something in my teeth?" She asked at last with a laugh.

But he didn't answer. Instead, he picked her up in his arms.

Her breath caught in her throat in fear.

He carried her back to his bed. It was a narrow mattress tucked into a low-ceilinged alcove, and gently he laid her down. There were windows along the side, and she glanced out to see the darkness and enormity of the sea. The ferocity of the ocean and confined quarters frightening her.

In a flash, he removed his shirt, and she stared at his bare chest. His eyes were glazed with lust as he began to fondle her breast and kiss her.

Finally breaking free from a kiss, she begged, "I cannot."

"Yes, you can."

"No," She stared up at his handsome face, tears stinging her eyes. "I want a life, I want a husband, children and a home."

"Josianne, I want to be with you."

"And you think I don't?" She struggled around him to sit up. "What happens to me if our little...*tryst* gets me with child?"

He was gently brushing back her hair from her face, "It won't, there is a thing we can do."

"And you'll be halfway around the world in bed with another woman."

He was insulted. "No, I *won't* be with another woman. Josianne, you have *hypnotized* me, heart and soul." Grabbing her hand, he placed it against his chest. "Feel my heart, it is pounding with desire for you."

Timidly, she pulled her hand away. "I'd like to leave, please." Awkwardly, she got to her feet. On her way to the door, she picked up the sailcloth. No reason for her friends to suffer.

Sighing, he stood up and walked to the door, opening it. In the doorway, she stopped. "Thank you for the water and cloth. I appreciate it."

He sighed with frustration. "Please don't go. What can I do to make you stay?"

Unable to stop herself, she blurted out, "Could we not...be married?"

"I cannot give you what you want."

"Is what I want so difficult?"

He knew it was not but said nothing.

"I have hypnotized you heart and soul... but you will not *marry* me?" she asked, her heart hammering with brittle hope.

"I doubt I will ever marry anyone." He looked down at the floor, crossing his arms across his chest. He seemed annoyed, and this hurt her all the more.

She wiped a single tear from her cheek, and straightening her back walked away and back to the bowels of the ship, her wounded heart slowing it's beat as she walked.

"Here, I have some cloth," Josianne said, crawling over Suzanne and Maélle's legs to hand them pieces of cloth that had been sheared from a sail. New, *clean* cloth.

"Where did you *get* this?" Hélène marveled.

Josianne blew a strand of hair away from her face. "From the boatswains, mate," she lied.

"Who?" Maélle asked.

"How did this happen?" Hélène asked, incredulously.

"What did you do, Josianne?" Maélle asked, still wondering why the ship's captain reconsidered and removed all their chains.

Josianne shrugged, forcing a smile. "I got us cloth, and at least every other day, a bit more food."

"But...how?" Hélène asked, although, in a way, she did not care. They would have fresh cloth; it was a blessing. It was bad enough to have your monthly along with fifty other women (and it happened to all of them at the same time) and have nothing to soak it up with.

Josianne pressed her hands against her large breasts. "I let him touch."

"You did what?" Suzanne asked, and Maélle shushed her, coaxing her to go back to sleep.

Hélène looked down at her own flat chest and could not imagine anyone giving her *anything* to simply touch them. "He gave you cloth for...*touching* you?"

Josianne forced a smile, "But of course. I made him think it was the most scandalous thing in the world and that I had such perfect breasts that sculptors would make naughty statues of me."

"You didn't have to—" Hélène began.

"Be a wanton woman?" Josianne forced a laugh, and Maélle shushed her, not wanting to wake the others. "No, even though they say we are all prostitutes. Besides, I am saving that treat for my rich husband." Even though she was not a virgin (she had her old employer to thank for that), no one needed to know. She knew men thought they could tell if a woman was "untouched" or not, but she doubted they would question her innocence when she gave them her performance.

Maélle fell over into the straw, hand over her mouth to stop her giggling.

"It's not funny, Maélle. It's not fair we are subjected to this humiliation."

"Hélène, it is fine. I did not mind, really," Josianne soothed, although nothing was fine.

Maélle choked on her laughter, her hands over her mouth.

"How can you be laughing? You're in the pit of a stinking ship, and you are *laughing*?" Héléne scoffed.

"How can you *not* be laughing?" Josianne admonished. "If we survive this godforsaken voyage, it will be a miracle. How can we afford *not* to laugh? I guess, Hélène, you would have us *cry* the whole way to Louisiana?" She leaned closer to her friends, "What I propose is that we all find husbands—"

Hélène groaned.

"Yes, even *you*, Hélène. That we all find husbands, have lots of children, and make this our new home. We can be anyone we want to be here; there's no one to look down on us. And... we are *free*. My husband will be the richest man in the territory. And I will live in a fine house, and all of us will be friends. I will be an aristocrat in the new territory, and Maélle, you can make me beautiful gowns."

"I would be honored," Maélle bowed, playing along.

"And my husband Henri will build you the houses," Suzanne chimed in happily.

"*What?*" Maélle said, spinning to glare at Suzanne.

"Henri, the one that undid our chains?" Josianne asked with amusement.

"Suzanne, you cannot marry a ship's carpenter," Maélle implored, having heard unsavory things about sea-faring men.

"But he's not a sailor. He is on the ship as a carpenter, and he is going to stay in the territory. He brought all his own tools and will be a great success."

Maélle had no idea how he managed to fill her head with these lofty ideas.

When at last they all quieted down, Josianne closed her eyes and let down the charade, and let the devastation and disappointment course through her soul.

# Seven

Hélène relieved herself by squatting over the piss bucket and felt immediate relief from the unbearable cramping. Every one of the women had dysentery. The clear soup they were being fed and coarse bread made the cramping and bloating worse, but that was all there was to eat. And the bloody flux was weakening them even faster than starvation was doing. The smell assaulted her, and she prayed that everyone would stay asleep. She was surprised that in these horrendous conditions, she could still feel a modicum of embarrassment. "At least we are still human," she whispered.

Hélène struggled over to the matted straw where she was sleeping, glad she had not woken Maélle.

She wiped her mouth with the back of her hand and noticed her gums were bleeding again.

Not only were all of them suffering from dysentery, but the "plague of the seas," which started innocently enough as swollen, bleeding gums. They were all finding it hard to chew the stale bread, and some of them were losing their teeth in the pieces. In the darkness, Hélène pulled up her skirt and looked at her legs. They were misshapen and swollen, glossy in the darkness, and there was a purple ulcer starting on her ankle. It had been but a small mark days ago but was getting worse.

Laying back down, she prayed. She had prayed little since she had left the forced prayer of *La Salpêtrìere*. There, it had been mandatory, and she had acquiesced to prevent punishment, but lying in the dark on the rocking ship, alternating with starvation, seasickness, and dysentery, she wondered if God had abandoned them. And prayed for it to end, thinking there could be nothing worse in the world than this voyage.

She was wrong.

# *Eight*

Nearly everyone was on deck, and Maélle was standing near the back and having trouble seeing over the crowd that gathered at the ships railing. When she caught sight of land, she felt tears prick her eyes, wondering if she was looking at her new home. Glancing to her left, she saw Henri, who was also jockeying back and forth, trying to see.

"I was not sure we'd ever make it," Maélle remarked nervously.

"Not much of a sailor, are you?" His brown eyes were mirthful. It had been a while since she had seen him.

"No, not really," Maélle looked away, trying to force down the sudden lump in her throat. "You must be excited to start building the new town."

He grinned, "Yes, I am. And I predict you will be the finest *couturière* in the town."

"You're teasing me." But it made her blush that he not only remembered but thought highly of her talent.

"I'm not. I build things with wood, and you build

them with cloth." He reached out and touched her shoulder to inspect the seam. But it sent a shiver down her spine. "Tiny stitches, tight buttonholes, the way you work with the fabric and make it drape," he glanced up with a smile. "What you do is no different than me working with the grain of wood. You are a master at your craft."

Feeling her heart stutter happily, she tucked her hair behind her ear.

"How did a skilled artisan like yourself end up here?" He had been wanting to ask her these things since he first met her. Glad that Suzanne was not around to interrupt them.

"My father and brothers dropped me off at *La Salpêtrìere.*"

"The old gunpowder factory in Paris?" He knew the remote place. It had enormous stone walls surrounding it that must have blocked out the sunlight, as well as the sights of Paris. It was bordered by a city dump on one side and the Seine on the other. A dilapidated cemetery made up the third side, and on the fourth, a putrid pool of waste collected from the nearby tanneries. In the summer, he remembered the cesspool teemed with mosquitoes, and he'd seen rats swimming in the filth.

"Dropped you off at that horrible place. Why?"

"My father wanted me to stay home, tend the fields with my five brothers, and help care for my little sister. But I was making money where I was. I did not mind sharing the money I made, but they wanted it *all.*"

He nodded as if he understood but did not. "But they were going to bring you back, surely?"

She hated to infect the lovely conversation, "Actually, no, you can be dropped off forever if they see fit."

He shook his head in disbelief, "I've never heard of such a thing."

"By the *lettre-de-cachet*, any male relative can be rid of an unwanted female. I know women who were dropped off because they had taken the Lord's name in vain. And they are certainly dropped off if they were going to inherit before a male relative. And it must be done before age twenty-five."

"Before you would have attained your own civil rights."

She nodded grimly.

"There's... *nothing* you could do?" He was shocked by the cruelty.

"No, nothing. No recourse. I can never return to them." She said bitterly, but knowing that other than her little sister, Suzanne, she hoped never to see any of them again. And now that she was an ocean away, she hoped her mother, who had not protected her, would protect her little sister.

He stared out at the ocean, "Then I am glad you are rid of them. I am glad you are here. I am glad you can make your own life." He smiled down at her. He began to speak again, but Suzanne wiggled in between them and urgently pulled Henri away from her.

The wind stole their words away, and Maélle could tell whatever they were talking about was serious because Suzanne's eyes were filling with tears, and Henri looked ashen and totally dumbstruck. Suzanne was looking up at him with such adoration that Maélle felt the ugly taste of jealousy.

Yelling yanked her attention away, and there was commotion on the ship and even as she saw the shore in the distance the ship turned sharply starboard. The rattling of the ship's anchor pierced the air.

Knowing she should not approach the captain, Josianne grabbed the boatswain's mate and pointed, "Why have we changed course? Is that not the shore over there?"

It looked like it pained him to speak, "We can't take you there yet." His eyes left hers, and she dropped her hand from his.

"But that's the new territory. Where are we going?" A shiver of fear snaked through her.

"We couldn't get ashore from here anyway; it's only fifteen feet deep."

Josianne waited for him to continue.

"We are about thirty miles from a settlement called Mobile, we will load you into *chaloupes*." He motioned to the impossibly small rowboats being dropped into the water, "These will take you to the island."

"*Island*? Why take us to an island? Take us to the territory, please." Her nails were digging into the flesh of his forearm. "It's just as easy to row us to the mainland rather than that...*island,* isn't it?"

"I cannot."

Letting go of him, Josianne watched as the women began lining up towards the front of the ship to board the smaller boats. She glanced out to the island in the distance. She looked over to the captain, who was watching her. Regardless of the impropriety, she approached him.

"What is on this island?"

"Truthfully, I have no idea," He took the opportunity to look her up and down. She had not come to see him since that night, and he missed her. "You may share my cabin if you'd like. I could take you to the mainland later."

She turned to go, and despite being on deck, he reached out and took hold of her hand. "Josianne, stay with me." There was a storm in his blue eyes.

She wavered for a moment; the feel of his hand on hers was warm, inviting. "As your wife or mistress?"

This made him angry, "As my guest. I-I can...rent a place for you."

"And drop in on me a few times a year?"

Even to his own ears, it sounded unappealing.

"I don't deserve that, you know it," she said, staring up at him. "Is that all you think of me?"

"Josianne, *please.*"

Her eyes met his again. "I cannot. I *will* not."

Dropping his hand, she turned and walked away. When he made no attempt to stop her, a burst of hot pain radiated through her chest.

The frigid water splashed up on them as a sailor rowed them out. The women huddled together for warmth. It was a cold, wet, hideous ride.

"I don't understand." Hélène turned to the sailor, "Where are you taking us?"

"*Ilé de Massacre.*"

"Why in the world would they call it *that*?" Hélène shrieked, her stomach lurching as the waves wreaked havoc with the tiny boat.

"Because they found bones, human bones, on that island," the sailor said, relishing that he got to tell them the gruesome details. "I have never seen it myself, but that's what I've been told. It seems there is nothing to eat on that godforsaken island, so they ate each other."

Hélène wrapped her thin arms around her even thinner waist. "Why would anyone want to eat us? We are nothing but skin and bones." The other women in the tiny boat gasped at her words.

"You're not going to leave us there, are you?" Angélique asked in a small voice. She had been two cells over from Hélène. It was alarming to see how bright and frightened her eyes were in her dirty face.

"Yes, all of you are going there. It's a barrier island, and it will take us all day to get the lot of you over there and the others from *Deux Fréres.*"

"There are others?" Hélène asked, twisting in the tiny boat to see another frigate in the distance, which was also anchored and unloading more women.

The sailor leered, "More of ya *debauched* women," he laughed then, revealing all yellowed and some broken teeth.

"We *weren't* prostitutes," Hélène admonished, then wondered why she cared what this filthy, despicable sailor thought. "What is a barrier island?"

He kept rowing, but because of the waves and wind, they didn't seem to be making much progress. "A speck of an island. It's a day's voyage there from New Biloxi, although it is only thirty miles, but you cannot see it from the mainland."

It occurred to Hélène that they would be hidden from the mainland.

"Surely there are people there?" Angélique piped up, pulling her tattered dress tighter around her scant frame, trying to protect herself from the biting February winds. The seawater splashed them every few minutes, making any reprieve from the bitter cold impossible.

He grinned at her, "No, no people."

"But the *Ile de la Citre* is close to the city. People come and go every day." The only islands Hélène had ever seen were urban islands like the *Ile de Saint-Louis* in the Seine, which were built right on the water's edge and had bridges that connected them to the mainland and Paris. What she was looking at in the far distance was like *nothing* she had ever seen.

"*Mademoiselle*," He began, his words dripping with contempt, "This is not like Paris. There is no *Notre-dame Cathedral* on the island to greet you. There will be no one there and nothing to eat." His words sent a shiver down Hélène's spine.


Somehow Hélène fell sleep with the monotonous rowing but was awakened when a wave almost displaced her from her seat. The other women were still huddled together in the boat trying to ward off the cold. She lifted her face to the gray sky, hoping mercilessly, it would not rain.

The sailor noticed she was awake and lifted his chin towards the island.

Hélène turned to look.

It was a scene inconceivable to her. Never in her imagination could she have conjured a more devastating sight.

It was a desolate, forlorn beachfront, where only scattered, straggly pine trees grew. And the shape of the trees was frightening. Buffeted as they were by the constant wind on the island, they grew in grotesque, other-worldly shapes.

Listening to the slap of the water as the sailor rowed them closer, she saw a shack that looked as though it had been abandoned years ago. What was left of the wood, was weather beaten and pitted. The roof had fallen in, and the sand that blew in drifts along the beach was piled five feet high on what was left of one wall.

Stepping out of the boats, Hélène realized how cold the water was. She had no shoes, and her clothes were nothing more than rags. She lent a hand to the other six women who stepped out of the boat.

Thank God Captain de Martonne had allowed their chains to be taken off! It was a relief to stand unfettered and without the weight of the chains around her waist. When the last woman disembarked, they all huddled together for warmth, like they had had to do when they were chained together.

Angélique began to cry, and instinctively, Hélène

pulled the woman against her chest. Resting her chin on the top of her head. "Don't cry; tears will do us no good."

The young girl looked up, the tears making clean lines on her filthy face.

More *chaloupes* arrived and when Hélène saw the boat that carried her friends, she darted out again into the sea to greet them. "Maélle, Josianne, Suzanne!" She saw her friends, and looking up, saw Henri.

Everyone's reaction to the deserted beach they were deposited on was the same. The long stretches of lonely beach, with dotted twisted marsh pines and scrub oaks. It occurred to Hélène that they were not good trees for fuel, and then, looking at her hands, she wondered how she was to cut one down and, without a flint, how she would light it for light or warmth.

The more *chaloupes* that arrived, the more the panic in Héléne's chest grew. How long were they going to be left there? How would they keep warm? What would they drink? What, if anything, could they eat?

When the last boat was leaving, Hélène spotted Henri still with Suzanne. He had his arms protectively around her, trying to keep her warm. But she didn't get out of the boat, and it was suddenly obvious Suzanne was not staying with them.

"Goodbye, *mon ames*." The sailor who told them the gruesome story, shouted. He then had the audacity to happily whistle as he rowed away.

Hélène ran out into the surf after Henri as he began to row away. She fell once, the saltwater stinging her eyes. She did not know how to swim, and feeling the soft bottom beneath her feet give way, she struggled back, terrified. "You are going to *leave* us?" She screamed, the wind muffling her words, spitting out the hair that made its way into her mouth. "We have no shelter, no food, no water. Is there another boat coming to supply us with...*anything*?"

Henri hurled an animal skin flask at her. Héléne desperately hoped it held water, scrambling towards it, she grabbed it.

"There's nothing else I can give you," he shouted back, "I will be back. I promise."

Suzanne was shivering in the boat, and although Hélène could not hear what she was saying, she could tell she was crying.

A hideous bile rose up in Héléne's throat. "When, *when* will you be back? When we have all starved to death, and the birds pick at what's left of our flesh?"

Maélle realized, with a gasping catch in her heart, that he was taking Suzanne, and they were leaving the rest of them on the hideous island. That he had taken *Suzanne* and left her.

"I'll come back as soon as I can," he yelled to Maélle, then mouthed the words, "I'm sorry."

Hélène stood watching the boats row away, paralyzed with astonishment. She slumped down into the wet sand then and put her shaking hands over her eyes. She wanted to howl at the injustice, at the cruelty.

Instead, she looked back up and stared unblinking at the merciless sea until she could no longer make out the boats.

· · ·

When the sun went down on the island, the wind took on an eerie moan. It was as if the island was whispering ghost stories to them. With a shivering Louise in her arms, Maélle was relieved when, at last, Louise fell asleep. They were all huddled together, trying to share their scant body heat.

Maélle stared up at the inky black sky, studded with so many stars that there was scarcely a place in the sky not lit up. She had not seen more than glimpses of the night sky for years at *La Salpêtrière*. Sometime during the endless, cold night, she saw not one but three shooting stars, and although she made a wish on all of them, wondered if good luck was meant for people like her.

When she finally slept, she was assaulted with nightmares of Suzanne smiling at her as they rowed away.

They woke up the next morning cold, hungry, thirsty, and stiff. No one knew what to do, and Hélène reluctantly became the leader because the women of *Deux Frères* seemed even more timid. All but one who eyed Hélène with suspicion. The two of them had already gotten into one disagreement about how many sips of water everyone could have, which Josianne put a stop to by shouting at them, "We must work together, or more of us will die."

The women from *Deux Frères* had also been sent by *Madame* Pacletain and were no better treated than the women of *La Mutine*. They traded stories of being rounded up, incarcerated, and then shipped off.

They griped about the merits of France's "experiment" with finances. Unanimously, they decided that if they were ever alone in a room with the men who decided such things, they would strangle them with their bare hands.

"I don't think it's a coincidence that all of a sudden, Madame Pacletain needed to get rid of all of us. Seems to me it all started when Paris had 'Mississippi fever,'" Héléne said.

"Are you blaming what she did to us on *that*?" Maélle asked, thinking it absurd. She knew Paris was in turmoil and well-remembered the gangs of thugs looting the shops.

"I don't know, but out of nowhere, she must make up lists for *'bonnes pour les iles; why* all of a sudden?" Héléne asked.

"Did *Madame* Pacletain get...money for doing it? She, too, lived at *La Salpêtrière*. It's not like she was rich," Josianne asked, joining the conversation.

"It is because of the greed in Paris and the bad men in power. It gave her a way to get rid of us. Us women of the sedition," Marie Denise said, her eyes boring a hole into Héléne's face.

Several of the women glanced around warily. No one liked to talk about the 'uprising' at the hospital in November.

Only a few women in the prison had taken part in the skirmish. They were revolting against cruel treatment and wanting more food. But Madame Pacletain sensationalized the minor incidence, saying the 'creatures' involved had slashed guards with knives, set fires in their cells, that there had been several injuries. That it took the police to put down the unrest, which *Madame* Pacletain made notorious by calling it a 'sedition.' It was what gave the women involved life sentences at *La Salpêtrìere*. In truth, only, four women were involved, and they had neither knives to slash with nor the strength to 'bash in heads.', and no way of setting their cells on fire.

They flocked together throughout the day, trying to shield their bodies from the sun, trying not to think about their thirst, and hoping their friends who had gone to explore would find something. But as the afternoon shadows fell across the Island, the group returned without food or water. The water Henri had given them, to be shared with so many, would not last long.

"*Mademoiselle*, you are from Paris?" a tall, dark-eyed woman from *Deux Fréres* asked Héléne; the same woman Héléne had argued with the day before.

"Yes, I was rounded up."

"My name is Marie Denise."

"Héléne." They grasped hands briefly.

"We must find food."

"I know."

"And water."

Héléne was unnerved by the woman's unwavering gaze.

"How many of you died and were pushed over-board?" Marie Denise asked.

Héléne's stomach rolled. It was not something she wanted to remember or talk about. "At least twenty."

Marie Denise's dark eyes eerily reflected the moon-light. "I have counted thirty-one."

The next day, Marie Denise and Héléne headed out to explore the island.

It was laborious walking in the sand and then the tall grass. The island was difficult to navigate, and at one point, they realized they were lost.

"How did you end up here?" Marie Denise asked, plodding behind Héléne.

"I was a laundress. They said I stole clothing. You?" But Héléne did not want to talk. Talking required mois-ture in her mouth, of which she had none.

"I am *Bohémien*."

Héléne had heard of these people, People the French government had been trying to eradicate for years. As a people, they had dubious reputations for being wander-ers, fortune tellers, *gypsies*."

"My family was arrested by a river in eastern France. We were all lumped together without even separate charges or files. It was said we women were guilty if our husbands had been sent to the galleys. Even though we did nothing wrong."

Sighing quietly, Héléne digested this. "We have made it through the prison, the awful voyage, and if we get off this island," she looked into the distance, "no one will know who we were."

For a second night, they huddled together while the cold wind whipped the sand against them, tearing at the rags they wore. The incessant sound of the surf lulled them to sleep despite their hunger. The small sips of water barely quenched their thirst, and Héléne wanted to cry when the flask was returned to her empty.

Sometime during the night, Maélle awoke and had the oddest sensation: something was nibbling her toe. She moved her foot.

Then she felt something biting her toe and, looking down, saw movement. Furiously, she kicked at the rodent and realized, to her horror, that there were rats around them. She had seen her share of rats in the alleys of Paris, but this was a swarming pack.

"Wake up!" She cried.

"What is it?" Josianne asked. And feeling the rat rooting in her hair, she jumped up and kicked at the scurrying animal. "Oh no, not my *hair*!" As the rats fled, they kicked up wet sand on Josianne. "Nasty pests, not my *hair*," she bellowed, picking up a fistful of sand and hurling it uselessly at the fleeing pack.

Everyone was awake now, yelling and jumping up; it was pandemonium for a few seconds.

Hélène watched Maélle squeezing the wound on her toe, but only a bit of blood oozed from it.

"Are you all right, Maélle?" Josianne asked, at her side.

"*Oui*, I am fine. It was only a small nibble."

"Rats chewing our toes, rats in our hair. I'd eat one of those bastards if I could catch it!" Hélène screamed.

"Maybe we will find something to eat tomorrow," Maélle soothed. "At least the air is fresh.... we have space and solitude. We will be all right."

"I agree if they don't leave us on this island too long--" Hélène said softly, calming down.

Looking across the group of women, she caught Marie Denise's black gaze and shivered.

# Nine

"I see it," Josianne whispered, walking ahead of Hélène, Angélique, and Louise. They were venturing again to see if they could find food or water. One of the girls, Beátrice, wild with thirst, gorged herself with seawater and vomited so long that Josianne half expected to see her organs come up.

The temperature was bearable during the day, but the sun's setting unnerved everyone. As the sun's rays sunk into the ocean, the temperature dropped thirty degrees, and the wind picked up. In France, Josianne remembered that the wind slowed down at night but blew incessantly on *Ile de Massacre*. When the sun disappeared into the ocean, the darkness brought a bone-chilling cold and eerie moan that contributed to everyone's nightmares and ruined sleep.

"It's a pond. It might have sweet water in it," Josianne said, taking off at a run. But the tall grasses with sharp leaves snagged her skirts and painfully scratched her flesh.

Reaching the water, Josianne dropped to her knees, panting.

When Hélène dipped her hand in and licked it, she realized the water was spoiled with salt.

"*Oh, mon Dieu! Oh mon Dieu, On mon Dieu!*" Louise wailed, clenching her fists and uselessly splashing at the saltwater pool. She fell back on the gritty sand, her hands over her chapped and windburned face, and began to cry. Her French had improved, and although she was still challenging to understand, they knew what she said.

Josianne gagged on the water and felt it hurtling around in her stomach. She rolled over on all fours and vomited a yellow bile. Strings of saliva hanging from her lips.

Hélène watched her friends heave their guts out and barked, "Come on, ladies. We must push on."

"Push on to *what* Hélène?" Angélique challenged, "they have left us here to die!" She glanced around at the desolate Island. The grotesquely twisted trees, the long grasses that cut her legs, the rats, and the ever-present wind. "How will we survive; *how will we survive*?"

"What were you in Paris, hmm?" Hélène asked, wiping the sticky sand from her hands. A nasty sunburn on her nose, as dark as the port wine stain on her cheek.

"I was a miller's daughter. That's why I know how bad the flour they sent us was and how it spoiled quickly; the bran was still intact. And it was already full of weevils."

"So, you can bake, can you also cook?" Hélène looked past the women, but only Josianne noticed.

"*Oui,* I love to cook. When I have something to cook

that is. I fed my entire family once for two weeks on a single chicken." She smiled with pride. "I plucked it, removed the organs, and simmered the chicken in a pot. I cooked the organs too and sliced and served with a thin gravy when all the meat was gone, although my father, because of his teeth, could not chew the gizzard. I saved the stewing water and dropped bits of flour into it. Although the stock got thinner and thinner because I had to keep adding water, it did last us." The memory caused her to smile.

A loud crash startled them. Hélène was on her hands and knees in the surf with a small rock, smashing it on a crab running sideways away from her. Seeing what might be their only meal escaping, Josianne scampered to her feet and grabbed the rock from Hélène. Josianne lunged toward the crab, smashing the rock against its shell.

Liquid squirted out of the leg and into Josianne's face. Hélène picked up the dead creature, turning it over. She had never seen such a crab. It was five inches wide and a beautiful shade of blue. Its black eyes on antennae stared back at her. She grabbed a pincher and twisted until the claw broke free and sucked the juice. She scraped out the moisture-dense flesh, using her fingernail to scoop the meat from the crevice. It slid down her throat. It was tasteless, wet, and slimy. The most delicious thing she had ever eaten.

Josianne came forward, and twisted off the other pincher, and sucked at the gooey flesh, letting the juice drip into her mouth. Hélène took the crab out of the surf and, grunting, snapped the tough shell apart. The sharp sides of the shell tearing at her fingers until they bled. She fell back as the others picked at the wet, gummy flesh.

"This is how we will survive," Hélène panted, thinking they had been lucky to find such a large crab. But there would be others, and she was determined to find the crabs.

Hélène was particularly good at finding and killing crabs. She scoured the beach every day from when the first rays of light pierced the horizon and laid on the ocean like gold ribbons until those same gold ribbons turned pink and red, and it was too dark to see. Josianne refused to let her go alone, and together, they explored the Island.

Maélle stayed with the group because some women still tried to wander off, sick from hunger and thirst, and Maélle had a talent for calming them down. Six had already died, and no one knew what to do with them. They resorted to burying them in the sand, not realizing the ever-changing tide would eventually lift them from their shallow graves.

Josianne struggled to keep up with Hélène as she climbed a small hill; they stopped when they reached the top, panting.

"It's not fair," Josianne teased, still trying to catch her breath. "Your legs are longer than mine, and I can barely keep up with you." But then she stopped talking.

As far as they could see, there was nothing but beautiful blue sky and sparkling ocean. Although the wind was worse at the top, they turned to each other in awe at the spectacle of sunshine hitting the water, so bright it was blinding.

Tired from the hike and wanting to inspect how many bloody scratches they got from the wild grasses, they sat.

"It's beautiful, actually, and big." Josianne said, shaking the hair out of her face. When she smiled at her friend because her lips were so chapped, it hurt.

"Yes, very big and very mean."

Josianne understood. "Hélène, you are tougher than the world, and I admire you."

Héléne laughed.

"No, really, I do. You organized us into groups. You found the crabs. You have even found a way for us to sleep to reduce the attacks from the rats. And I know it is hard on you that they all come to you with questions."

"Yes, but I have no answers."

"But you make them feel better. You are a resourceful, tough woman. One that I am glad to know." Josianne knew Hélène was just as frightened and worried as the rest, but she was a master at hiding her feelings.

Touched by her friends' testimony, Héléne smiled.

"Yes, so far, you are right. The world had been very mean to us." Josianne glanced up at a gorgeous shade of blue that she had never seen before in France. "But it's not over yet."

Hélène smirked, "Isn't it?" She picked at some of the grasses and gently slipped it through her fingers.

"We thought we would starve, and you found the blue crabs. You must have faith, Hélène; it will all work out."

Hélène stood up disgustedly, "I hope you are right, but it depends."

Josianne stood up as well, and they made their way down. "Depends on what?"

"If they leave us here too long, how many blue crabs we catch won't make any difference."

Josianne understood. The solitude, the darkness, and the relentless wind played tricks on everyone's sanity. And day after day, it only got worse.

The days on the Island without shelter meant no relief from the sun. All of them were sunburnt; even the part of Maélle's hair was sunburned. The salt and sand got in what was left of their clothes, aggravating their tender skin. When they tried to walk, the grass cut their legs and arms. Their lips were cracked and peeling. And all of them had the "plague of the seas" with their bleeding gums and loosening teeth.

The nights were no better, with the rats creeping towards them, nibbling on their tattered clothes. They tried taking turns at night to shoo them away, but it did not always work.

But worse than the rats was the biting cold and relentless wind. It always felt damp, even if their clothes were sun-dried during the day; when the sun disappeared into the ocean, the humidity at night was severe and they slept even closer together than when they were chained. It was a miserable existence. The wind never stopped, the drone of the ocean never stopped. Other than a scant odd bird flying by, they were alone.

Maélle thought she might have lost her mind at night if Josianne had not started to talk. At first, no one responded to Josianne's stories about her life in the house of *Monsieur* Pettelier. How wretched he had been, how hideous it had been to empty and clean his chamber pot, how the ugly son tried to feel up her skirt. But the more Josianne talked, the more they listened.

It was better than Marie Denise's stories about the spooky folklore of her grandparents in Romania. Honestly, Maélle had never heard such frightening tales featuring gruesome monsters, most of which she realized were aimed at keeping unruly children from misbehaving, yet the stories were still terrifying.

The women begged Josianne to continue her tales. Josianne talked about the rich husband she would marry, the fine house she would live in, and the pretty clothes she would wear. She spoke until everyone fell asleep, and exhausted she would curl up and close her eyes. Once she dreamed Captain de Martonne came back for her.

A day later, when Maélle first spotted a boat on the horizon, she said nothing. Fearful that her desperate eyes were playing tricks on her.

Blinking, she glanced out to the sea again. It was just getting light. It was indeed a boat. Her heart sped up in her chest.

"Hélène," she said quietly, "I see a boat."

Héléne looked to the horizon, then turned back to her friend with joy.

"They are coming back for us and did not forget us.

*Mon Dieu!*" Maélle dropped to the sand, clasped her hands, and prayed. But she gave thanks not only to God but also to Henri because he kept his promise.

"We are close enough," Henri said, jumping out of the tiny *chaloupe*. He landed knee-deep in water and began wading to shore.

The rest of the women could now see boats coming to take them to the mainland. They all hugged each other and waved.

"Henri," Maélle choked out, running towards the beach. She smacked into him, and he took her into his arms. She held on to him as a lifeline. Looking back up at his handsome face she noticed his beard was trimmed and he seemed taller than before. "I am so glad to see you," she gushed madly up to him.

There was horror on his face, aghast at how much they had changed. He glanced at the other women crowding around him now and forced a smile. "More *chaloupes* are coming. And we have water and hard crackers."

They had been thin on the boat, but they were skeletal now, and it was unnerving to see their bright eyes in the gaunt, sunburnt faces.

Maélle reached up and kissed him, then held his face in her hands. "How is Suzanne?"

She was confused when his face, "I am so sorry about this, Maélle." His eyes drifted guiltily down, "Suzanne and I are to be married."

Maélle stared up at him, then slowly let go of his face.

It was as if all the air had left the world. Maélle could not breathe, nor did she want to. Henri wanted Suzanne, Suzanne, whom she loved like a sister. It occurred to Maélle that despite all the horrors of the last few months, the humiliation of being banished from France, the hideous voyage, the inhumanity of being stranded on a desolate island with nothing but their wits to survive. The knowledge that Henri wanted Suzanne and not her, was worse than all she had endured.

# Ten

"How long did you leave them on that island?" Clément Heriot murmured to the first lieutenant from *La Mutine*. Unfortunately, Captain de Martonne had already returned to France, and Clément was disappointed because he and the captain were friends, and he enjoyed his company.

They were seated on small folding chairs under a mended tent in New Biloxi. It was the finance manager's job to record the information about the women who were temporarily housed on the Island. But he was unavailable, and the task had fallen to Clément Heriot. A man who had once been the understudy of Paris' financial minister Antoine Crozat and was now one of the colony's finance officers. A job that Clément no longer wished to be associated with when he realized the men at the top cared little for the colony. Clément believed in the new territory and was disappointed in the colony's progress.

The women brought from the Island were a hideous

sight. Cadaverous faces looked back at him. They were nearly naked, the clothes disintegrating on their bodies, caked as they were with filth, sand, and vermin.

Ironically, Clément had been looking forward to this assignment. When he first heard they were sending boats of able-bodied, marriageable women, he wanted to see them. He had dealt with the West Indies Company before and knew they were in the habit of not adequately outfitting their ships. He and Captain de Martonne agreed that the West Indies Company was dishonest and close to criminal.

"They were thin when they boarded, and I honestly did not know there were no provisions on the island," the first lieutenant said. He scanned the women, "there is one, however, that I would like to get to know better."

Ignoring him, Clément put his pen firmly against the coarse paper as the first woman approached him. "Name, age, town, and previous occupation, please," he waited then, poised to write.

"Suzanne, fourteen, Paris. I-I did not work yet."

It was the softest, loveliest voice he had ever heard, and he could not control the desire to see what creature was making the sound.

She was on the cusp of womanhood, and even clad in rags, filthy, and emaciated, it was apparent she would be gorgeous when she matured.

"Did you say *fourteen*?"

The corners of her mouth produced a dimple on one side as she nodded, completing the angelic picture. "I turned fourteen during the voyage."

"Your last name, mademoiselle?"

"I don't know it. I was at the *La Maison de St. Louis.*"

He rested his wet pen against his other hand. "The orphanage in Paris? Were you born there?" It occurred to him that things were still deteriorating in Paris.

"No, but the sisters say I was dropped off soon after."

"So, you have no idea who your parents are, and you have no surname?"

She shook her head.

He looked back down at his parchment. He understood the difficulties of life in Paris in the last few years. Paris, sadly, had lost its mind. The country was bankrupt even before John Law's outrageous schemes made Parisians crazy with mania and greed he had never seen before. But this young girl was fourteen, and her parents did not give her away because of the current turmoil in Paris. He wondered if her mother and father wept when they had to give her up.

"You will be Suzanne Martin," he scratched on the paper, giving her a common last name. Angry when he paused, a small ink blot made the S too large. "Next."

"Hélène Francois, twenty-seven, Paris. Laundress."

Glancing back up, it occurred to him that these women went from one extreme to another. Even though women were scarce in the territory, he wondered if anyone would marry this one. She was tall, skinny, and had a pointed chin. And the poor thing had a large port wine birthmark on her cheek, and if that was not bad enough, it had a nasty scar running through it. Did heaven have no *conscience*?

Clément smiled at the woman, "It will be good to have a laundress in the territory."

Hélène glared at him incensed. "I will *not* be a laundress. You think I traveled halfway across the world in chains to come here and again be the lowest of the *low*?" Her dark eyes bore a hole in his face.

He forced a smile. Not only unattractive but a shrew. No wonder the woman was twenty-seven and still unmarried. He contemplated writing "harpy" by her name to discourage any potential suitor.

"You think because by some accident of birth, that I was born poor, and you were not, I am lesser than you? I will prosper here, and my children will prosper."

With a tongue like that, he doubted she would need to worry about children. But Clément Heriot was a kind man. "*Mademoiselle*, I meant no disrespect. You are right; you are free to do as you wish." Pointedly, he looked back down at his paper, relieved when she moved away.

"Marie Louise Letellier, sixteen, Auvergne, farmer's daughter." It was still new to her speaking this French, and not her native dialect, and she was proud of how well she had done.

Clément nodded.. The line of women was long, and he dipped the pen in the inkwell as the next in line approached, wondering if this one, like the former, would have swollen, bleeding gums.

"Angélique Mandre, nineteen, Paris, a *pommes cuites au four*." Clément looked up, and it occurred to him how young and innocent these women were. He hated that France was abandoning them this way. He wondered how a Parisian bread seller would survive in a colony where little wheat was being cultivated.

Sighing, he waited for the next one in line.

"Josianne Daudessot, seventeen, Paris."

He waited for her to finish, and when she didn't, barked, "Occupation?" How daft were these young women?

Josianne twisted her fingers, "A lady's maid."

Clément Heriot glanced up with annoyance but was then dumbstruck. How was it possible that attired in rags, covered in filth, she retained her exceptional beauty? He noticed that her eyes could not decide whether to be brown or green, and her dark reddish-brown hair slipped out of its knot and cascaded down her shoulders. Her heart-shaped face was charming, and he felt a sensation in his groin and shuffled his legs to discourage it. What was the matter with him? He was more than twice her age. By God, she was only seven years older than his daughter Clara!

"This is the one," The lieutenant whispered, his eyes flicking up and down Josianne.

"Welcome to Biloxi, *mademoiselle*," Clément breathed, simply wanting to continue gazing upon something so lovely.

Josianne smiled her prettiest smile, "*Merci, monsieur*. Are there any rich men in the territory?" She remained where she was even when she knew it was time to step aside. She did not dare ask about the captain's whereabouts, worried that if she did, it would destroy her.

Clément shook his head, "Not many *mademoiselle*, but you will find ample suitors, no doubt."

She breathed in deeply, which made her breasts swell

against her bodice, forcing him to drop his gaze and clear his throat.

"*Monsieur*, do you know any rich men? Because I would like to make their acquaintance."

He sat back in the folding chair. "Surely, *mademoiselle*, you will find an adequate young man in the colony." As much as he did not want to, he motioned for her to move along.

"Are you rich?"

The lieutenant smirked, "*mademoiselle*, you are speaking with a *Monsieur* Clément Heriot. He is the comptroller on the Island here." But when the word made no impression on Josianne, he continued, "He is one of the richest men in the colonies, and he has a vision for a city west of here. A city he will build with tobacco money and rule, no doubt."

Clément turned to the lieutenant, "I've told everyone that tobacco is not suited to this climate. It will be a fool's errand to try and grow it. Tobacco needs dry, not *submerged* land. But the territory has other bounties."

The lieutenant grinned and nodded toward Josianne, looking as ripe as a peach in late June.

"Oh, I suppose you are married, *monsieur*," her disappointment evident.

"I am widowed." He noticed her hazel eyes had flecks of gold, and her lashes were exceptionally long.

"I am sorry *monsieur*. I am sure you miss her very much." Her condolence struck him as sincere. It was the first time anyone had mentioned Monique to him in a long time. Even though life was hard in the colony, and no one had time to dwell on misfortune, he still missed

Monique and had no one to share his grief with. He did not want to burden his daughters with his sadness. Besides, he feared his daughters had more of his departed wife's delicate constitution. A constitution not well suited to the wild, untamed world, and he worried about them incessantly.

"*Oui,*" he tried to continue, but a lump formed in his throat because this young woman was consoling him in a way he hadn't realized he craved.

"How long has she been gone?"

"Two years." He spent two long, agonizing years trying to keep his business running, keep Governor Jean Baptiste Le Moyne de Bienville and the settlers happy, and keep his daughters from despair.

"And you have children?"

"*Oui*, Clara is ten, and Celeste is twelve."

Her pretty face clouded. "They must miss their mother. I, too, lost a mother at a young age. It is not good for daughters to be without a mother. You should marry again and soon."

She shocked him by touching his hand. Their eyes met.

"*Mademoiselle* Daudessot, my apologies. We must move along now." He was flustered and wished she would take her hand off his.

She smiled sweetly at him, "Please call me Josianne."

Clément looked down at his paper, knowing she would not last long in the territory, and was jealous of the man that would win her.

# Eleven

M aélle pulled her arms tighter around her as she and the other women lumbered to the Old Biloxi Fort of Maurepas barracks, studying the land that would be her new home. She stared at the odd trees with the eerie moss in their branches nicknamed 'Capuchin's beard.' The moss waved in the wind, trapped as it was in the leafless branches of the trees. And unfortunately, some of the trees were also spookily twisted like they had been on the Island. Walking past them, she made the sign of the cross and recited two *Our Father's* just in case.

There was not much to New Biloxi, which had been designed as a military outpost and not equipped to deal with the masses of immigrants that kept landing on her shores. The soldiers had at least felled some trees and constructed crude housing with the bark still intact, acting as shingles. But they had only cleared enough land for soldiers, including a pavilion for officer barracks, quarters for the commander, and a storehouse to protect what food and supplies they had from the elements. When Maélle realized there was no settlement, her hopes sunk even further, knowing that making pretty clothes would be impractical in this strange new world.

She kept wondering if she had heard Henri correctly, his mention of marrying Suzanne still echoing inconceivably in her head. She would have to talk to Suzanne.

The landscape was a tangled mess. The unruly rushes, canebrakes, and palmettos were so dense she realized it would take a herculean effort to clear the land for planting. She always thought farming a noble pursuit, but because it depended on the weather and God's good or bad graces, never wanted anything to do with it. Looking at the untamed wilderness, with vines threaded through the mess she could not imagine anyone farming there.

Closer to the beach now, the howl of the wind stole her breath away. The water lapping at the shore was brown, not the deep shades of blue she had seen during the voyage.

The place they got ready to spend the night in was a building constructed of posts, logs, and palmetto fans. It looked like a strong wind might level it. It was an improvement over the straw on the floor of La *Mutine* and far superior to the elements of the Island. After a meal of strange yellow bread and fish soup, Maélle got ready to sleep.

Suzanne put her arms around her friend. "I am so glad you are my friend Maélle. I am so sorry you had to be on that Island."

Maélle hugged her back, noticing Suzanne had

already claimed the spot next to her. Again Maélle wondered if Henri had spoken out of turn.

"Have you found your husband yet?" Suzanne asked, having to stifle a yawn so big and childlike that Maélle's heart warmed.

"No, of course not. We just got here." So far, Maélle was not impressed with the strange foliage, the murky brown water lapping at the shore, ironically missing the deep green-blue water she'd stared at for weeks. "And you should not either, Suzanne; you should not make your decision to marry so hastily. What is this about you marrying Henri?"

Suzanne continued as if Maélle had not spoken. "When we get married, we will build cottages next door, bake our bread, wash, and raise our children together."

"I've barely seen a tree large enough to cut down for wood, much less make a house," Maélle smirked and glanced up at the palmetto roof, realizing that it did help stop the wind, but if heavy rain came, they could get wet. "Maybe when we go to the bigger town, there will be some shelters, stores, or town. Something other than this, wilderness." Maélle stopped then, realizing Suzanne had fallen asleep.

Maélle emptied a water bucket the next day when she saw Henri enter Governor Bienville's office. Although she knew she should not, she crept to the doorway and listened.

"What brings you here, Henri?"

"*Bonjour* governor, I'm here to ask one of the girls to marry me, Suzanne."

The governor rolled out the precious paperwork that Clément Heriot had carefully written up.

"*Which* Suzanne, we have three."

"Suzanne Martin. That was a name she was assigned."

"Ah... the young Suzanne," Governor Bienville said, his bony fingers touching the medallion around his neck.

"She turned fourteen on the voyage," Henri added, although her age embarrassed him.

"And Suzanne, why is she not with you to make her acceptance known?"

"I-I am not sure; she said she would be here this morning." He looked towards the door, expecting Suzanne to appear, but it was Maélle that did.

"Ah, good Suzanne," the governor exclaimed. This was the first man asking for a bride, and the governor was glad to be getting the process started. He hoped to have them all married and settling the land in six months. The sooner they were married and off his hands, the less he had to worry about feeding them.

"I'm not Suzanne," turning to Henri, Maélle whispered, "You should be ashamed of yourself," Maélle said under her breath, noticing that the governor uninterested had gone back to his list.

Henri's tortured eyes met hers, "I have no choice."

"What do you mean you have no choice? You're an adult. She's a *child*."

"Maélle?" At the sound of Suzanne's voice, Maélle and Henri turned to see her standing in the doorway.

Maélle had carefully finger combed her long blonde hair only this morning. As it fell across Suzanne's shoulders it made her more angelic than ever.

Going to her, Maélle took her by the hands. "Suzanne, you barely *know* him. How can you get married already? You are still a child."

Suzanne stared at her, "I'm not a *child*, Maélle." Her worried eyes turned to Henri: "Have you changed your mind?"

Guiltily, Henri's eyes dropped to the floor. "No."

"If there are no more impediments, we can proceed with the marriage this afternoon."

"This preposterous. She's a child, and you are a grown man with nothing to offer her!" Maélle burst out.

"Maélle, please—" Henri began.

Maélle ignoring him, directed her words to the Governor. "Can you condone this Governor, marrying this young girl off to a man none of us knows anything about?"

"What sort of work do you do?" the governor asked suddenly.

Offended, Henri spoke. "I was sent as the assistant to the chief engineer for the colony. And I have been promised a cottage in the new city west of here, and we will be moving there." Henri handed the papers to the governor.

"This *cannot* be!" Maélle spat.

"*Mademoiselle*, this is not France; we are lucky to have a leaking bulrush roof over our head and shoes on our feet." He glanced down at Maélle's bare feet. "Survival is of the utmost importance. We do not have the luxury of posting banns and genteel sensibilities. If I am not mistaken, you have crossed a perilous ocean to make a new life for yourself?"

Maélle lifted her shoulders indignantly knowing she had made no such choice, but said nothing.

"This is not your concern," Suzanne announced again, angry that Maélle and the governor were deciding her fate as if she was not standing before them.

"If I am not mistaken, that is why all of you made this trip, is it not?" Governor Bienville smirked.

"Can we just...wait a few *months* before we marry this girl to a man we know little about?" Maélle implored weakly.

"*Mademoiselle*, you make excellent arguments," thinking that if the world were different, she would have made a good *advocate*.

He sat back in the chair, hoping Henri was not one of the salt smugglers or galley slaves that loitered about the colony. Again, it was not his responsibility who they married, but simply *that* they married.

Angry with all of them for ignoring her, Suzanne spoke up with a conviction that surprised them. "Governor, I am ready to be married now. I chose Henri. I understood that I can make these decisions since I am no longer in France." She neared Henri and took hold of his hand. "And besides, I am pregnant."

"*Suzanne*!" Maélle screeched, whipping around to stare at Henri, whose eyes were on the floor.

"Then we should proceed without delay," the governor said, looking back down at his papers. He was glad they got the matter settled.

Silently, Maélle backed out the door, pressing her spine painfully against the wall, wishing she could simply disappear into it, as painful tears flooded her eyes. Not only was her precious Suzanne moving away, but what Maélle wanted with Henri was never to be. Clamping a hand over her mouth, she darted away, humiliated.

Angélique was the next to be married in New Biloxi. On a Tuesday, she met a soldier named Jean Pierre. They decided to marry the following Friday, and on Wednesday, they stood in the square to be wed. There was no priest to marry them, so instead, she had Maélle and Josianne stand up as witnesses.

It was essential to Angélique and the six other women who were married that first month to ensure their marriages were legal and that their children would be legitimate. The only way for them to do this was to ensure they had witnesses. The French government and the Catholic church, knowing that they neglected to supply the colony with priests, paper, or ink, deemed the 'witnessed' marriages legitimate.

Despite the crudeness of the surroundings when fifteen of the girls had been married, the settlers decided to have a town party under the direction of Josianne, who convinced Governor Bienville to have the celebration. It was early twilight, and the sky was lit by a gorgeous display of dying purple, blue and coral lights. There were no refreshments, but two men in the village made music well enough for the bedraggled inhabitants to have a bit of fun.

Josianne had found no one more prosperous in the territory than the man who had taken their names, Clément Heriot. And with her face, hair, and clothes washed, she made her move.

Standing beside him, she gently touched him on the arm. "We are going to dance now, come *Monsieur* Heriot."

Clément knew he should politely decline. Besides, how ridiculous did a man of his age look dancing with a girl like Josianne. But her soft, round face was tilted up at him, her brown hair stuffed under her cap looked full, and he imagined it tumbling down to her waist. Before he knew it, she led him to the dusty ground where two pitiful sailors played their fiddles.

"Have you been in the colony long?"

Looking down at her, he realized her eyes would change from hazel to green. "I came as a much younger man. And I have been back and forth a few times, " he said, trying to impart how old he was, although he feared his graying and thinning hair would be a testament to that.

"And you are happy here. Is it a good place?"

A smile lit up his face. "It is different than France. I came here as an understudy with *Monsieur* Crozat," Clément decided not to use the man's notorious nick-name, *Crozat the Rich*, "He was a financier of King Louis XIV. Through the benevolence of the almighty, I have been able to provide well for my family. I believe in this colony, and I want it to succeed. It truly is *L' Esperance de Mississippi,* but it needs people. And you *mademoiselle?"*

"I am an orphan. I became a lady's maid, and after that I lived at the Hospital *General de La Salpêtrière."*

"And how was that for you?"

Josianne shrugged. "It is not a good place. We worked there all day, every day. Cleaning, spinning, weaving, sewing, or embroidering-there was no talking at all. That was hard for me. They told us hard work was necessary because we needed to repent. That we needed to choose virtuous, productive lives." Josianne sighed quietly, feeling like she always did, that she had done nothing wrong. The husband of the house had been after her, *not* the other way around.

Clément laughed, enjoying the feel of the lithe young woman in his arms. Already deciding that when the dance was over, he would make sure and leave her to one of the many suitable young men that were no doubt, cursing him for monopolizing her time.

"The worst was that the women in charge read from the bible to us all day long, *every* day. I mean, I love the Lord, but don't you think he approved of a little break occasionally?"

Clément chuckled, agreeing with her.

"And the 'sisters' at the hospital are not even Catholic nuns, but rather women who got room and board for life. And they wore those awful habits and cut their hair short. They were bitter and mean and enjoyed doling out punishments for the littlest of things. Can you imagine *wanting* to hurt others?"

He could imagine someone as beautiful and vibrant as Josianne being positively stifled in a harsh environment like that, yet she appeared incredibly untarnished by the ordeal.

She smiled up at Clément, "Which is why I am so glad to be here with you."

Clément wondered if his ears were playing tricks on him.

Unable to think of anything to say, he asked "how was your voyage?" Noticing her hand fit neatly into his own.

Wrinkles formed on her forehead. "I had never seen a ship so big, and even though there were three levels, we were to stay at the bottom. But the sea was huge, some days it was beautiful, some days frightening, some days boring." She didn't want to talk about the squalor, the stench, hunger, and desperation. As for Captain de Martonne, she promised herself to *never* think of him again.

The fiddlers stopped and Clément dropped is hands from hers, not sure what to do suddenly. He thought about what brought this young woman to the Louisiana territory that he and Antoine Crozat had been responsible for colonizing, and so far, was proving to be a daunting task. At first Crozat suggested they send prisoners and criminals to the new land. The cost of supporting the criminals was weighty on the Kings treasury and sending them killed two birds with one stone. But it had not worked out. There was a scarcity of ships, which caused the men bound for Louisiana to be incarcerated for a year in the dank prisons in Lorient. The few that survived were further weakened by the voyage. At the end of the ordeal the sick men that finally staggered off the ships did little to grow the population.

It was Governor Bienville who later appealed to the counsel in Paris, saying that sending criminals, was impractical, and begged they send no more vagrants, and only those that chose to come and stay in the colony. It was indirectly from this appeal that *Madame* Pacletain hatched her plan, and why Josianne stood before him now.

"And how did you make your fortune, *Monsieur*? Were you born to it?"

It was a forward question, but he was proud of his successes. "I inherited some of it in France, then was granted land by the regent *Duc D' Orleans.* Tobacco is a cash crop, and it was thought to grow here in the sandy soil." He shook his head thinking of the money the blunder cost him, "But the quality was inferior and if not dried properly it also spoils on the way."

She waited, watching him.

"Then there is salt. And I started with one ship, then bought two more. I do pay the king his taxes though," he said wryly, knowing how many *faux sauniers* were sent to the galleys for that very thing. He left out that the taxes levied on the rich were *lower* than lesser men had to pay.

"*Free* land?" It was a concept unheard of to her. In France, the aristocracy owned all the land. "How did you get land?"

"It is very...muddled here. What we have decided to do is if one is to get a petition requesting a lot, and vow to clear it, and build upon it, it would be yours. So I signed petitions, cleared more land, and acquired more. Or rather, I paid men to do it." He thought of the Africans that came, the soldiers that France had not paid in months. Both groups were starving. Although he did not believe in charity, he had fed and housed them while they cleared the land. He had even given them lines of credit at the only warehouse in town, where on his good name, they got supplies and could make, if they chose to, a life for themselves.

"Where is this land?"

"In the territory just west of here, and I am hoping that someday perhaps I can make it the capitol city, although there are those that want to keep it where it is now in Biloxi."

"And you live in a grand house?"

He thought of his house on the arpents of land set back from the delta. But he slept easier at night knowing that his daughters slept in a home that was bolted with a four-inch hardwood door.

"No," He wondered if this young girl had been fed romantic notions about life here. He thought of the black and white pamphlets the West Indies Company made up. A leaflet touting the richness of the soil, the land grants for any soul hearty enough to clear it. How it showed well-kept houses, workers toiling with tools in front of their neat, shingled houses. It was a fallacy.

"But it is *yours*," she said, leaning near him and again surprising him by touching him. "It is a place you can keep; it is not a place that houses hundreds of people. I would like to see it *monsieur*."

This shook him. "Why on earth would you want to see it?"

"I want to see if I want to live there." The song ended and they both clapped politely. She looked at him, "Do you think I am pretty?"

Clément had to swallow hard, perspiring in his suit. Ah this was it, she wanted money for favors, or something equally distasteful. It was rumored that all these women coming on these boats were prostitutes, which was why France was so ready to be rid of them. But he would play along with her game, "Yes of course."

"I like you." She smiled sweetly, "Shall we get married then?"

He couldn't have been more shocked if she had slapped him.

"*Marry you*? Why, I'm an old man, *mademoiselle*." He looked around at all the younger, more suitable men, "There are several other choices."

"I know that, but I don't want them. I would like to marry you."

Clément laughed and rubbed his face with his hand, waiting for her to give up the ruse.

"Surely you are...*joking*, my dear. I am old enough to be your father."

Josianne shrugged her shoulders, "Maybe you are, maybe you are not. I never knew my father. How am I to know how old he was when I was born?"

"*Mademoiselle*, I am sure you can ply your trade with someone else."

He saw her nostrils flare, saw indignation color her cheeks. "I am *not* a debauched woman *monsieur*. There was a woman at *La Salpêtrière, Madame* Pacletain. *She* listed *all of us* as debauched women. Simple girls, flower sellers, bread sellers, a lady's maid such as myself. It is *she* who is a *debauched* woman. A woman who hated her own kind and conspired to hurt them." He watched her work to visibly calm herself. When she regained her composure, she smiled at him. "I forgive you for your ignorance if you promise never to say such a thing again."

He laughed nervously, still expecting her to give up the ruse.

"You want to be married?" she implored, looking up at him.

In truth, he had never thought of re-marrying. Monique's death had left a hole in his heart. When he thought of her, he was overcome with guilt because she never wanted to come to the territory, and her delicate constitution should have warned him she would not survive. The summer she contracted the illness and died, he realized it had all been his fault.

Holding his hand, she stroked his palm with her fingertips, "A man needs a woman. Someone to talk and sort out life's woes."

It occurred to him that even given her young age, she knew intimately of life's woes.

"I will be your partner, and your daughters need a mother. Let me mother them."

It was uncanny how she keyed in directly to the deficiencies in his life. It made him wonder if he was underestimating her intelligence.

Regaining his senses, he pulled his hand away. "It seems to me *mademoiselle*, you are only talking to me because of my wealth, certainly, these other young men are more to your liking."

She shrugged, "That may be true, but I want a rich husband. I will not lie. Is it any worse than a man wanting a beautiful wife? Would you be talking to me if I were not young and beautiful?"

As the question hung in the air, Clément found he could not contradict her.

"Make me your wife, I promise you will not regret it."

It was madness, but also tempting. He had acquaintances, and business associates, but no one to sit with around the fire at night and simply talk. Then he imagined going into his bedroom with her, and flushed purple.

"This is absurd." He said finally, looking around for someone to rescue him from the quicksand he was falling into.

"First, I am a prostitute now I am *absurd*?" The indignation made her voice raise, and people turned.

"No, no, not at all." He smiled nervously, thinking it was time to put a stop to this inane predicament. "*Mademoiselle*," he began, "You are a silly young girl, who has romantic notions about love and marriage."

Her eyebrows rose in irritation. "Really? I am a *silly* young woman who was orphaned, who worked eighteen hours a day, who got a bit of bread and a tiny piece of a herring once a week. A silly young girl who had to fight off the disgusting advances by the husband of the house, then the son, and suffer the wrath of the jealous wife. A silly young girl who was chained at the waist for months on a flea and lice-ridden boat, and left on a barren island to starve. I am *silly*? Do you think I have *romantic* notions? I want a rich husband. I find you pleasant. And no doubt, because I will be good to you, *you* will fall in love *with me*. And I will mother your daughters Clara and Celeste, and they will call me *Maman,* and come to love me. And if you want more children, I will give them to you. And do not underestimate how valuable a good hostess could be for your business. You will build a grand house, and we will all live there. And if they do place the capitol to the territory west of here, you can influence them and see that they do it right. Through all of this, I will be your ally." She had already decided they would wait till the warmth of spring to be wed.

He was speechless, all the moisture gone from his mouth.

# Twelve

Hélène was not surprised she was still single; she always knew she would be the last to be married if she ever did. In her most private moments, she did wish to marry and have children but was careful no one suspected it. If she were going to survive in this unforgiving world, she would have to be tough.

And if marriage was not in her future, she did, however, need to find a way to survive. Both she and Maélle had been moved from New Biloxi for the other territory to the west. There was no shortage a new brides showing up in New Biloxi and there was a subtle pressure from the governor that these "leftovers" move on. Besides, it was where Suzanne and Henri had gone and where Josianne and Clément were going to go after they married.

The only job Hélène could find was to help the warehouse owner count and keep inventory of what little provisions they had. Although Hélène's reading was questionable, numbers made sense to her, especially when they had money attached to them. He had no money to pay her, but he gave her food and allowed her to sleep there.

Although Hélène vowed she would never do laundry again, the shopkeeping job was not enough to support her. Besides, it was a way to make herself valuable to the struggling settlement and earn at least enough to keep the hunger from possessing her every waking moment. That along with her work at the storeroom was keeping her fed and housed, at least for now.

It was late in the afternoon, and she knew she should not tarry long at the beach, but enjoyed wandering along the desolate shoreline. There was something about seeing that quiet, barren beach that made her feel not so alone. It was curious, on the Island she felt the desolate beach had been a torment, but now, it offered a bittersweet solace.

She stared at the water and watched as a wave crested the beach and saw the stain in the sand of the wave before it, and it occurred to her that the ocean was constantly changing, and that no two waves were identical. Curiously, she glanced out to the sea again. The rolling of the waves was both monotonous and yet spontaneous. It could lull her into a kind of trance or be exciting. She realized the sea had been putting on this show for centuries. And that the people of the Bible must have stood dumbstruck, as she was, at its entrance.

The April wind was warm and blew her plaited hair into her eyes. She shook the strands from her face and glanced up at the birds.

She had not seen many birds in her life, and never seabirds. Astonishing to her that they could fly magically for minutes without flapping their wings caught on some invisible current of air. Worried she held her breath until at last, they flapped their wings. She saw white, yellow billed birds diving into the sea gulping down a fish. Feeling paradoxically triumph for the bird, and sadness for the fish that would be swallowed whole. She noticed other gray birds skimming the water, so close to the waves as if to touch them.

She stopped walking to watch the tiny gray birds that skittered along the beach. They ran across the sand toward the surf when a wave receded. Making good their seconds to see what bubbles rose, exposing what critters they could devour. They ran so fast on tiny legs, her laughter bubbled up.

"Are you laughing at the sea?" A man's voice said behind her.

Turning, Hélène saw a rough fisherman. "I don't know, I guess so. At the little birds."

"Sandpipers?"

"I suppose so." She had trouble repressing a smile when the birds repeated their antics on tiny legs. She braced herself for the wind that blew so hard it sometimes made her eyes tear.

"They are deceivingly fast, and more often than not, they find a meal." He kept his bright blue eyes on her longer than was polite. Hélène was not so vain to think he fancied her but he did seem interested.

Birds cawing drew their attention. Two white and

gray birds were fighting in flight, pecking, and shrieking at each other.

"Gulls, they are hell when you are cleaning your fish on the dock," he said shaking his head. "Pests of the ocean,"

She looked at the birds skimming the water, that then dove into the sea, surprised at the splash the large birds made. "Don't their wings get wet?"

"They do, but are covered with oil and dry off quickly. And if you watch them, they fly *into* the wind."

"Wouldn't that just slow them down?"

"No, they can maintain their speed and hold flight while they look for fish." They both laughed when, as if the birds hearing him, demonstrated his words. Leaning near her, he pointed. "Look out there, where those birds have gathered, they've spotted a school of fish. Just waiting now for a straggler to wander too far."

Seeing it in the distance, she smiled.

"There's a storm out." He turned his face to the wind. The gale blowing his black hair straight back. His face was lined even though he did not look old. Although his face was tanned, there were white marks in the crinkles around his eyes, forehead, and mouth. In the afternoon light, it was difficult to tell his pupils from the iris. "Do you see it?" he asked, "That green haze there, it's raining out in the ocean, and no doubt headed this way."

It was a marvel, she thought, that one could be standing in the dappled sunlight and see it raining in the distance.

"A pelican." He pointed to one of the birds she had

seen earlier, the ones that swallowed their catch in a single bite. "If only I could fish that well."

She was surprised to see the tenderness in his eyes when he smiled.

He picked up a stick and began drawing elaborate swirls in the sand. "What's your name? I've seen you a few times before but don't know what to call you."

"Hélène."

He nodded as if finding the name acceptable. "I am Michel Clavier, Mickey. You are from Paris?"

She nodded.

"What part?" He asked, still drawing in the sand.

" *La Salpêtrìere,* the prison that pretends to be a hospital. "

He smirked, "No *mademoiselle, bicêtre* is a prison."

She looked up at him, hoping her face did not betray the uneasiness she felt.

"*Oui, mademoiselle* I am a convict."

"A murderer I suppose?" She challenged.

He laughed, "you think highly of me." He hurled the stick into the ocean. He was tall, his torso thick and the muscles in his arms flexed. If there hadn't been a hardness and danger about him, he might have been handsome. "No, not a murderer. Nothing but a lowly *faux-saunier.* "

She tried to tame her tongue but could not. "You *knew* better, why did you do it, why did you not pay the king the taxes for his salt? I did nothing *wrong* and I had been incarcerated, and you *willingly* broke the law!"

His eyes narrowed, and then he glanced back out to the sea and the approaching storm. "Our king wanted too much of the profit. There's barely enough to go around after everyone is paid. I do all the work, I take all the risk, and then the king is there with his gilded hand out wanting a payoff too. I've had too many setbacks to let a greedy king take that for which I have broken my back. Besides, the *gabelle* was twenty times higher in Paris. And yet, the *rich* who deal in salt do not have to pay the taxes at all."

She didn't know much about these things, only knew the whispered remarks people made about these dangerous and unscrupulous men. She glanced out at the ever-stretching sea, watching the slow waves seeping up to the shore. "How long were you in prison?"

"Not long. A king must feed and house a prisoner. Why not make them earn their keep in the galleys rowing?" His life sentence had been commuted to rowing. "I was chained together with other men. We made the trek on foot, from Paris to the southern port of Marseille."

When she did not react, it occurred to him that she had no idea how large France was. "That is a distance of over four hundred miles. More than half died."

"What were the galleys like?" she asked, wondering if it was as hard as *La Salpêtrière*. Besides the only ship she had ever seen had been *La Mutine*.

A sort of pall came over him, and Hélène wished suddenly she had not asked.

Reaching out he touched her shoulders, pushing her firmly into the sand.

"Do not move. This is your space. Where you sit and row, day after day, year after year. Where your legs cramp and your hands blister and bleed, where your back aches until you think it will break in two. Where you eat, sleep, piss, and shit. There are five of you on the line, you row every 3 seconds. When the chained man next to you dies, a sailor comes over and throws him overboard." He let go of her, finally. "And die they did. Most men don't make it more than four years."

Mesmerized by the tale she asked, "how long were you there?"

"Six years." There was a sort of macabre pride in his voice.

Hélène had to swallow hard.

"You like the sea?" He asked changing the subject, hoping he hadn't frightened her.

Hélène nodded, "I'd never seen it before in France. Then I was on *La Mutine* for three months and saw nothing *but* it. It's different here though, the water is...strange."

"That's because it is not only sea water that you gaze at, but the Mississippi river that flows into it bringing mud along. Have you ever tasted it?"

She shook her head, never having contemplated doing such a thing. He dipped his meaty hand into the water.

"We don't drink it but taste it." He gently put his dripping hand to her lips. It was an odd, intimate thing for him to do.

It was not salty like the ocean, nor did it taste like mud.

"Not salt water or fresh water but both, brackish. Until you get farther out, and the ocean swallows up the river and they become one. And the shelf here, it goes on for a long, long ways, you can walk for ages until it gets deep, until the depth is... unfathomable."

She stared at his profile at how he studied the sea. It was exhilarating.

A flash of white lightning zig-zagged across the sky, followed by an ear-splitting crack of thunder.

"We better run. It's going to soak us." He put a heavy arm around her shoulders and ran away from the beach to the cover of scruffy trees and bushes that tried to anchor the sandy soil from the merciless wind.

Despite their sprint the rain pelted them and within seconds they were wet.

He hauled her in after him to a shelter under the trees and branches. She felt her dress and sand sticking to her as she crawled in after him. It was surprisingly dry underneath the brush, damp, and warm. They were leaning against a particularly twisted tree, and she could feel her spine against its gnarled trunk.

Another clap of thunder exploded her eardrums, and she buried her head against his shoulder. She could smell the dampness of their clothes and his earthy scent stirred up by the humidity. His shoulders and knees were touching hers as they huddled watching the storm.

She turned to him.

Rain collected in her eyebrows and because she had sand on her palms, he brushed the raindrops from her face. Smiling, he said, "This won't last long. It's just a spring shower. It's come from the west, but it will run out of fury."

The lightening continued to dart across the sky, bringing with it the inevitable thunder. The previously calm ocean's waves were wild now, and the color turned to murky green with waves of bubbly foam crashing onto the beach.

She thought about the birds suddenly and hoped they had roosted somewhere and were safe from the storm.

"Here," he said, handing her a round pale object as big as a grape. As she rolled it between her thumb and forefinger, noticed the iridescent colors, and small ridges. Although the surface was shiny, it was not reflective.

"What is it?"

"It's a pearl. I found it in an oyster a few days ago. To some, they are precious."

"How pretty. Do all oysters do that?"

"No, only if a bit of sand gets in forming an irritant," he grinned.

She thought about how Maélle spent hours sewing on sequins and other embellishments. Hélène wondered what she could do with the pearl. There were people she realized in the world that desired such extravagances and had money to pay for them.

He looked down at the pearl in her hand, and shrugged, "I don't really know what they are good for."

"Isn't being beautiful enough?" She thought of Josianne suddenly and smiled.

"I suppose it is," He paused, then added, "All your friends have... married?"

"No, not all."

"You don't.... *want* to marry?" He asked, and brushed the hair from her face, tucking it behind her ear.

Surprised by his familiarity, she pulled back.

Although she was strong, sometimes she wished she could be vulnerable like Suzanne and have someone else take care of her. It would be a relief to at least shoulder the worries with someone. She wondered then, why did she pull back when someone touched her.

"I suppose I will have to." She focused out at the storm.

He laughed and glanced away from her as if he were embarrassed suddenly.

"You are a fisherman?"

He shook his head, "Not anymore. I am a *voyageur.*"

"I don't know what that is."

"I fish and trade the waters of the upper Mississippi. The bayous, the streams that feed into it."

"How do you know if they...connect?"

"Trust me. They all do *not.* And there are hundreds of them. It takes a certain skill not only to navigate the ever-changing waters, but dealing with the swamps, mosquitoes, the alligators, which is mild compared to dealing with the people I encounter."

"People?"

He nodded. "I trade with the Choctaws and other indigenous tribes even the Spanish that have settled up north near Pensacola."

Her brow creased, "but there is so little in the territory, how can you make a living doing it? What do you sell?"

"Beaver pelts, deerskins, rum, bear oil. Anything I think I can make a profit off."

"I am sure you do," she said under her breath. She felt the damp sand seeping into her clothes and wanted to get away. She would have to find a husband, but decided she was not so desperate as to associate with an ex-galley slave, who was obviously not above stealing in his occupation.

As if he read her thoughts, he asked, "are you accusing me of cheating my clients?"

Hélène felt the color burning her cheeks, knowing that soon her whole face would be as red as her birthmark.

"To tell you the truth, I can't cheat or steal. The only protection I have out there is my reputation. If I am not a man of my word, I might as well turn over my own pirogue and let the alligators eat me."

He had meant it as a joke, but Hélène shivered. She had heard about the hideous beasts and never wanted to encounter one. "Have you seen an alligator?"

He nodded, "lots of times. And if you leave them alone, they will return the favor. Just don't bother them in the spring when they are trying to mate. It is a spooky noise to hear them bellowing, trying to attract a female. They will fight for her too." He thought about adding that he'd seen older alligators missing an eye or even a leg because of their fights, but thought better of it.

He was sifting the sand through his fingers, "besides, it is a whole new world here. And I lived another life." His voice trailed off. "And I know I do not want that life anymore. Not for my sons."

"Are you married?"

"Not yet." He answered.

"It sounds like a difficult life being a *voyageur*." She

remembered now, she had heard about these men, they were gone weeks at a time.

Mickey shrugged, "what is not difficult here or in France? Besides, without us *voyageurs*, life in the settlement here would stop. Crozat the Rich and the rest of his crooked friends don't send the boats with supplies regularly." It was rumored that Crozat was levying a 300 percent markup, further burdening the already faltering economy.

"Why don't they send the boats?"

"Greed, indifference. We are misfits of France, an afterthought."

"Then it's good you are here." Without knowing why, she smiled at him.

"I suppose." Even Mickey did not know how the entire settlement depended on the travelers to keep the faltering economy from failing. "I'll be leaving soon."

She was disappointed. She didn't often have conversations with men, and this one was turning out to be oddly pleasant.

He leaned near, "perhaps you will miss me, wait for me."

"Wait for you for what?"

Mickey looked at her and shrugged, "I did without a woman for more than six years of my life. And I would like to share my bed again, share a meal, make a home for a child. I am hoping to make a new start."

She was confused, "Why would *I* wait for you?"

"We are both misfits. Perhaps we could make a go of it." He pulled her to him, and kissed her. His lips were chapped, and she could taste the onions from a meal.

"Mickey, don't--"

"Why not? You want it, I want it. We can get married before I go." He found her mouth again.

Her hands were on the damp front of his shirt and pushed him away. Awkwardly she stood up thrusting the pearl into her pocket.

Just like he prophesized, the rain let up, and the beach was once again bathed in sunlight as steam rose from the wet sand. Scrambling from behind the damp undergrowth, she walked away from him, kicking up wet sand behind her.

"Hélène wait, please." Following her out, he met her on the damp beach. She looked pitiful with her hair plastered against her face and nose running. Not knowing how self-conscious she was, he tried to touch the birthmark, but she batted his hand away. "Where are you going in such a rush? I'll walk back with you."

"No, it's fine, I can find my way." But the wet sand slowed her down.

He quickly caught up to her, "Can we... talk again?"

"*Talk* with me?" Stopping she faced him. "Because I'm ugly you think I'm desperate. You think I could do no better than a stinking fisherman who's a convict? I'll make my own way."

Anger bubbled up in him like soup on an open fire, "You can do *better* Hélène, really? We are both *misfits,* even in this new world we are. I thought we could make a life together. Do you have any other *prospects*?"

Embarrassed, she had to look down.

"And while we are at it Hélène, you are no prize either."

Instinctively her hand went to cover her cheek, some-thing she had done her entire life. "That's a *despicable* thing to say." Tears burned her eyes. How she hated that birthmark.

He reached out and touched the birthmark, "*This* is not your problem Hélène," He grabbed her chin then and forced her to look up, "Your *damn* mouth is!"

He left her alone on the beach.

## Thirteen

On the first day of May Josianne and Clément were married. She insisted Clément use the back of a receipt to record the marriage. Because she could neither read nor write, signed it with a mark, and seeing her husband sign his name with ease, made her eager to learn.

Josianne's feet were tucked neatly underneath her skirts, and her wedding bouquet of pink willow herb and yellow buttercups was clasped tightly in her hands as they rode down the narrow, rutted path towards the house.

She had shoes on, the first shoes she had worn in months, and delightedly wiggled her toes inside the soft leather. She had no idea how he had finagled it, seeing how everyone in the territory was struggling getting even the barest of necessities, but she was thrilled to have them.

She had never been this far from the shore and noticed how thick, tangled, and green the foliage was. The air was heavy and because she was nervous, felt lines of perspiration trickling between her breasts and down her spine.

The horse was plodding slowly along as the unruly vines and branches scraped along the side of the wagon. Several times, she had to untether a wayward branch that snatched at her clothing. As if the forest was reaching out greedy green fingers to grasp her, reminding her of the eerie tales Marie Denise told on the Island.

There were things blossoming in the woods as they drove along. Purple clasping bellflowers that were attracting small butterflies, as well as yellow centered white daisies, and they must have crushed a variety of mint as they drove along, because she could smell the pungent aroma.

Clément was silent as he guided the horse, and she knew he was worried what his daughters were going to think. When he proposed, he was nervous and had a coughing attack followed by a hiccupping fit. Neither of which would stop till Josianne made him sit down and drink a glass of water.

Josianne swatted at a mosquito that landed on her face and seeing blood on her hands wondered what her face would look like when they finally reached the house. She wiped the dead mosquito against her skirt, and was careful not to stain her clothing.

"You are quiet husband," Josianne said looking at her groom.

He was dressed in the same coat she had first seen him in. His knee-high leather boots were old, but polished. Hélène had laundered his white shirt, but it was thin due to multiple washings. She wondered if the tightness around his throat was choking him because his face was flushed.

Clément tried to think of something to say. He could not even turn and look at the lovely young woman beside him, and wondered what madness had possessed him to marry her.

"Is it much longer?" she asked, eager to get to her new home and meet her stepdaughters.

"No, not much longer."

"Tell me about this man, John Law," she asked suddenly.

Clément turned to her skeptically, "My dear, I am sure you do not want to hear the complicated tale. I am afraid it would bore you."

"Does it bore you?"

"No, but I am much older and more...*acquainted* with such things."

"Are you saying I am too young to understand or too female?"

He laughed lightly under his breath. His new wife was proving to be more of a handful than he thought. "Neither."

"Is John Law a good man?"

He caught himself before he laughed again, thinking it was not so easy to say simply if a man was good or not, but then wondered if he was wrong. Perhaps it was that simple.

"Depends upon who you ask, I suppose. All right, I'll tell you what I know. There was an explorer by the name of La Salle that came four decades ago now to this Mississippi territory. He claimed the entire region for Louis

XIV. When France was in trouble financially after the Kings death, Law came along and convinced the French regent *Philippe, Duc d'Orleans* that this territory would be France's salvation. Law acquired stocks of other companies and was a master promoter. He renamed the companies he received as the Company of the Indies. Law claimed the territory was as rich and bountiful as the garden of Eden, that veins of silver in its hills rivaled those of the Bolivian silver mines. A Frenchman even described the place as 'enchanted, where every seed sown multiplies a hundredth fold.' But all this exaggeration of the territory's bounty had an unfortunate consequence for the French people. It created a frenzy of stock buying. But what the buyers did not realize, was that Law's investment was intrinsically tied to the Mississippi territory being prosperous and settled quickly. And he had, as I am sure you can guess, *grossly* overestimated the potential wealth. In a plain house on #65 *rue Quinampoix,* Law made Parisians millionaires overnight. Before 1719 Paris only had a single stock exchange, and merchants with foreign clients, and monies were not publicly traded. But Law talked the finance officers into implementing his new economic ideas and things got worse, and quickly. This wild speculation caused normally sensible Parisiennes to stand in line and eagerly hand over their money to be invested. However, with this newfound wealth also came an inescapable crime wave."

Josianne remembered Maélle telling her about Madame Oudart shouting at the men to leave her store. None of them realized that the poverty and shambles France was currently in had anything to do with the gilded lies John Law sold to the beleaguered finance ministers.

"And because there was a frenzy buying the stocks, in no time at all, Law could not pay their dividends."

"What are dividends?"

"The cash given to the shareholders, or those that bought into it."

"The people lost their money?" Shock widened her pretty eyes.

Clément nodded, "Millionaires on Monday, and paupers on Tuesday, and inflation at sixty percent overnight. That is when I had had enough. Besides, I am getting too old for politics and games. I want peace."

"But we must have money too, what happiness is there in peace with no prosperity?"

He nodded.

"He does not sound like a good man to me," she said.

"Although he was a goldsmith's son, he was somewhat of an outlaw. Rumor has it, he participated in a duel over a pretty face and ran a sword through his opponent. He was to be hanged, but the charge was amended to manslaughter, and somehow, he escaped to Amsterdam."

"Was he really this...mastermind of finance?" She wondered why the supposedly savvy regent of France would trust such a character.

"More of a gambler really. Some say he was a master at finance but seems to me he was just a gambler who was lucky in the beginning. And it's not *all* his fault; France was already on the brink of collapse, and in walks a tall savior with new ideas, some of which worked. But he did some curious things, he made gold coins illegal in favor of paper money which unfortunately led to a stampede that killed over forty people. He had to reverse the edict days later."

"A womanizer, a gambler, *and* a thief."

Clément chuckled, "He did have *some* good ideas, such as the centralized bank. And it does make sense to untether money from gold and silver. He argued that the very velocity of money, of it changing hands often, would stimulate the economy. And it should have worked, however what he did *not* take into consideration was there would be no limits for the paper money, and that increasing the availability of it, only caused rampant inflation and the rise in the cost of everything."

They fell silent.

She looked around at the wild surroundings and realized that things grew fast. She stared at an enormous cypress tree with its wide base rising from the water. She had never seen such a tree and had to shield her eyes to see all the way up to its narrow top. There were sweet gum trees, hardwoods, magnolia, and the graceful swamp willows bending to the ground. "It is a rich land," she commented, "things do grow here."

Clément shook his head, "Not tobacco. Nothing grows at the rate Law said it would," knowing that tobacco grown in Louisiana had been part of Law's downfall. He mused for a moment, then added, "Cotton and rice do though."

"What about wood, what about that tree?"

He craned his neck to look back at the old cypress tree looming out of the delta's lowlands.

"We could sell.... logs, to build things with," she offered.

"Timber."

"Timber, we can grow things in the fields that live in this marsh world."

"I think those trees are older than I am, it would be a shame to cut too many of them down," Clément said looking up, but he was impressed with his wife's enthusiasm.

"Well, then we should not force things that do not want to grow, but let things grow that thrive." Her face was flushed. "What are those round fruits?" she asked, seeing the tangle of vines up in the dark canopy of the trees.

"Muscadines. It's a wild grape."

"What's in that tree?" she asked, pointing to a fine white sac in the branches of a lush tree.

"Silkworms. They like the white mulberry tree."

This excited her, "We could make wine from the grapes, grow fibers for cloth, and make silk." She touched her bodice her eyes shining at him brightly. "Tell me when we are on our land," She twisted in the seat to look behind her.

"We are on my land. We have been for half an hour."

"*Our land,*" She corrected agreeably, as if he had forgotten their recent nuptials. She looked at his profile because he was still too nervous to look at her.

He had been handsome once, but his looks along with his physique had softened. His face was lined, and the ones around his eyes got worse when he squinted as the wagon kicked up debris. His nose was well formed, and she wondered if his daughters inherited their father's pleasant features.

"All this?" she asked, looking at the semi-tropical forest. The road was little more than an overgrown path. Glancing up, she saw a bird swoop through the branches. It was five inches long and had the most iridescent blue feathers she had ever seen. Furthering its beauty, the indigo feathers were tipped in a gorgeous gray.

"*Oui*, I imagine someday this land will be valuable. It's nothing now, but it's at least something for my daughters after I am gone and can no longer look after them."

"And your sons," Josianne said, still looking up at the peculiar moss she saw in the trees. In the growing twilight the trees with their dripping moss made her shiver.

"Can we not plant all this land?" she asked, but looking at the snarling undergrowth, knew it would take a mighty effort to clear it. The soil she had already noticed was sandy, if tobacco did not thrive, wondered why they were not planting cotton.

"I may clear the land one day, grow cotton, but it's labor intensive to clean the fibers. My concerns now are to form a settlement, some kind of city. Map it out in orderly plats. Create something lasting, that makes sense. Figure out a way to make the settlers not just survive but thrive."

"Why can they not thrive now?"

It took Clément a long time to answer. "Our regent has too much on his plate. France has been involved in many wars, and wars are costly, especially when they are not won."

"Who were we at war with?" Josianne asked, realizing anew how sheltered she had been at the hospital.

"Most of the world, I'd say." He chuckled bitterly, "at one time the English, Dutch, Austrians and Germans. In recent history, all of them have been in wars against France."

"I don't know where those countries are." Josianne admitted and bit her lip, hoping Clément had a globe at home and he would educate her further on these matters.

"And if that is not enough, our King saw this territory as a way to thwart Spain and England and be a buffer between his enemies. He was also convinced the area was teeming with gold, silver, and precious stones, or whatever other madness he fancied, at the moment."

"And is it?" Josianne asked, wondering if there were indeed hidden treasures in the ground.

Clément shook his head, "no, not at all."

"So that's it then? The king wanted riches, and the territory is failing because of that?"

"My dear, there are so many reasons. The men that at first like Crozat sent boats here, expected when the boats came back, they would be full of tobacco, wood, animals' skins. Problem is the tobacco from here is inferior, the wood was too moist and rotting, and the pelts had all but deteriorated on the trek back."

"So, they were not good on their word and didn't send more things?"

"You could say that, but they were losing money, a lot of money. Even if they had good intentions few businessmen can stay solvent when there is not return on their investments, as I have done."

"We are ...poor then?"

"Not yet." He wondered if he should tell her he was one of the highest paid in the colony at 1,200 livres a year. "I was commissioned to build a city, and I am going to do it. I did however lose a substantial amount of my personal wealth on this...dream." Clément turned and smiled at her, liking that he had someone with which to discuss things that weighed on his mind.

"The territory is doomed because of... supplies?"

"Unfortunately, it is still not that simple. It really is a land of Indian nations. The Choctaws, Chickasaws, Creeks, Chitimachas, Houmas, Natchez, and even *more* don't want us here, not that I can say I blame them particularly. There is a lot of fighting and unrest. Not only do they fight amongst each other, but with the settlers as well."

"I've heard bad stories about them, scalping especially blondes." Josianne thought of Suzanne's golden mane and shuddered.

"Not all indigenous people do that, and not all of them are evil, just like not all white settlers are good. We attempt to live in peace with them, but in truth I don't think it will work. Our cultures are too different, and I feel for them really because I fear it will be their demise. We do not understand them at their core, nor do they us."

"You know them?" She asked her admiration for the depth of her husband's knowledge, growing.

"When Monique was sick with that fever, we had no

medicine. I had no idea what to do. But a Natchez woman came, and although I still lost Monique, that Natchez woman made Monique more comfortable. Whatever she gave, Monique stopped the coughing for a few hours so she could rest. And for that gift, I hold the indigenous people in high esteem."

They fell silent for a moment.

"So, the territory is failing because France is in debt, has silly wars, trusted a scoundrel like Law, and the native people don't want us here?"

"The climate is also unforgiving. In the spring it rains so much it's as if it will never let up, then the sun comes out, hot and fast and the steam rises from this forest like a mist. And with it comes the fevers." He shook his head in memory. "But even with all of that, all of that working against the success of the colony, man's greed is still the worst. The boats that never come, and when at last they do, the cargo is rotten and useless. They won't even send the metal fillings for windows and doors, never even a simple plow."

"Why do you stay, why not go back to France with your daughters?"

"I will never go back. France is too corrupt and cannot fix it. But here, in this wild place, there is still a chance I can do some good."

The house in a clearing was smaller than she thought it would be. It was a story and a half and made of rough wood, one side of which was so shaded from the sun, it was covered with a green, spongy moss. The roof looked new, at least, and the windows were covered not in deer skins or glass but *pastille*, a cloth that was wearing thin. Although Josianne was disappointed, she did notice there was a nice brick chimney jutting through the roof.

Josianne started down from the wagon when Clément put a hand on top of hers, to stop her.

"Perhaps I should go in first and see my daughters," his worry palpable.

Josianne's brow furrowed, "but why, I am your wife now?"

"I-I know but--" He did not know how to tell her that at seventeen she was only five years older than Celeste. That ten-year-old Clara still cried for her mother. And if he did not figure out his finances, they would all be ruined. That he had done a nonsensical, absurd thing in marrying her. In that moment he was thinking that he should have continued his lonely life with his daughters and Alisa the cook that lived with them.

Josianne jumped out of the wagon, straightening her skirts. "No, I will not wait outside like a servant girl." Before she could knock, a young girl opened the door and peered out.

She had dark hair and eyes, and looked as waifish as the street children in the slums of Paris. She was wearing a blue blouse tucked into a brown skirt, and because it was too long for her, caked sand clung to the bottom.

"Are you Clara?" Josianne asked smiling brightly thinking it must be the ten-year-old.

The young girl shook her head. "No, I am Celeste."

Looking past Josianne, saw her father and ran to greet him. "Papa, I missed you so."

"Now, now Celeste, it's only been a few hours." He stroked her hair, "you are all right. I told you I would be back before dark."

As Josianne watched her husband comfort his daughter, saw an even smaller girl dart out of the house, joining her sister.

"We missed you papa. We are so glad you are back before nightfall."

"I promised you I would be." He reached around Celeste, who was clinging to him like a kitten. He placed a kiss on Clara's silky hair.

Josianne waited for Clément to introduce her as he answered the girls' questions, and when he neglected to do so as the threesome made their way to the door, Josianne took the opportunity. "I am Josianne. Your papa and I were married today. I am happy to be your new friend."

Celeste looked Josianne up and down silently.

Josianne's clothes, patched so many times took on a quilt like appearance, were at least clean. Previously the left elbow had a gaping hole, but it had been expertly patched by Maélle. Josianne had washed her hair, and it looked shiny and healthy. She had no pins to put it up and instead braided the long tresses. She smiled at the girls.

Tears shimmered in Celeste's dark eyes. "You are very pretty, *mademoiselle*."

"Celeste, my dear, it will be all right," Clément soothed.

"No, no it will not," Celeste squeaked, and had to wipe her face free of tears. And between ragged breaths said to Josianne, "And I do *not* want you to be my friend."

Clément hated himself suddenly when Clara too began to cry. He had seen it before, Celeste was the more emotional of his daughters, but Clara often followed her older sisters' lead. Now, his two precious mother-less daughters were sobbing at the folly of his marriage.

"Celeste—" Josianne said, her eyes too beginning to tear. She could imagine their heartache, losing their mother in a place like this. And she would love them, she *knew* she could. She had always known her heart was big and that she had an abundance of love to share. She'd had lots of friends at *La Salpêtrière* and the other servants in the house had confided in her, because they knew she could be trusted. Josianne would love these girls like her own, and she would love Clément despite his fear, and give him a son. She would make the house a home again and help Clément with his business. If only these girls would give her a chance, she knew she could make it all happen.

"I don't want you to be our friend," Celeste interrupted, the tears wet on her face making her seem again to be the younger of the sisters. "I want you to be our *mother*," She dissolved into tears and Josianne gathered both girls into her arms.

"Clément, please get my things," Josianne said over her shoulder. Stupefied, he watched then as his new bride asked the girls questions, holding them close as they walked into the house. He even saw Josianne place a kiss on Clara's temple as the threesome made their way to the house.

As he got the bundle that held the meager belongings of the former Josianne Daudessot, he looked up to see the twilight sky streaked with pink, blue and gold, and it occurred to him that he was the luckiest man in the Louisiana territory.

Clément could hardly believe it. A half hour later Josianne had worked happily beside the black cook Alisa and managed to make a meal out of stale bread, lard, and a corn. She found some leeks and green onions in the garden and even coaxed the girls out to help her gather them. She laughed when they said they could not cook and taught them how to break up the bread and drop it into the bubbly concoction, all the while keeping up a cheerful chatter. He even saw Celeste smile once and Clara had laughed, a sound he had not heard from his daughters in an exceedingly long time.

Josianne insisted on helping the girls get to bed. He could hear them talking from behind the door, although what Josianne could to talk about with two girls she had met a few hours before, he had no idea. And he found himself looking around the living room of his own home as if he were the newcomer.

He sat in the velvet armchair, noticing that the threads were getting thin on the armrest. Monique would not have stood for that. He traced his hand along the thinning fabric, listening to the night sounds of tree frogs and crickets, sounds that would drone on for most of the night.

Leaning back, he closed his eyes, luxuriating in the comfort of his own home. His thoughts wandered to a meeting he would have next week with Governor Bienville and the ship that was due, and he desperately hoped a storm would not delay their arrival. Not only did it delay his profits, but he worried about his friend, Captain de Martonne. He feared one of these hellacious storms would send the young captain to a watery grave.

"Husband."

Opening his eyes, he saw Josianne standing in front of him. Swallowing hard, he sat up straight in the chair.

"Are the girls asleep?" He was surprised when she neared and touched him gently on the chest.

"*Oui,* they are settled in for the night. Come to bed." Turning, she ascended the stairs. Following her up the steep stairwell, he noticed how delicate her hand looked along the banister.

She allowed him to enter the room first and closed the door behind him.

"Thank you for being so good to my daughters." He said, his insides shaking.

"You are welcome. They are good girls. We will be fine." She pulled down the covers neatly, which he appreciated. He felt a sudden flutter in his heart, realizing he was alone with this lovely creature.

"How did Marie Magdaleine come to be here?" she asked about the silent French maid living there, along with the cook Alisa's two daughters and son.

"She was Moniques nursemaid from France. Frankly, I hardly remember before she was in our house."

Josianne nodded, "why does she not speak?"

"I am...not sure, really. I am told Madeleine is simple in the head and that she had ...unfortunate things happen to her in France. Monique's parents employed Marie Madeleine's mother. They had to take the daughter in as well. And Monique was attached to her."

Josianne could well understand the "bad" things that could happen. "Did she speak to Monique?"

"Yes, but never to me. Never to any man that I know of. And she rarely speaks to the girls. After Monique died, I did not know what to do. I needed someone to help care for my girls, but Marie Madeleine was like a child. Frankly, I would feel guilty for sending her away."

Marie Madeliene's eyes were empty, and Josianne hoped that, in time, she would find out what had caused this woman to go silent. But if she could not, Josianne vowed to make her life safe.

"It's getting dark, husband." Leaning up, she kissed him.

He had not kissed anyone since Monique and had thought that part of his life was over. But suddenly, with this young woman in his bedroom, he was delighted it was *not*.

"I've never been kissed like that before." It was a lie. She had been thoroughly kissed by Captain de Martonne but pushed his handsome face from her mind.

"No?" Clément asked, breathing heavily, his heart beating double. "Never, by anyone?"

She tilted her head in thought. "There was a boy once

that delivered the wood for the hospital. I was weeding the garden, and he told me a dumb joke, and then he leaned down and kissed me. It was soft and nice, but it did not last long because the sisters never left us alone." She briefly touched her lips, pulling back, "does that bother you?"

Clément smirked and lowered his head. "No, not at all." But he laughed, "I do, however, suddenly find myself jealous of some boy in far-off France." He gathered her close then, young, and nubile in his arms, her large breasts pushed against his chest. He touched the loose braid, thinking it was the color of exotic mahogany that came from tropical rainforests. He'd never bought it before because it was so expensive. Grabbing her face between his hands and pulling her mouth up to his, decided he would furnish the entire house with it.

She stepped back after the kiss and began to undo the buttons on the front of her bodice. He saw the thin white chemise underneath as she carefully folded the discarded bodice on the chair. She undid the button at the back of her skirt and placed it on top of the bodice. The chemise was next, and when she stood there in nothing but her thin shift, she moved towards the bed.

He was undressed and beside her in a moment, uncharacteristically letting his clothes fall where they may. Anxious and perspiring, he rolled on top of her, hardly able to believe he was permitted to.

"My husband," sweetly, she stroked his bare back.

"Josianne, I-I," he stuttered, overcome with disbelief that she was his. Relieved, his daughters appeared happy again and willing to accept Josianne into their lives.

Incredulous that his life, which he thought was resigned to sadness, had hope. He wanted then to make love to his gorgeous wife, and not merely for the physicality, but because it would unite them as one.

Clément wanted to show his bride how much he cared about her. Because she had been good enough to marry him, he would spend the rest of his days proving he was worthy of her.

The pressing need to couple was growing, but it had been years since he had sex.

"Josianne—" he whispered, his hand shaking as he felt her breast.

She smiled up at him in the twilight, all giving, all welcoming.

But when he tried to consummate the union, he realized, to his horror, that he was losing his erection. As much as he wanted to make violent love to her, he could not. In this most inopportune moment, his body betrayed him.

*"Mon Dieu!"* Slamming his eyes shut in mortification, he fumbled below and felt his body go limp.

"Shh," Josianne breathed in the darkness, pulling his trembling, feverish head against her breast. Stroking his cheek, she whispered, "It'll be all right. We will in the morning, then." She caressed his face until he stopped trembling and fell asleep.

When the soft light of morning dawned, a renewed Clément did too. When he saw Josianne's beautiful face smiling up at him, his body betrayed him no more.

## Fourteen

### ⤴⤵

Maélle dressed as well as she could and knocked on the door of one of only three businesses in the village, which was supposed to be *Nouvelle Orleans* but was nothing more than a swampy, mosquito-infected marsh. Waiting at the door, she felt the damp sand under her still bare feet. Hearing the hum of a mosquito in her ear, she slapped viciously at the insect when the door opened.

"*Bonjour*, is *Monsieur* Godefray here?" she asked the mercantiles' short, pregnant indigenous wife. The woman didn't understand but smiled, showing a missing right canine.

The wife said something Maélle did not understand, and a moment later, she was staring into Pierre Godfreys's brown eyes. He motioned to Maélle to come in, turned to his wife, and spoke to her in an Indian language.

"Sit," he said.

Maélle moved to the far end of the shop where a

small table was pushed to the corner with two benches. "Little Moon will be bringing us some brew."

"You speak her language?"

"*Oui.* I had to learn, because otherwise, the winter nights would have been far too quiet." His brown eyes were mirthful.

"Does she speak French?"

He shook his head, "No, and she does not want to learn."

Digesting this, Maélle smiled when Little Moon returned with two tin cups of brew and a small plate of flat bread made of corn. She watched Pierre tear a piece and stuff it into his mouth.

"Is she..." Maélle racked her brain to remember the names of the Indigenous people who occupied the territory. "Natchez?"

"No, my first wife was Houmas, but she died. So many of these poor Indians die from maladies they've never faced before. They are resilient people until another race comes along and subjects them to their illnesses. This one here is Choctaw."

"How did you come to know her?"

"The whole Choctaw tribe was being decimated with raids from an enemy tribe, the Chickasaws. Luckily, I found her before the Chickasaws did, or she'd have been murdered or made a slave. It's amazing to me, man's inhumanity to man. I thought it was just a French or English trait to kill people who are different than you or enslave them. Turns out, it is universal."

He seemed well educated, and as if he read her thoughts, he said, "I was educated by the Jesuits in

France. But in France, the government is so corrupt that I would rather live with the unknown than live with that." He smiled, "But I know you didn't come here to talk to me about my marital status. I hear you are a seamstress and need a place to live."

Maélle nodded, wanting to make a good impression. "With so many settlers coming, I thought I could work here in your store and make garments that could be sold. I didn't know if you carried anything like that," Maélle looked nervously around. Although the place held items for sale, they were dusty.

"No, I do not and it may be a good idea if the boats come in with any fabric."

Maélle knew of that unfortunate fact but plowed ahead with her plan regardless. "I would ask for a discount on the fabric that comes in and live off the sale of the clothes. And I have a friend who has given me a bolt of cloth to start." Dear sweet Josianne, "but I need a place to live."

He chewed the bread carefully, watching her. "No man here strikes your fancy?"

Maélle looked down and blushed, knowing the man she wanted was not available. "No, not yet."

He sighed wearily, "frankly, I don't have any idea if this will work or if you'll be able to feed yourself."

Maélle nodded, her stomach rumbling. She had been half hoping that at noon she could share in their meal, and now, fearing that it was no longer an option, felt her hopes fading.

He eyed her speculatively, "If we do this, you can help me too. Little Moon is a good woman but afraid of most things... *French,* shall we say." He watched Maélle's eyes flit to something on the wall. "Little Moon's people are masters of *typishuk* or basket weaving; they are not only durable but works of art. They use *uksi* or canebrake grasses, and some are woven so tightly they will hold water. The one you are looking at has a diamond pattern, meant to respect nature and the rattlesnake."

Admiring it, Maélle agreed; it was indeed beautiful.

"As much as I appreciate the weaving, Little Moon does *not* wash the clothes or keep house, which I understand because she has never lived like this before. If you help her, I can help you too."

As if on cue, Little Moon came nearer to her husband. Maélle had no words for what she was wearing. It was made of some sort of hide, and its wrapped skirt looked comfortable and practical. The long-feathered necklace that was resting against her chest was pretty. Her black hair was pulled back tight, and her ears laid nicely against her head. Her dark eyes were huge in her round face. She looked young, perhaps fourteen, but already weary from a hard life.

Ignoring social customs, Pierre slipped his arm around her waist and pulled her against him. He placed his other hand against her middle, fingers spread, and, looking up to Little Moon, had a conversation in a language Maélle did not understand.

Maélle hoped it would work out because she did not know what she would do if it did not. She was relieved when Little Moon innocently grabbed her hand and held it, smiling.

# Fifteen

Maélle looked up when the bell over the mercantile door sounded, She saw a blonde soldier walk in. Seeing her in the back, he nodded as she resumed sewing. She heard Little Moon come in to wait on him. It was impressive to her how he spoke her language.

Pierre Godefray worked out an arrangement with Maélle, and she was at least surviving. She had a corner in the mercantile and sewed every day. The light was poor because there was no window, and after getting blinding headaches for the first two weeks, she earned enough to buy a lantern. Trying to be frugal, she only used it when it was dimmest, the early morning and late afternoon.

She enjoyed the banter of the settlers who came in, the smell of Little Moon's cooking, although she did not eat with them, the freedom of getting up and using the outhouse whenever she wanted and being able to look at the sky from the front window of the store. Although her only paying customer so far was Josianne, she had hopes that soon there would be others.

Maélle watched the blonde solider touch one of the white cotton shirts. It was a simple design, with wide sleeves and an adjustable drawstring collar. She had challenged herself to get twenty-five stitches per inch and was proud when she had got twenty-two. But it was exhausting work, and she decided to save the tedium for women's clothes where her fine stitching would be more appreciated.

"*Mademoiselle*?" The man said suddenly, holding one of her shirts, "these are for sale, no?"

"*Oui*, of course." She tried not to blush at the thought of someone buying one.

He looked down at the shirt. He unfolded the stiffly ironed garment, inspecting it. "I'll take it. It will be a joy to have something new and clean."

Maélle felt her mouth go dry when Little Moon turned to her and smiled in appreciation.

Maélle told him the amount, hoping it would not be too dear. After all, she knew the cost of the fabric, the thread, and the hours it had taken her to craft it.

Happily, he paid her the sum, dropping a rarity, a coin in her hand. She felt it hard and smooth in her palm. Money she had earned, earned as a woman in this new land. She wanted to run back and tell Hélène, Josianne, and Suzanne. She wanted to tell Henri, wanted to see the pride in his eyes that poor, uneducated Maélle Mercier was a seamstress in the new French territory.

"What is his house like?" Maélle asked as she straightened the piece of blue muslin, carefully smoothing out the edges before she cut. There was a subtle stripe in the fabric, and she could not afford to make a mistake. Josianne had come to her with a bolt of fabric and ideas for a dress. It was only the second bolt of fabric that had made it to the territory, and Josianne had already told her she would give her the rest of the fabric when the dress was finished. Although Maélle hated to accept charity, she was grateful for her friends' generosity. And with that in mind, Maélle was determined to create a masterpiece.

"It is not as grand as I thought it would be. Only three rooms with a loft above. But it is wonderful to sleep on a decent mattress, and I fear I've gained weight in the few months I have been there." Josianne, never shy, pulled up her bodice to inspect her still-flat midsection.

"And the girls?"

"They are timid little things. When I laugh some-times, they wince because I make too much noise! And I cannot help it; I feel sorry for them, *pauvres petites filles*. Sheltered, then motherless, and knowing nothing of the hardships of the world. I sometimes think it is better to have suffered some; that way, when things go wrong, you aren't unprepared."

"What an interesting way to look at it." Maélle nodded in agreement but did not take her eyes off the fabric.

"There is a maid there that tended to Monique. She does not speak, and some think she is simple in the head."

Maélle shrugged, having known a few throughout the years.

"Clément thinks something bad happened to her in France, and she has never spoken to him."

"Lots of bad things happened to a lot of us," Maélle said, "But the strong survive. And men—" she stopped her cutting to look up at her friend, "can be awful."

Josianne changed the subject, "how is Hélène?"

Maélle, cutting the length of fabric, was slow to respond, "The same. Angry as ever." She nipped out the notches to mark the places to stitch.

"She is still working as a laundress?"

Maélle nodded, "She's making even less money than I am, and I am afraid it won't be enough. She's going to find something else to do...or get married." But Maélle had not seen a man in the territory give Hélène so much as a second glance. And it was not just the birthmark; it was the scowl she perpetually wore. The joke was that she had even scared off the convict *voyageur*, who was as rough as they came.

"And our Suzanne?" Josianne asked, surprised to see Maélle's demeanor change.

"She's fine. Henri rebuilt the cottage. It's sparse, but he did manage to put in an actual wood floor. The roof is redone, and he's busy, which is good. Not that everyone here has any money to pay him for his work. Maybe the next time ships come, they will bring something we can use as money, as it is; coins are so scarce we must barter and trade."

Josianne's back stiffened. There was still wild speculation in the territory that cotton would save the failing colony. Others said it would be oysters or fishing.

So far, the unforgiving, overgrown wilderness was

not producing a bounty of *any* kind. It was late spring, and no one was concerned yet, but Josianne worried how hard things would be in the coming winter. Although no one said it directly, she knew most settlers were blaming their beleaguered deceased king, John Law, Governor Bienville, and finally, *Clément*.

"I'm going to see Suzanne next week. Do you want to come with me?" Josianne stopped Maélle's sewing by touching her hand.

"I cannot," the pain in those words was deep.

"She is your friend, and you love her. Do not abandon her, especially when she needs your guidance."

Maélle, able to get her hand away, resumed her stitching, "She did not need my guidance when--"

Josianne sighed, "they are married and soon to have a baby. It is time to put away the anger." The silence in the room was loud. "Fine, then, Hélène and I will go. And we will tell her Maélle, whom Suzanne loves like a sister would not come, would not see her."

Maélle jerked her head up and, taking the bait, begrudgingly agreed to join them.

# Sixteen

It was late May, and yet it was already steamy and hot. A four-month pregnant Suzanne stopped to catch her breath, resting against the stump where Henri cut wood. She tugged at the sweat-dampened clothing, fanning it against her skin. It was so hot that the sweat drenched her eyebrows and stung when it rolled into her eyes. Wiping the moisture off her forehead, she glanced up at the brilliant blue sky—so intensely bright that she had to look away.

She brushed her wet hair from her forehead with the back of her hand and stretched her aching back. It was humid, and she had to pull the thick air into her lungs, noting the monotonous drone of insects.

Maintaining a garden was difficult. Even though Henri had done the hard part of turning the soil, she had to constantly hoe it to bat down the weeds. She didn't enjoy the backbreaking labor and hoped Henri would soon be making more money.

She wasn't sure what was wrong, but Henri was quiet. She did not know if it was because of his work, or the humidity, or wildness of the place, but he seemed unusually sullen. She hoped that when the baby was born, things would improve.

*Home*...it was a word she had no memory of. Glancing at her chapped hands, she remembered how Henri had bandaged them when the blisters opened and seeped the clear pus.

Suzanne hoped the squash, beans, and pumpkin Little Moon had told her to plant would grow. She was excited at the prospect of preserving them and, if she could get her hands on any glass, canning them in the fall. She loved the idea of next year mashing them up with water to feed her baby when little pearly teeth told her it was time.

Their house had one room and once belonged to a trapper. Years of neglect made the roof cave in, but the walls were still strong. Henri had redone the roof and promised Suzanne that someday they would have glass in the windows. As it was now, *pastille* covered the windows, but in the heat and humidity of the coast, the fabric did not last long, and Henri had talked about putting animal skins up instead when the weather got cold.

And she was proud that Henri was acquiring land grants, especially since the commission to be one of the designers of the city had been rescinded. Suzanne had been beside herself with anger and outrage. Henri had merely shrugged, knowing if he had kept the position, he would have to deal with dishonest men. Besides, he was already making a name for himself, crafting frames for doors, windows, and even furniture. He was hardworking, and she was glad for the many sailors she had known on the ship, she had chosen him.

Suzanne leaned on a wooden hoe when she caught movement of a snake on the ground. "Are you the friendly black snake or the not-so-friendly cottonmouth?" She asked, trying to remember what Henri had told her. The snakes looked alike, although one was venomous and to be avoided, the other harmless and good and keeping rodents away. If it had slits for pupils and a divot behind its' eye, it was dangerous, but the snake was gone before she could inspect it. She was relieved, not sure if she had averted a dangerous situation or been with a friend.

Grabbing a wooden hoe, she raked the sandy ground, which was hideously prone to weeds. She was looking forward to having her friends over, especially Maélle, who she knew was still angry with her for marrying Henri. The truth was she had not thought much of Henri until Maélle showed interest in him, and then, well, the rest happened.

There was a small table, and since there were no chairs, she asked Henri to cut thick pieces of stump for them to sit on. If the two hens would keep laying, she was going to bake a small loaf cake. The poor things had been so ridden with fleas that she sprinkled ashes around their coop, it helped to inhibit them.

She named the hens Coco and CeCe, and they were

better now, especially since Henri nailed the loose boards of their coop, and Suzanne hoped the fox she saw at twilight would stop tormenting the hens.

A few days later, Coco and CeCe did their duty, and Suzanne was taking a sad-looking little cake out of the makeshift oven when she realized her friends had arrived. She was not sure how the cake would turn out since there was no flour, and she had used ground corn instead. At least it was golden on top, and she hoped, edible.

She wiped her hands on her apron and smoothing her hair, darted out the door to greet them.

"Maélle," Suzanne laughed, then turned to the others, "Josianne, you look so pretty. Hello, Hélène."

"What a wonderful little cottage," Josianne said, placing her hands on her hips. She had on a new light blue skirt and matching bodice of brushed cotton, and the white blouse peeking out from the bodice had a small insert of lace. "It's very pretty, Suzanne."

"Oh, thank you. I know it's much smaller than the house you have with Clément, but it's home."

"And a garden. That's wonderful," Hélène said impressed. "The plants we put in near the mercantile don't look as good as these."

Suzanne beamed at the compliment, and she turned to Maélle, wanting to show off her house.

Josianne handed Suzanne a parcel wrapped in an old sailcloth but tied with a lovely blue ribbon. "A house-warming gift. It's from all of us." Hélène and Maélle turned curiously to each other. They knew of no such gift but realized it was merely Josianne, again sharing her good fortune.

Taking the package, Suzanne was surprised at how heavy it was. Pulling back the small piece of fabric, saw an eight-inch looking glass, a decided luxury. "Oh, it's *wonderful*! I'll be able to see how fat I am getting!" She laughed, "I will have Henri make a lovely frame for it."

"Maélle and I brought you soap," Hélène said, hoping their simple gift would be appreciated after Josianne's gesture. It was wrapped in a large amount of cloth.

"Where did you get this cloth?" Maélle marveled, inspecting it, wondering if Suzanne would let her have it.

"I-I don't remember," Hélène fibbed. It was from Mickey and she could not wait to divest herself of it. He sought her out from time to time, and she did her best to avoid him.

"*Je l'ame! Merci beaucoup.*" Suzanne laughed again, looking at the mirror. "Maybe someday I'll have a chest of drawers to put it on."

"Someone as pretty as you should be able to see herself," Hélène said, "something smells good, Suzanne."

"I baked a cake, or at least I tried to. Come in, come in. Although we'll have to sit on stumps."

"No chairs?" Maélle ducked into the low-framed door, her eyes needing to adjust to the dimness of the interior. The first thing she noticed was that the ceiling was low enough that someone as tall as Hélène would be able to touch her head if she were on tiptoe. There was a dilapidated table that, to her surprise, did have four rough-cut stumps surrounding it as chairs. There was a crumbling fireplace, and Maélle could not imagine how difficult it would be to cook on it, falling apart like it was. There was a tiny bed nestled into the corner with a painfully thin straw mattress.

Maélle busied herself by arranging the three plates stacked on the table as Suzanne began cutting the dense cake into small pieces. None of the dishware matched, and all three of the plates had chips.

"I don't know what it's going to taste like. I didn't have any flour and had to use mashed corn, although I did add a little honey," Suzanne said.

"Can I get the tea for you?" Hélène offered. Nearing the fireplace, she did not see a hot pad, so she gripped the handle with her skirt, brought it to the table, and filled the pot with water to steep. They all laughed at her ingenuity and how little she cared for fashion.

"I only have two cups. We'll have to share."

"That'll be fine," Josianne said, sitting on the stump, although she hoped the roughness would not snag her new clothes.

"How is your house, Josianne?" Suzanne asked, "And your new daughters?"

"The house is good, smaller than I thought it would be, but I asked Clément to build me a bigger one. The girls are timid; the little one Clara still cries at night for her mother, but at least she lets me comfort her. Clément has been teaching me to read, and since the girls already can, I spend time with them snuggled under my arm as they tutor me. I am learning to write, too."

Hélène scoffed, "You are lucky they did not throw stones at you marrying their father."

Josianne shrugged, "I know, it could have been terrible. But I was not worried. I would have managed it, whatever happened."

"I believe you. You do always seem to get your way."

Josianne's brow rose, "you sound as if you disapprove. Are you jealous, Hélène?"

"Actually, no, impressed is more like it."

They all laughed as they sat and ate the strange cake with their hands, laughing when bits would slip through their fingers. They teasingly fought over the two teacups, chattering about how strange the weather was in the territory and how the humidity made them sweat more than they ever had in France.

"And when are you going to get married, Maélle?" Suzanne asked. I heard a rumor about a particular blonde soldier who has been hanging around the mercantile." Suzanne giggled.

"Oh, I don't know," Maélle blushed and looked down. She had only walked with the soldier one time, but it did nothing to diminish her feelings for Henri.

"Better get married before you two are old maids!" Suzanne snorted.

Maélle calmed her breathing and looked away.

"Yes, Maélle and I are the leftovers. At least we are making a living, meager though it is."

"What about the fisherman, Mickey?" Suzanne asked.

Hélène looked down. " Oh I don't know." Reaching into her pocket she fingered the pearl, amazing how it warmed up at her touch.

Suzanne reached forward and squeezed her friend's hand consolingly. "You will find someone, Hélène. It is so wonderful," Tears filled her beautiful blue eyes. She turned to Maélle, "I have all of this, I have a house to call my own, I have a handsome, wonderful husband, and if that is not *enough*, I will have a baby in the fall!"

Maélle tried to smile.

# Seventeen

*September 1720*

"Thank you, Pierre." Hélène counted the change she got from selling soap in the mercantile. At least it was something. The last time she sold soap, Pierre had not been able to pay her and had given her food instead. She was excited to have actual money and hoped to buy shoes when the next ship came in.

It was Saturday evening, and although she needed to be up early for mass in the morning, she took the long way home to gaze out across the ocean. Of the fifty-three that survived the voyage, island, and heat of summer, there were only two of them left unmarried from *La Mutine*.

And although Maélle and Hélène laughed that they would be the last two old maids, it looked as though the prophecy was coming true. Hélène did not mind, she never had romantic notions. Although the men from the governor's office reminded her that her passage and prior board in the barracks *required* her to marry, she worked around it by doing the wash for a few of the landowners in town. She especially disliked Jacques Perot, a city planner who could barely bring himself to acknowledge her presence. And since she was not pretty, she went between her two jobs largely unnoticed and forgotten.

Hélène suggested she and Maélle live together as two spinsters, reasoning that they could live better together by pooling their money, but Maélle was distant and aloof and would agree to nothing. Hélène was still pondering when looking up, saw Mickey blocking her path.

"Hélène."

It had been months since she had seen him. His skin was so brown it made his blue eyes more intense. His beard was full, but she could see his lips and could not help but remember he kissed her once.

"Hello, Mickey." Without meaning to, she smiled, glad to see him.

"It's been a long time. Did I...miss your marriage while I was gone?" Despite being said in jest, he still glanced at her hand to see if there was a ring, although rings were a luxury few could afford. In fact, the only bride she knew that had a wedding band at all was Josianne. Nervously, Hélène covered her bare finger.

He cocked his head curiously and laughed when she did not answer. "Have I waited too long to find a wife?"

"Maélle and I are not married." She hated herself for admitting it. It was as if he knew she would be last picked, knew her insecurities. There was an awkward silence. "I've got to be going."

He blocked her way again and, reaching out, touched

her arm. His hand was warm. "There's no hurry. Could I buy you some wine at the tavern?"

There was one tavern, if you could call it that. It served overpriced wine, rum, and tafia. It was not a terribly successful venture, but it stayed open because it was the only business of its kind in the territory. Hélène often thought if she ran it, she could make it turn a profit in no time.

"Thank you, but I don't think so."

They fell silent again.

"My *pirogue* is here, and I've not had the chance to show it to you. Would you like to see it?"

"No, thank you."

He was running out of reasons to talk to her, "a walk on the beach then?"

"I've got to go back. I have clothes to iron."

"Ah... I see a washerwoman again. You and Maélle, the two last stragglers. The one in love with a man already taken....and *you*."

She stared up at him, knowing Maélle would be mortified if she knew. "I'm going."

He yanked her arm up against his side. "Why do you *continue* to refuse me? Am I *really* not good enough for you?"

"Let me go, Mickey."

He dropped his hand, and stared at her as if assessing what to do. "Was my gift not good enough?"

Hélène looked down, fingering the pearl in her pocket. Relieved he would never know how she had given the fabric to Suzanne.

"Did you forget that afternoon, Hélène?" He was close now, and she could feel the warmth of his breath.

She had not forgotten. In fact, she walked on the coastline half hoping, half fearing she would someday run into Mickey.

"You *want* to be a spinster?"

Anger erupted, "Why are those my only two choices, marry or be doomed a failure? It's none of your concern, Mickey, what I do." She turned to face the water. The gently receding tide rippled along the murky, shallow shoreline. She noticed something gray in the water and wondered if it was an oyster. Wondered if it too held a pearl like the one Mickey had given her.

He, too, looked out over the sea. Squinting so that the white lines within the tan disappeared. His curly black hair was long around his ears, and his chin was thrust up. When he spoke suddenly, it was in a tone she had never heard him use before.

"My family was from Romania, but I was born in a Paris slum. I had a father, but I have no memory of him. I had three older brothers who used to take me with them when they pickpocketed. They taught me at a young age to be a criminal. And I was good at it. Better than them."

The fact that he was not only a convict but also a gypsy frightened her. She remembered breathing an odd sigh of relief when Marie Denise married and moved away. Marie Denise had a way of knowing things she should not. "What happened to your brothers?"

He grinned at her, but not with joy. "All hung in the town square." He looked again towards the water. The gray clouds skirted the horizon, the sun falling below them, making a band of orange. "The bodies hung for days in the sun, bloated and covered with flies."

To hide her shock Hélène looked up as a giant bird flew over them. It's five-foot wingspan blocking out the sun for a moment. They listened to its cawing and watched it swoop past them and to the water in search of prey.

"I have a boat, and *Monsieur* Heriot gave me land. All I must do is clear it, and it can be *ours*. I am going to build a house, and I must marry, or they can send me back to *bicêtre*." His eyes did not leave hers, trying to impart something that he could not bring himself to say.

The hairs were up on the back of her neck, afraid to hope. "Then get married. There are a lot of women that came, you could have married any one of them."

"Maybe I...want *you*."

There was a part of Hélène that wanted it to be true. She remembered the morning they were docking at the territory, how he'd caught her eye—the afternoon on the beach, the pearl, the fabric.

He thrust his chin in the direction of the twisted growth next to the beach that encroached every year, only to be battened back by the sea. "You aren't like other women, Hélène."

Hélène smirked, "really?"

"I mean that as a compliment. You don't care what you look like, and you don't have stupid ideas about marriage, and you are a hard worker. We have both been dealt a bad hand. Together we can have a better life."

"There will be other boats of women. Why not marry one of them?"

He shrugged, "I'm tired of waiting."

Hélène tried to keep her voice steady. "Why not marry Maélle? She's prettier than me."

"She loves another."

Mickey was staring at her, and Hélène was running out of excuses. Even though she knew love was a luxury not meant for her, he was telling her she was an odd, unattractive misfit and that he wanted to marry her because he was tired of waiting.

"I can make a living doing the laundry."

Annoyance stamped his face, "you would rather wash other people's shit-stained clothes than be the mistress of your *own* house?"

"I will survive."

He turned away, disappointed. "I do not doubt for a moment that you will. But I was hoping to do more than simply survive." There was a wounded look in his eyes that she was surprised to see. He left her then, alone on the beach.

She opened her mouth to call him back, wanting him to prove to her that even *Hélène Francois* was worthy of love and affection. But he did not turn around, and if she had known it would be a year before she saw him again, she would have run after him.

# Eighteen

"Clément, my love," Josianne breathed, sliding into the room, her feet invisible under her pale blue silk nightgown. It was tight around her waist, and he could tell she had nothing underneath because he could see the roundness of her breasts and the outline of the areola pressing against the silk. "It is late. You must come to bed."

He was seated in the keeping room, which Josianne had already found ways to add womanly touches. For now, she agreed to keep the threadbare furniture but insisted on a new rug to cushion Clément's feet, worrying as she did about his frequent bouts of gout. The walls had been freshly whitewashed, and she kept a crystal vase of colorful wildflowers on the table.

Clément did not mind the money she spent, which was not often given how unpredictable the boats were. But he enjoyed how well she dressed and how well his daughters were outfitted and reveled in the fact that his house was once again a home.

"I've much work to do."

She put her arms around him, forcing his face up to her. "You work too hard," She kissed him and then snuggled herself on his lap, tucking the nightgown around her thighs. "Tell me what worries you."

He marveled that Josianne knew instinctively how to comfort him.

"There are fewer ships with provisions coming than last year. Fewer ships and yet more people arrive. The storehouse has supplies, but not enough to last us another year. There is no meat except for wild game, which is fine if you can find it. The *coureurs des bois*, or the men that hunted it, did find wild turkeys, deer, and other wild game, but it was not easy. The corn the Choctaws and others grow still has to be crushed by hand because we still have no mill to grind it. The Chickasaws and Choctaws can catch fish, but the average Frenchman, for some reason, fails at that." He paused, wondering how much more he should tell his wife, knowing there was a real possibility that the settlers would starve in the next few years if conditions did not change.

"We can preserve the beans, squash, okra, and whatever else. We can hunt what game we can, why even I have seen wild turkeys and pheasant, and when we get deer, we can dry the meat to last. Portion it out. Maybe Mickey can teach these settlers to fish when he comes back. Can we build a mill on a stream to grind the corn?"

He admired his wife, who was unwilling to admit defeat.

"These are.... good suggestions, but it takes time,

resources, someone to take the reins and get things done."

"We do not have much time. The nights are growing shorter. I will have a meeting with the women in town. We will preserve what we can, be careful with it, and make it last. I don't know which berries and nuts are edible, but I can ask Little Moon. You will call an emergency meeting and get the mill built on our land near that stream."

"Josianne, there is *no way* to get all these things accomplished." But as he said the words, he realized he was telling a woman who had so far beat all the odds that something could not be done.

"It's just that this whole colony is scarcely two decades old, and it's already decaying."

"What do you mean?"

"Fort Louis in Mobile is falling apart. Mobiles encircled by swamps and marshy bogs, cane breaks, and muddy streams. Everything here that is made of wood is rotted in a decade."

He had taken her along to Mobile a few weeks ago, and she felt the need to defend the settlement. "But it is mapped out well and the streets are straight. You are too hard on our Mobile."

"It is, you are right. But there are still no monuments, no churches to speak of."

"But the houses built now are sturdy. They now have roofs built of shingles, not bulrushes, and you started the brickworks at the edge of town."

But she suspected his real worry was the Louisiana territory, where they were. It had been mandated to be built in 1718, but as of now there were still only fifteen residences built. It had been decided that although Mobile was much farther along as a potential capital city, its proximity to the Spanish port of Pensacola made it a dangerous liability. "Old Biloxi," which was the site of the original settlement, had been moved to "New Biloxi" and then back again. All the while, the city Clément was most interested in floundered in Louisiana. And since his money was invested there, it floundered as well.

"None of these men want to put their hearts or money into this new city."

"We should have a party."

He laughed, "Josianne, my love, have you lost your mind?"

She ignored the slight, "Not at all. We should invite everyone, including Governor Bienville, his friends and other landholders, and the businesspeople. They will sit and talk in your house, drink your wine, and eat food. While I am making sure everyone has what they need, you will be presenting your ideas and thoughts. You will make your case for this town. We will show them that this territory can be a great civilized place and that the capitol should be here."

Clément paused a moment. "I would love to, my dear wife, but I do not think Alisa could oversee a large party, and besides, we do not have a room big enough to accommodate them."

"I know Maélle and Hélène will both help, and I will plan a menu that makes sense not only for what is growing in the garden but what we can prepare beforehand while being respectful of not consuming too much.

And I will show our daughters how to make little crepes. And since we do not have chairs, I will ask Henri to make us stools. We will bring out the rug from the keeping room into the yard and double the space for our guests."

Like she had countless times before, Josianne amazed Clément. She could figure out the logistics of a problem and tackle it like no woman and scarcely any man he'd ever known. And he adored that she referred to Clara and Celeste as "our" daughters. In the time Josianne had been there, he watched his daughters blossom, felt the absence of their mother melt away, and knew it was all because of Josianne.

"I can start the menu tomorrow and get word to Henri about the stools. Can you start making the verbal invitations?"

Clément realized all he had to do was nod, and it would all materialize. His young wife was taking it upon herself to help him with the territory. His affection for her soared, and he realized now that what he had once felt for Monique was minuscule in comparison.

"*Oui,*" he looked at her, and felt emotional tears form in his eyes. "Josianne, I-I don't know what to say."

"You are welcome, husband."

# Nineteen

S eptember was still hot, and Josianne, wiping the sweat from her forehead, wondered if the territory ever cooled down. The mornings were at least bearable, but by 10:00 every day, the merciless sun would bake the house and grounds, and the only respite she could find was near the ocean where the slightly cooler breezes blew. The nights stayed uncomfortably warm, and she found herself wanting to sponge bathe more than once a day, but refused to allow herself such an extravagance. The mosquitos were a constant annoyance, and she did not like the lizards that hid in the corners of the room, raising and lowering their heads. Although Clara enjoyed catching and taking them outside, giggling as she felt them wiggling in her hands.

"*Maman*, lizards in the house are good luck!" Clara said.

Josianne laughed, "then we should all be having a *great* deal of good luck."

Even with the shortages and heat, Josianne forged

ahead with her party planning and hoped that the heat would abate by the beginning of October.

It was going to be a grand event, and if she had anything to say about it, the first of many. Josianne had already decided to throw a *Joyeux Noel* party every year and a spring party too, perhaps the *fete de la Saint-Jean* celebrating the longest day after Clément got the big new home built.

*"Madame* Heriot?" One of Clément's workers asked, "Henri Genest is here with the stools."

"Splendid," Josianne grabbed her long skirt and dashed out to greet Henri, who already passed the two new posts she had Clément commission to mark the front of the drive to the house. "Henri!" she pulled him down for a long hug. "How are you, and how is little Suzanne?"

"I am well, and little Suzanne is *not* so little these days; she's out to here," he motioned to illustrate her advanced pregnancy.

Josianne glanced towards the wagon, expecting to see Suzanne. "I was hoping she would come with you."

"She said to tell you she would see you at the party." He began lifting the stools down. He had made two actual chairs, though, and Maélle had made covers for them and stuffed them with horse hair. Josianne had even gotten her hands on a few tacks, and Hélène, handier with a hammer, had offered to finish the uphol-stery for her.

"Thank you, Henri. It's always good to see you," Josianne said as he got back into the wagon to leave. When he was gone, Josianne surveyed the ten stools and two chairs he had made, proud to be able to offer actual seats to her guests.

The day of the party Josianne was a bundle of nerves as her guests began arriving. It was curious; everyone, including her friends and her husband, assumed she would be a natural hostess. In reality, she had been an upstairs maid and didn't have the faintest idea of how to throw a successful party. All she had to rely on was the grumbling of the maids in the house about how much extra work it was.

But as she donned a lightweight yellow silk dress and arranged her hair, she was determined not to let anyone realize her folly.

Governor Bienville was one of the first to arrive, and Clément greeted him as an old friend. The governor obviously did not remember that she had come aboard *La Mutine* in rags and starving because he welcomed her to the territory and 'hoped she had a pleasant voyage.'

Josianne greeted his wife, Etiennette.

"*Madame*, it is so good to meet you." Josianne gushed but noticed that the woman pulled her hand away quickly and that something must be foul smelling by the look on her face. "Have you met Elisabeth Vallet? You may remember her husband Marcus is the black-smith in town."

If Etiennette's greeting to Josianne was cool, the greeting the governor's wife gave poor Elisabeth was arctic. It was obvious to Josianne that some aristocratic superiority had come over from France as well.

To mask the stall in the conversation, Josianne noted Elisabeth's new blue bodice. Maélle had delicately embroidered the squared neckline with sand colored thread. The effect was understated and elegant. It still amazed Josianne Maélle's skill that she could transform simple items into masterpieces. "You look very pretty, and I like what the dark blue does to your eyes." Josianne gently cupped Elisabeth's chin. It was true Elisabeth was probably not the intellectual equal of Etiennette, but it occurred to Josianne that the real mark of intelligence was realizing someone's weaknesses without being condescending.

Elisabeth's eyes brightened. "Thank you, Josianne, and you know who made it." She turned hopefully to Etiennette. "Maélle Mercier is a fabulous seamstress in town. I can introduce her if you are not acquainted with her."

Etiennette grimaced at the woman's naivete. "I know who she is." She smirked and made her way back to her husband.

Josianne was relieved when her friends showed up minutes before each other.

"Suzanne, you look like you are about to burst," Josianne laughed and sent Clara for a chair for Suzanne from Clément's study.

"It wouldn't be so bad if I wasn't so hungry all the time. I bet it's going to be a boy with that big appetite."

"Who are all these people?" Héléne asked, seeing new faces.

Josianne neared her, "That short one is Pierre Louis Le Bond. He is one of the men sent to build the new city, and the other one, with the darker hair is his understudy, Jacques Perot."

"Yes, I know him," Héléne said under her breath, "I do his laundry and he finds me difficult to look at!" She chuckled, "and when are they *starting* this new city?" Because in the months they had been there, little construction had been done.

Trying to hold back her laugh, Josianne gripped her arm. "I know, I know, but I'm also trying to get a mill built on a stream to grind the corn, and if I leave it up to these men who keep *changing* the location of the capitol, it will never happen."

"Ahh, *Madame* Heriot," Jacques Perot said, nearing them. He took Josianne's hand and kissed it a second longer than was customary.

After kissing Maélle's hand next, Héléne had to stifle a laugh when Perot, upon seeing her birthmark again, apparently decided it might be contagious, and made a short bow instead.

"How are things progressing with the mill?" Josianne asked.

Perot sighed, standing Héléne thought, too close to Josianne.

"It will be difficult, and we may need additional funding."

"Really? The funds my husband and I have already pledged will not be enough?"

Before Perot could answer Governor Bienville, his wife, Clément, and a few merchants joined them.

"Governor, I hear there is a delay in the mill again?" Josianne asked, going right to the source.

Bienville flushed. He was not a tall man and the fact that he was a Canadian and not a Frenchman had been an issue she knew in the territory. Even though they spoke the same language, the French and French Canadians did not always get along. "I am sure, Madame Heriot, it will all be sorted out in time."

Although Josianne nodded, her friends could tell she was not impressed.

"You see, it is not my fault; the Indies Company defaulted on all their loans months ago; they are in the midst of bankruptcy and selling their assets, including ships for trade with our colony," the governor said.

Josianne wrinkled her brow because she knew this was not totally true. If it was not bad enough that seemingly everyone who dealt with the colony was a scoundrel, Bienville himself had critics who pointed out his sloppy bookkeeping. The report from La Chaise, a commissioner sent from France, even went as far as to say Bienville was 'profiteering and engaging in improper commercial transactions.'

"Why does what is happening in France have to affect our building a mill that my husband and I agreed to finance?" She wondered who among the men that were surrounding her were squandering the money, and blaming it elsewhere.

But Josianne was also worried what would happen

next. If no boats were coming with supplies, she wondered what the impending winter would be like.

"Bankruptcy? That's absurd. Aren't they the ones that are financing this whole Louisiana—" Josianne fought for the correct word, "Experiment?" She glanced at Clément, who avoided her gaze. She then peered questioningly at Etiennette to see if she had an ally.

"Privileges afforded by The Indies Company are being defaulted on, such as land grants, and all bank accounts have been eliminated."

Josianne was incensed, not only at the French government for continuing to listen to the Scotsman's idiotic schemes but at Clément for not mentioning this to her.

"Law is nothing more than a common criminal in dandy's clothes," Héléne murmured under her breath, and hearing her, Maélle nodded in agreement.

"I am sure Governor Bienville will have this all in hand, my dear," Clément said, trying to tamp down the flush of worry and rage he saw on his wife's cheeks. He was glad then that he had not mentioned to her that Law's schemes did more than jeopardize financial stability for the colony and France, but it had rattled the markets in London, Hamburg, and Amsterdam.

But no one believed him.

A half-hour later, Maélle was getting ready to leave when she overheard a conversation with a merchant complaining about fabrics that he had to transport with no one to buy from him. Shoring up her resolve, she introduced herself. She never thought of herself as a woman of business but realized since the man she wanted was gone, she would have to make her own destiny. And what would be better than dealing with clothes, something she loved.

*October 1720*

Suzanne was squatting on the ground, pulling weeds. Although they came out easily in the sandy soil, if she missed weeding even a few days, it was as if she had missed a month. She hated that the weeds made long cuts on her hands, hated that she had to work so much, and wondered again when Henri would earn more money.

She was tired of being pregnant, tired of the heat, tired of the whole stupid territory. She had her eye on a ship's lieutenant that stopped to talk to Henri last week. She knew the lieutenant thought she was pretty, even though she was round with child. She wondered if his lips were as soft as they looked.

She felt a sharp, painful pinch.

"*Mon Dieu!*" Jerking her hand back, thinking she had gotten hold of a particularly thorny weed. But when she saw blood begin to ooze from the two small puncture wounds, realized something had bitten her. Annoyed, she ducked into the house to tend it.

Grabbing the only cloth she had, pressed it to the wound, holding it at her side, waiting for the pain to stop. She wondered if she squeezed the wound like a splinter it might expel whatever was in there. But when she did so, an odd watery blood leaked out.

She was suddenly ridiculously hot and felt sweat trickling down between her breasts and buttocks and weakly moved over to the bed. With her hand throbbing now and dizzy, she laid down. She dozed for a few minutes, but the pain in her hand woke her.

Sweat was dripping off her face now, and cramping, she curled up in a ball, but a sudden nausea bubbled up, and she vomited where she was all over herself. Sweat was now dripping off her face. Glancing at her hand, she was horrified to see the swelling.

By the time Henri got home, Suzanne was drenched in sweat, covered in vomit, and in full-blown labor.

It was as if something had burst inside her, slashing her womb from within, and the thin mattress she laid upon was soaked with blood.

"*Suzanne*!" Dropping to his knees, he had no idea where to start or where all the blood had come from. Her pregnancy looked grotesque on her tiny form. As he knelt beside her he felt the mixture of liquids seep into the fabric at his knees.

"*Mon Dieu* what *happened*?" Pulling up her hand he saw that it was swollen more than twice its size, and it was already bruising purple and black. If that was not horrifying enough, large puffy blisters were forming around the wound. Henri touched her sweaty face; her eyes were no longer able to focus. Mucous ran from her nose and saliva leaked out the corners of her mouth.

Later that night, she gave birth to a tiny daughter who shocked Henri with her lusty cry. As if Suzanne knew her work was done, she died soon afterward. Never lucid enough to respond to Henri's desperate pleas to get well, unable to acknowledge the birth of her daughter.

"Henri," Maélle said, tears stinging her eyes as she knelt near a distraught Henri, holding the infant, who had only stopped crying because she was exhausted from screaming so long. "We have to do something."

The house reeked of vomit, urine, and blood. It was all she could do not to gag as she entered. Combined with the heat, the smell was as putrid as the sewers in the summer near *La Salpêtrière*. Suzanne's dead body still lay on the bed. Even though Henri had closed her eyes, they were slightly open, and the effect was chilling.

"*Petite Suzanne* must be cared for," Maélle said.

The eyes that despondently met Maélle's were rimmed in red and Suzanne's blood was dry on his hands.

"What.... what should I do, Maélle?"

Hélène looked up from her washing of the floor, wiping her sweaty face with the back of her hand. "You can start by digging her grave."

Henri looked over at Hélène, on all fours, cleaning up the mess that was his home. Wordlessly, he got up. He stared down at Suzanne's lifeless body. Leaning down, he kissed her forehead and left.

"Have you no decency, Hélène, no feeling?" Maélle hissed, still holding the sweating sleeping infant, knowing that she would awaken more ravenously than before.

Sweat dripped into Hélène's eye, and she brushed it away with the back of her hand, leaving the sodden rag on the floor. "I have feelings, Maélle, *and* decency. We must bury her. If you haven't noticed, it's hot." She continued to scrub the floor, "he has to get over this and move on."

"I cannot believe you are saying this. It was our *Suzanne*." Tears blurred Maélle's vision.

"Yes, our Suzanne. And to honor her, we must keep her baby alive."

They heard violent noises from outside. Hurrying to the door, they saw Henri with the largest knife they had ever seen, hacking at the encroaching forest like a lunatic, as if he were trying to root out the snake responsible for Suzanne's death. His howls chilling Hélène and Maélle. The baby woke then, and Maélle cried new tears as she held the squalling, hungry baby against her breast, with nothing to feed her.

The next day was worse. *Petite Suzanne* had been crying nonstop since the moment of her birth. Maélle had taken to wetting a cloth and letting *Petite Suzanne* suck, but the force of her hunger was so violent Maélle had to pull it out of the baby's mouth, afraid she would choke. They tried soaking the rag in molasses, and it had done some good to satisfy her hunger, but they soon ran out of it. No one close enough to them had a goat, and Maélle was desperate to find something for the poor baby to eat.

The next day, Hélène came by with a precious cup of broth. But *Petite Suzanne* consumed it so furiously, no sooner had she finished it, than she vomited it up all over Maélle.

"What should we do?" Maélle cried as she opened her bodice to wipe the vomit off, as the infant frantically rooted around on her chest.

Hélène stared at her. "Take her to your breast. Let her suckle you."

Aghast, Maélle's eyes met Hélène's, "but I've not given birth. I've got no *milk* in me."

"Until we figure out something else, until we can find some food for her. Try at least."

Maélle fumbled and brought a screaming baby to her small breast. The baby was crying so fitfully and turning red that Maélle burst into tears. Suzanne was dead, and her baby would die too.

"Come on, poor little thing," Hélène whispered, stroking the baby's feverish head, trying to guide the toothless gums to Maélle's breast.

"It won't work," Maélle cried as her tears dripped down onto the baby's face.

"Maybe not. Sit down. Try and make her take it."

Dumbfounded, Maélle did as Hélène suggested. Miraculously within a few minutes, the screaming stopped as the baby sucked fitfully against the dry breast.

"It hurts, it really *hurts*," Maélle wailed, never having felt such odd pain. The baby's mouth was a tiny vice pinching her flesh.

"But she's quieting. We'll think of something. There must be a goat or *something* around here." Hélène breathed, looking around the tiny house. She left when they both fell asleep, not knowing what else to do.

The baby woke a short time later, screaming from hunger, and Maélle again tried the wet cloth so that the furious infant would suck until it was only wet from her saliva. But the momentary satiation of water would only last for a brief time; then, the exhausted baby would fall asleep.

"I don't know what to do, *I don't know what to do!*" Maélle cried, her face as red as the baby's. As she wiped her tears from her face, she noticed that the baby's' face was still dry.

"No tears yet for you. I hope you have many days without tears. I hope you *never* have to cry." Maélle moaned, rocking the infant. But the baby was having none of the talk, rooting fitfully against Maélle's chest, and when she latched on, Maélle shrieked in pain. But the crying stopped as the poor baby sucked fitfully. "I am so sorry. I am so sorry, little one," Maélle whispered, and then noticed an uncomfortable tingle in her breast and realized that the baby was swallowing.

"*Mon Dieu!*" Maélle looked down at her small breast, realizing that her maiden body was producing milk for Suzanne's baby. It was a miracle. Maélle dissolved into tears of gratitude as the baby hungrily nursed.

"Maélle," Henri whispered, but still startled her awake. "She's asleep. How did you get her to sleep?" It was, after all, the first time he had seen his infant daughter not red-faced and howling.

"I nursed her."

Henri stared at her with disbelief, "how?"

"I don't know, but I am."

"But you've never been pregnant. How could that be?"

"I-I don't know, but it happened. Nature, God, *angels*. She was starving Henri. We might have lost her."

Henri nodded despondently, realizing it was true.

# Twenty

With the collapsing of the financial scheme in France, the beleaguered nation was licking its wounds, and any thoughts of their countrymen an ocean apart occupied little of their time. The boats that were bringing desperate supplies stopped, no more soldiers were sent, and even the formally profitable indigo trade dried up. And the soldiers who had worked *months* without pay simply deserted their posts and disappeared into the wilderness.

Stock rooms that were already running low became empty, and the last reserve they had sent from The Indies Company was the hardtack biscuit. But it had not been baked correctly and had spoiled.

If this was not all bad enough, the rains came ferociously that year.

Devastating rains washed away the plants that had not been harvested. Rains also drowned the plants the cows, pigs, and other livestock ate, so they were sick and starving as well.

It rained for thirty days in a row, swelling the streams and turning the sandy soil into bogs teeming with mosquitoes and other insects.

Everyone was weak from hunger, and only the bare minimum of work was accomplished in the capital as the bedraggled inhabitants fought to survive.

If it were not for the relationship with the Indigenous peoples like the Natchez and others, they would have all starved.

Life in the colony was already difficult, and astonishingly, it was getting *worse*.

"Maélle," Josianne called, jumping from the cart, ignoring the unladylike move. It was a day of rare sunshine and Josianne was glad to get to town.

Maélle waved, adjusting the sleeping baby in her arms.

"Isn't she precious," Josianne cooed. The baby was in a sling against Maélle's chest. "What have you got on to hold her? Isn't that clever?"

"Little Moon taught me to do this. She's been such a help. I've never been around a baby before," Maélle gushed, looking at the adorable pink and white face snuggled against her chest. The fuzzy down of blond hair on her scalp, the tiny lashes against her lightly flushed cheeks.

"She looks so like Suzanne, such a beautiful baby."

Maélle's eyes filled with tears, "She does; she's as pretty as Suzanne was."

Josianne touched Maélle on the shoulder. "And how are you?" Maélle's face was drawn, and her eyes were rimmed in red. "Where is Henri?"

Maélle looked away towards one of the boats docking in the distance. A boat had *finally* come, bringing much-needed supplies. "I have not seen him since yesterday."

"It's not fair he is doing this to you. You can barely afford to feed yourself, much less a new baby." Josianne did not understand why Maélle had taken baby Suzanne out of Henri's house in the first place. It was unnatural.

"She's not much trouble," Maélle said, nuzzling the tiny face. "And I love her."

"Of course you do. We all do. But she won't nurse forever and will need food, clothes, and a roof over her head. Can you expect to stay at Pierre's house with another mouth to feed? She is Henri's responsibility. Has he even.... *named* her yet?"

Maélle shook her head, not wanting to meet Josianne's eyes.

Two days later, Josianne showed up at the mercantile, and Maélle dropped her sewing to happily greet her. "Twice in one week. Did you tear a dress or something?" But her frivolity evaporated when she saw Henri walk in, and behind him and a Jesuit priest, who was new to the territory.

"What's...going on?"

"He has come for *Petite Suzanne*."

Maélle starred at Henri. He looked terrible. His hair was matted, and his clothes were stiff with dirt. It was as if nothing brought him joy anymore. "I want my daughter back in my home."

Maélle's eyes darted from Henri to Josianne to the priest. "But who will take care of her, who will feed her?" Her voice rose with growing hysteria.

"You will, Maélle, if you accept Henri." Josianne's hands were firmly on Maélle's shoulders.

"*What*?"

"Henri has agreed to marry you," Josianne continued. "And you can care for *Petite Suzanne*. You can still make things for the mercantile and me and your other clients." Josianne smiled, doing what she was a master at: making difficult situations palatable.

It was three heartbeats before Maélle could speak, "when?"

"We can do it now if you have no objections," the priest said, moving forward.

The room was spinning, and Maélle felt sick. She loved the baby Suzanne left behind, and she was still in love with Henri and had prayed fervently that he would someday be hers. But never in her life did she dream God would answer her prayers so hideously.

Maélle and Henri joined hands, and as the brief wedding was performed, Maélle could not think, could not speak, felt as if her untethered brain was bouncing loose inside her skull.

The priest spoke, "we should also baptize the babe. What is her name?"

When neither Henri nor Maélle spoke, Josianne leaned forward, placing a tender kiss on the baby's temple, "her name is Suzette, for the precious mother who died birthing her."

# Twenty-One

T he winter in the territory was harsh. The cold came in with battering winds off the coast. Although Paris had winter, it had a more temperate climate than the colony, and Josianne was already tired of being cold. The bitter wind blew damp off the ocean incessantly, and gray skies filled the days with gloom.

No matter how bright the fireplace was in the house, it always seemed cold. She was relieved Clara and Celeste seemed to be immune to the frosty temperatures and took to wearing extra undergarments to warm herself.

Clément was gone all day, every day. Overseeing the continuation of the building of the new city of *La Nouvélle Orleans*, which Josianne still thought was a terrible place to build a city.

It was near the mouth of the Mississippi River and prone to flooding. But as Clément explained, it needed to be there because it was close to the Natchez tribe whom the settlers were trading with. In addition, it was still on higher ground, which produced a natural levee. It was also a trading route between the Mississippi Territory and Lake Pontchartrain via the Bayou of St. John as well as offering access to the Gulf port of Biloxi. Often when she thought of the river, she wondered how Mickey was doing and hoped somewhere in the vast wilderness he was safe.

"Why are we calling it *La Nouvélle Orleans*?" she asked Clément one day. "Why are we naming a new city after old rich men who made a mess of France in the first place?"

"Because he was the regent in France, *Phillip II, Duc d'Orléans* when we were first trying to build the city. You are right; however, he is the man, along with others, who made such a mess of things." He knew she did not like his answer.

"We should keep the capital city in Biloxi." But she realized it would never happen, "Besides, all these men do is change their minds, and the *names* of things, and move the capitol around. First, the capital was to be Biloxi near Fort Louis, *then* they wanted to move it to New Biloxi, rename the fort there, *then* rename the post at Mobile, Fort Conde, and they have even tried moving it to Ocean Springs. And poor Mobile, which was to be the site of the capitol all the while, is forgotten. It's so confusing I cannot keep it all straight. And before you defend them, saying one port was better suited than another or because English or Spanish ships are there docking in the ports. None of you men can make up your minds, pool resources, and get *anything* accomplished!" She knew if she had not forced Clément against Governor Bienville's wishes to build the new mill to grind the corn, they would all still be doing it by hand.

Josianne never ceased to amaze him, and he laughed, agreeing with her.

# Twenty-Two

*C*eleste giggled when Josianne mispronounced the word *statue* in a book Clément had in his study. Self-conscious, Josianne tried the word again, only to see Celeste dissolve into laughter, hiding her face with her hands. "*Mademoiselle* Celeste," Josianne said, closing the book. "I suppose that is enough for today." Miffed, Josianne stood up. It was not just that Celeste had laughed at her, but among some of Clément's correspondence, Josianne found a letter from Captain de Martonne. Just seeing his bold handwriting across the page made her heart stall. The maroon wax seal was broken, and she was tempted to read it.

"Oh no, *Maman*! But we have barely started. It was only that you made a mistake." Her laughter evaporated when she realized Josianne was serious. After all, it was her favorite time of the day, tucked in the keeping room with a blanket across both their legs as she helped Josianne sound out the words. Frankly, Celeste was impressed with her stepmother's progress and enjoyed the closeness and one-on-one attention Josianne was able to give her, even though Celeste was the one teaching.

"We all make mistakes," Josianne said, fluffing out the folds in her dress, "and it is not kind to laugh at another's expense."

"But *Maman*, I meant no disrespect," her alarm grew.

"As I did not mean to mispronounce the word."

It was clear the discussion was over, and Celeste jumped off the couch and threw her arms about her stepmother. The laughter was replaced with tears, and Josianne was amazed at how volatile her moods were.

"I am so sorry, Maman. Please, *please* forgive me! I could not bear it if you were upset with me."

"Calm down, Celeste," Josianne soothed, stroking the young girl's back, and realized she was trembling. "All is well." She pulled back and cupped Celeste's face in her hands. "Be kind, be fair, and forgive. That is all you need to do in this world." She kissed Celeste on the forehead then.

Later, when Josianne was alone, she tossed the letter from Captain De Martonne into the fire, and watched it burn.

# Twenty-Three

*January 1721*

"There now, my love," Maélle soothed four-month-old Suzette, laying her in the cradle. Suzette was a good baby who slept when Maélle wished, took her breast without complaint, and rarely spit up. Maélle had fallen in love with the child more so because it was *not* her own and because she was the last link with Suzanne.

"I miss you, Suzanne," Maélle said quietly in the small room, stroking the baby's soft face. Suzette's eyes focused now, and she smiled up at Maélle, who had changed her diapers. The golden down was still on her head, and Maélle hoped she would be flaxen-haired like her mother. But then again, it was possible her hair would darken like her father's because babies changed, and one could never tell.

Henri was busy as a carpenter and spent hours away. Remarkably, her sewing clientele was growing. It was amazing to Maélle that some months, the colony would seem like it was improving, and just as quickly, a promised boat would not come, or the volatile weather would change.

Despite those variables she was making money with the few people who did have the means to buy her wares, and ever since she met *Monsieur* Massicot at Josianne's party, they had an agreement. Massicot needed someone to unload his French textiles to, and who better than a woman who excelled at making fine garments? Making new garments was not the only place Maélle shone, and she was also a *fripier—someone* who could take second-hand clothing and reshape it into newer styles.

A gust of frigid wind blew some dried leaves under the door, and Maélle put Suzette in her crib and replaced the old rug she had folded to keep the draft out.

It was a dark day, and everyone was anxiously awaiting spring, but it was apparent as the gray clouds hung thick in the sky, reflected by the ever-rolling sea, that it was not there yet.

Maélle turned the wick up a quarter inch on the lantern. The paltry flame grew brighter and threw eerie shadows on the wall. She sat down in a chair Henri had made and brought out her sewing again. She tried to do the fine work when Suzette was asleep.

Maélle's stomach rumbled. Food was in short supply, and for two weeks, they had eaten nothing but corn porridge that Little Moon called *sagamité*. She also added some squash that had survived the frost, and it was a welcome change.

She licked the end of the thread and, leaning closer to

the lantern, squinted to thread the needle. Successful on her third attempt, she knotted it and began to stitch a shirt.

The wind blew again, and Maélle held her breath. She wondered why, when she was alone, she often felt Suzanne's presence. It still bothered Maélle that they had used what little honey and molasses they had to feed Suzette rather than using the open jar of honey by Suzanne's body.

The honey would connect the deceased person's soul to other departed souls. But Maélle supposed that feeding that molasses to Suzette was more important than completing rituals born of old superstitions.

A light, cold rain started. Maélle could hear it against the roof and smell it in the air. Sighing, she put the stitch-work on the table and, leaning back, closed her eyes. The small fire in the hearth gave a bit of warmth, and Maélle wished she could feel more of it.

She awoke a few moments later and heard Suzette. Suzette was simply lying on her back, cooing quietly. Reaching into the cradle, Maélle held her lovingly against her chest. Suzette's head was still a little wobbly, but her neck would support it.

"There now *mon doux bebe.*"

Suddenly, Suzette held her head up straight, staring at something behind Maélle, and then giggled. Maélle turned to see what Suzette could be looking at. There was nothing but a blank wall. Maélle kissed Suzette's cheek. The baby looked at Maélle, smiled, and then again looked past her and giggled.

"What are you giggling at?" Maélle laughed and spun

around, holding the baby. Although Suzette enjoyed the antics, she continued to face the spot on the wall. An uneasiness came over Maélle as Suzette continued to smile and coo at nothing.

A few nights later, a lonely wind tore at the logs and bousillage of the cabin, and Maélle huddled under the covers. It was an inky night with no moon, and it was dark inside the cabin, except for the dying flames in the hearth.

She shivered and was glad for the heat of Henri asleep next to her. Maélle had taken one of the blankets from their bed and put it with Suzette. But now, with teeth chattering, Maélle moved closer to Henri, pushing her body against his warmth. She heard him sigh in his sleep and scared she had awakened him; she didn't move until she heard his steady breathing again.

But a few minutes later, she felt Henri turn towards her. The warmth emanating from him was so delicious she could not stop herself from moving into his embrace. His arm was around her; his hand found her breast, still plump from nursing, and Maélle's breath caught in her throat. She touched his chest. Then he guided her hand lower to his groin. Groaning weakly, he rolled on top of her. She had never been kissed before, but in the darkness of the little house, she had no trouble opening up to him.

His hand was underneath the covers to get the offending clothing out of the way. It was overwhelming and wonderful, and she found herself arching up to him.

It was not comfortable, but she dared not cry out even though her groin ached. When Henri climaxed, he laid against her for some seconds, just breathing in the warmth of her neck, then softly rolled over. In a little while, she heard his soft snores.

Maélle was up and at the hearth when she heard Henri turn over. She was coaxing the fire to life, Suzette in her free hand. She was not sure what she should say to him; but unable to delay any longer, Maélle faced him.

His hair was tussled from sleep, and his shirt was not buttoned properly. Standing up, he pulled on his trousers and grinned at her.

A flash of love seared through her.

Nearing Maélle, Henri took Suzette out of her arms. "*Bonjour* Suzette, *mon chere*," Henri said, kissing the baby.

Not sure what to do, Maélle went back to the stove, kneading together the last of the mashed corn to fry in the skillet. She skipped eating yesterday, and as her stomach painfully turned over, she promised herself that she could have a bit of food today. When it was finished, she brought the sparse meal to Henri at the table.

"Thank you." He ate the scant patty quietly, holding a gurgling Suzette. The way he looked down at Suzette with adoration made Maélle's heart swell. Maélle would do anything for Suzette, and if that meant living only for her adopted daughter, she would.

"Maélle, was it...all right last night?" His eyes were unsure, and Maélle had to look down to calm the disappointment drumming in her heart.

"Yes, I mean, I did not mind." Realizing he remembered what happened, began to wring her hands, assaulted with shame, unable to believe she had said such a thing to Suzanne's husband.

"Then, we can be...husband and wife?" He asked hopefully. He had been unsure how to approach the subject, and was relieved it was out in the open.

Maélle's heart thumped painfully in her chest. She forced a smile, "it does not bother me."

Henri's face flushed with a smile. "We are *married*, after all. And I appreciate you taking care of Suzette." Looking up he met her eyes, "I don't know what I would do without your help."

Maélle's heart clenched. It was obvious to her that Henri did not love her. She was nothing but a nursemaid to her deceased friend's child. It was then that Maélle closed off her heart to protect it.

# Twenty-Four

Hélène stoked the fire to heat the water for the laundry. She stirred the enormous pot carefully with the paddle. The water was scalding, and she had a whole pile of Le Bond's clothing to sort and wash, as well as the other architect, Jacques Perot. Perot had trouble looking at her and she figured it was because he had never seen a birthmark that large before. Knowing this, she made sure to *always* show him her right side.

She added a small amount of lye soap and waited for it to dissolve when Le Bond's housemaid, Edele, appeared.

"Hélène, I am afraid I have bad news."

Hélène clenched her hand inside her pocket, rolling the misshapen pearl between her fingers. Just touching the pearl calmed her. Sometimes, she wondered how many more Mickey had found during his trips.

"We are going to have to let you go. *Monsieur* La Bond does not have the funds to keep you anymore. You can still do the wash, but we cannot feed you anymore. I'm afraid you'll have to make other plans." The owner of the storeroom had told her the exact thing a few months ago. No one, it seemed, had any room for Hélène Francois.

Even though Edele and Hélène were not close, Hélène knew it pained her to break the news.

"Plans? What other plans am I supposed to make in this God-forsaken place? I was already thrown out of the warehouse. What am I supposed to do now?"

Edele frowned. "You were supposed to marry, not come to the territory and find work. Your work was to be a wife and populate the settlement." She sighed then, "I am sorry, Hélène. *Monsieur* Le Bond told me this a few weeks ago, and I've been trying to find another way for you."

Hélène nodded but couldn't help but think she was just another piece of Paris trash thrown away.

Edele handed her a small piece of cloth tied with string. "These are your last wages." She closed her hands around Hélène's, "I'm so sorry. I hear Mickey Clavier is back in town...perhaps you should go see him."

It drizzled in the late afternoon, and as Hélène walked along the sandy, wet path, deciding what to do, she noticed there was not much mud because the sandy soil greedily soaked up the rain. It was why she supposed a plant could grow six inches overnight, and realized how folklore about woodland deities, like faeries and sprites, began.

At the seashore now, she watched the gray clouds scuttle across the sky far out, where the sea became a flat line. Despite the clouds, it was still bright, and she put her hand up to shield her eyes. The dampness of the wet-packed sand seeped into her shoes. She smiled, wondering what was better, the damp beach she walked on now or the dry sand that kicked up into her shoes.

The wind was making frothy peaks out in the ocean, and she scanned the horizon for birds. Seeing them in the distance, she smiled. The day tasted of sea salt and dirt. The winter had been cold, but the sun was warm, and she was damp under her arms and at her waistband. When a breeze caressed her body, it chilled her.

She found herself standing outside Mickey's shack. It may have been a dark wood once, but proximity to the shore had weathered it to a dull gray. She assumed it had also been perpendicular, but now it leaned left.

She stood for a few minutes gathering her courage, then rapped on the door. Looking around the shack, she saw Mickey's skiff bouncing in the shallow water and, next to it, the pirogue. It was amazing to her that he could spend months on end in such a small watercraft. It was little more than a hollowed-out tree and looked like it would be difficult to steer. There was a long paddle lying at the bottom of the boat and a hard bench for the seat. Not totally unlike the galleys, she realized and shivered.

She rapped again, and the door opened a crack.

"Mickey?"

Realizing who it was, he swung the door open.

His hair was longer than she had ever seen, and was a tangled mess. His beard was unruly and covered more than half his face. He was shirtless, and she noticed the jarring GAL tattoo on his right shoulder. There were several scars on his body, and realizing he had gotten those in the galleys, her breath caught in her throat.

"Well, if it isn't Hélène Francois." Then he grinned. She noticed one of his incisors was gone and wondered if it had been knocked out in a fight. "Come in, come in. I've been waiting for you."

She hesitated, fear slithering like a reptile in her stomach. She winced when the door was shut behind her. Nervously, she glanced around the shack, and was surprised.

It had a neat brick fireplace, and one window that was covered by an animal skin. The light in the room was coming from a sooty oil lantern with a cracked glass shade. The walls, at one time, had been whitewashed, but it was wearing off, and Hélène could see the grain peeking through. There was a teak wood table and two chairs. A narrow bed against the wall was covered with a tattered quilt. Although she could still hear the ocean from outside, it was surprisingly a restful, calming place.

She turned to face him, "waiting for me, why?"

"You've lost the position at Le Bond's house. All the other brides are married. And now, finally, you have come to me." He uncorked a bottle and poured two inches of rum into two dented cups. Handing her one he said, "let's have a drink."

Holding the cup, she swallowed it anxiously in one

gulp, trying not to wheeze as the strong spirit burned her throat. "How are you doing?"

He tilted his head, "Good some days, bad the others. I am at the whim of the river and the weather and whomever I encounter."

This was not reassuring, and she wondered if she wanted to be tangled up with a man who blamed bodies of water and the weather for his failures. She nodded politely, having no idea what to do next.

He poured more rum into her cup.

"*Sante*," he said, upending his cup, then added even more rum.

"But you are trading, and I heard you turned a profit."

He put a foot up on the chair, leaning his elbow against his knee. He grinned. "Always the bottom line with you, Hélène, isn't it?"

Embarrassment burned her cheeks, "I don't think wanting to make money is to be looked down upon, do you?"

He shook his head, finishing the rum. "I suppose not. And if you are asking if I am rich yet, I am not. It will take a few years." He let his eyes wander over her face, happy she had come to him. "And what will you do now?"

She resented that he had the advantage, "I-I don't know."

"Then, why did you come to see me? There must be something you want." He waited for her to answer and when she did not, added, "you have no job."

"No, I can still do the wash, but I-I am to find other lodgings and meals."

"So, you have nowhere to live and nothing to eat."

She was defiant, "it's only...temporary."

"Only *temporary*? You are a laundress with no home who can barely feed herself." He let that sink in.

She took another drink.

"Why come to me?"

She swallowed hard, embarrassment and humiliation fighting to color her face. "You asked me once if you remember."

"I asked, what?"

She hated that he was making this so difficult. "You asked me if I would marry you."

"Yes, I did. And you said.... *no.*" He crossed his arms in front of his bare chest. He was heavily muscled from years at the oars. "Why should I marry you now? You're the last one, and you're not very nice or pretty, Hélène."

Anger seized up in her, "I *know* that!"

"And I was *a* gentleman. I came to see you. I brought you gifts. But you, *you* would not have me."

As he scrutinized her, she had to look down, knowing what she looked like. She was gawky, and her hair frizzed up in the constant humidity, and the birth-mark reminded her every day, that she was different.

She swallowed hard. "I'm sorry, Mickey. I realize now I was not nice to you."

He shrugged, wiping the rum from his lips, not bothering to contradict her.

"We could help each other. I can cook the fish you bring, and I can salt them. We could sell them in the marketplace." She paused a moment, wondering how best to present her skills. "I could wash your clothes and help you sell the things you bring back."

He was staring at her, occasionally placing the tin cup to his lips, washing rum down his throat.

She looked around the room helplessly, "I can keep the house while you are away." She touched the table, which was covered with sand and dust.

"Poor Hé-lène. It's such a pretty name; it does not seem to belong to you." He enunciated each syllable.

"Don't say *that,*" painfully remembering someone else had once told her that.

"You come begging now to a man you would not look at before."

"I know. I said I'm sorry." She hated that he was making her grovel. And since when was a convict such a prize? "I'll go," she moved towards the door, but his thick hands caught her by the shoulders.

"So soon? But we've barely finished our drinks." He sloppily refilled the little cups.

She wavered. If he was not going to marry her, she was not going to stay any longer and be humiliated. What could she do, though? Perhaps Josianne could take her into her home, perhaps she could live with Maélle at Henri's; perhaps she would starve in the streets.

"I will be gone for months at a time on the river.... you will be alone."

Hélène swallowed hard, "I can manage that." Thinking she would prefer the solitude to his ridicule.

"And when I am back? What will you do for me, Hélène, when you are my wife?"

She did not like the way he was looking at her, but bolstering her faltering courage, she stared back at him. "I suppose what any other woman would do."

"Have you been with a man before?"

Her ears went scarlet. What could she say? Tell him that when she saw dogs humping in the street, thought it disgusting. She was not *about* to tell him about the rape. "No, of course not. I lived in a hospital run by nuns."

"Would you like to find out what it is like... to be with a man?" Putting his cup down, he came towards her.

So this was her punishment for thwarting him. He was just as depraved as she suspected he was, but her choices were limited, and she vowed not to let him know how scared she was.

He stroked the side of her face, even touching the birthmark.

Uncomfortable with anyone touching it, she tried to move away. "Mickey don't."

"It's all right, it does not bother me," he said with a kindness that surprised her. His thumbs stroked her cheek, and leaning in, he kissed her. His lips were rough, his beard was scratchy, and, as always, he smelled faintly of sweat and fish.

Before she knew what was happening, he was backing her away from the door. She felt the side rail of the bed against her calf, then he lowered her down on the bed. His weight pressing her so deeply against the mattress, she felt the rope webbing against her spine.

"I've been waiting a long time for this." Straddling her, he undid the buttons to her bodice.

"Mickey, no."

He stared down at her. "Are we going to act like you aren't curious about this Hélène? Pretend this is not what you came here for?" He was undoing the thin string that did up her shift, "I want to see what I am getting."

Exposed, she shivered and modestly put her hands up to hide herself.

He scrutinized her childlike breasts, and shrugged, "they are small, but I don't care, they will be *mine*."

His breathing quickened, and his eyes turned dark with lust as he pulled up her skirt. "Spread your legs, and it won't hurt so much."

She had to grip the sides of the bed to keep her head from hitting the wall as he thrust against her. He was breathing like he'd run up a hill. His bare chest rubbing against hers, his face buried against her neck, was oddly erotic. It was thrilling to feel the power of him, the force, and she was ashamed to admit she felt disappointment when it ended so soon.

Getting up, Mickey nonchalantly pulled his trousers on.

Unsure what to do, she sat up and made up her clothes. She heard him pouring more rum and brought her the cup. He sat down then on the bed next to her like nothing had happened.

Hélène brought the cup to her lips and swallowed it. It occurred to her that she was not a proper maid anymore. All her life, she had heard whispers about the pleasures of the marital bed. As she sat next to Mickey, she wondered now what all the fuss had been about.

He wiped his mouth with the back of his hand, "I will tell the governor we are to be married."

There suddenly didn't seem to be anything else to say. She walked to the door and left without either of them saying goodbye, fingering the pearl in her pocket as she walked.

At their marriage the next week, neither of them looked at each other as the priest put the sacred garments across their wrists, uniting them.

When they walked back through the settlement after their marriage, it was embarrassing for Hélène to see how happy Josianne was, how Suzette cooed in Maélle's arms, and how happy Henri was for them. Maélle had made her a new bodice with the fabric Josianne had purchased. It was a pale green silk, and although beautiful, impractical for the life she would be living.

It was not until that afternoon, when she reluctantly followed Mickey into the shack, that it all sunk in.

"Where can I put my things?" Hélène asked. Although she had few possessions, she still wanted to carve out an existence.

"Wherever you want, I suppose."

Sighing silently, Hélène came into the room and moving a bucket with her foot, found a place near the bed to lay down her things. She had never seen so many fishing poles, lines, harpoons, and nets wondering why she hadn't noticed them before.

"I'll get water for you." He was dressed as nicely as he could, given that his clothes were old and faded. He had bathed, though, because his dark, curly hair was clean and shiny. When he stood next to her during the short ceremony, the smell of sweat and fish had been replaced with soap.

He opened the door, and a woosh of afternoon air and humidity flooded the room. Héléne could hear the ocean, smell the sea, hear the cawing of the birds in flight.

"Tide's going out," he said, his back to her. He glanced up at the sky, seeing the constellation patterns were changing with the seasons. "I'll be heading out soon." She was both relieved and scared. She had never taken care of a house before, never lived alone.

"I'm going to go check my lines," he said and left.

Unbuttoning the pretty silk bodice, Hélène replaced it with a practical cotton one, deciding if this were to be her new home, it would be clean. Pulling the cracked glass shade off the lantern she realized it would emit more light if it were clean. Finding a tattered piece of sail, she buffed the lens.

She dusted what she could and tidied the floor. To her amazement, she found a broom and swept the planked floor, realizing she had to sweep with the grain of the wood; otherwise, the sand merely collected in the grooves between the planks.

She dozed off later in the afternoon, but hearing something at the door, opened it to find Mickey winding up a rope into a perfect oval.

"Mickey!" She gasped, relieved to see him.

"I've caught us dinner."

He had a large fish in his hand. She watched him make a slit by the gills and a circular cut around the head. He then sliced it down the middle and peeled the skin off the fish like a snug piece of clothing. She heard a small crack then as he broke the backbone and pulled the head of the fish in the opposite direction, thereby removing the entrails and skin in one fluid motion. He threw the mess into the water. "That'll feed some other creature."

She reached out to take the fish having no idea what to do with it. "I-I don't know how."

"There's a frying pan on the stove. I can show you."

"What *is* it?"

"A channel cat. Blues, and flatheads usually get bigger." Removing his gloves, he walked in the house.

The table was dusted, the chairs tidied, the floor swept, the bed made, and the old stove scraped of grease. The house smelled of soap and fresh air. Even the skin over the window had been beaten clean of dust. He put the catfish on the stove.

"You *cleaned*!" Leaning down, he gently kissed the birthmark, softly stroking his thumb across the bumpy red edges.

"Please don't Mickey."

He continued to stroke the birthmark, "It's all right. It does not bother me. Don't let it bother you." He drew her near and kissed her again, a long, slow kiss—a kiss that opened the locked doors in Hélène's heart, doors she thought would never open.

He put his hands around her waist, squeezing gently as his thumbs brushed the bottom of her breasts. Hélène shivered, pushing herself against him.

"Now?" he asked.

"Yes."

He wavered a moment.

"I can't wait," she said, tearing at his clothes.

Breathing heavily, he bent her over the table. Eagerly she moved her feet apart, and he mounted her with a ferocity that excited her. It was primal and lustful and enjoyable, and she understood now why people did such things.

When he was done, he wrapped his arms around her, holding her against his chest. "I've never made love like that before," he said between ragged breaths, "always wanted to."

"What other ways are there?"

He pulled up from her, still sweating, and laughed. "Lots of ways," bending, he kissed her again.

She put her arms up around his neck, "I think I'd like to try them all."

"I just bet you would," he laughed and nipped a violent kiss on her mouth. "But you're going to need to give me a little while. I'm not as young as I used to be." Closing his eyes, dropped back onto the bed.

"Should I find a younger husband then?"

He cracked an eye open, "I suggest you don't. Are those your plans while I am away?" He asked with annoyance.

Héléne laughed, enjoying the playful banter, but then he caught her hand.

"You'll be faithful to me, won't you, Héléne?"

When she realized he was serious, a rare warmth spread through her heart. "Of course, I will be."

She knew they were not in love, but perhaps their odd, misfit marriage could work.

# Twenty-Five

By the time Mickey finished making the preparations for his next trip, Hélène was unsettled and cross. Everything was happening too fast and she was surprised how much she did not want him to leave. She hid it though, not wanting him to tease her or think less of her. The weak did not survive in this world.

"What else do you need?" she asked, even as tall as she was, she had to look up to Mickey.

His brow furrowed in thought, "that is everything. I will leave first thing in the morning." He closed the door behind him, and sat to take off his boots.

Hélène stood wringing her hands.

"Is there something...bothering you Hélène?" done with his boots he put his hands on his knees.

"No, I'm-I'm fine." A blur of tears embarrassingly came into her eyes, and although she did everything in her power not to, she sniffed.

He cocked his head at her suspiciously. "Are you... crying at the thought of me leaving?"

Hating the amusement she detected in his voice she looked down. "I've...never lived alone."

"Well, you'll have the bed all to yourself." He grinned, thinking about the pleasurable nights he had spent with her. Their lovemaking was rough and passionate, and neither of them was shy about asking and getting the pleasure they craved. He liked that she was adventurous and did not pretend she did not enjoy their coupling. Looking around he realized there was not a spot in the room, where they had not made love, and her eagerness for sex was an aphrodisiac. He knew they joked in town that he had married the "ugly one" but he did not care, they did not know what he did. "Would you like to... get back in that bed with me before you find yourself all alone in it?"

She forced a smile and angrily swatted at the tears. She had not cried much in her life, after all what was the point? But now felt as though she had something to lose.

"I know the currents are swift in the spring, you are going to have to be extra careful." She had violent nightmares of him drowned along one of the poorly charted tributaries, gruesome images of his body bloated on the shore, while birds picked at his flesh.

Nodding Mickey unbuttoned his shirt, tossing it to the chair. "You do realize I have done this before?" But he was taken aback when his sharp-tongued wife seemed to wither before his eyes. "What is it?" he asked finally standing in front of her.

Tentatively, she reached out and touched his chest,

touched the place where GAL was crudely tattooed. "Mickey--"

"What's bothering you Hélène?"

"Nothing. It's nothing."

Anger cartwheeled through him, "I wish you would tell me. Is the house not good enough for you?" Annoyed at himself for caring so much what she thought.

"It's a better house than I have ever lived in."

"Am *I* not good enough for you?"

She closed her eyes, "of course you are."

Mickey hung his head, "What do you *want*... Hélène?" he plead, his eyes met hers. "While I am gone you are free to do whatever you want. I never stop you from helping Maélle, you are free. What do you want?"

It was a moment before Hélène could gather the courage to speak. "I don't want to be afraid."

He leaned against the table and folded his arms in front of him, "What are you afraid of?"

Her voice was small. "You were a salt smuggler. You defied the King's laws and committed a crime. You were sentenced to the galleys, and now you are here."

"I am aware of my own history."

"But need I remind you of mine? I was kicked out of my house when I was eleven. I did the wash for soldiers, and merchants, where I am accused of stealing. Then I am sent to *La Salpêtrière* prison for years, and then sent to this God forsaken land for no reason. I did *nothing* wrong. And yet...here I am. I don't want to fear if someone is going to round me up, take away my liveli-hood. And what best calms my fears... is money."

Hélène was concerned about his silence. She had still

never witnessed the "violent" gypsy those in town warned her about, and wondered if they knew him at all.

He came to her and clumsily put his hands on her shoulders.

"I promise you; I will be a success; I won't drown, and I will come back to you. And I want you to know, that I would never let anyone take you away from...*me*." He bent and tenderly kissed the birthmark.

She leaned up and kissed him full on the mouth. A long, passionate kiss that spoke to him more than her words could. He had never thought she loved him. Knew the harshness of life people could ill afford such luxuries, especially in the territory.. But when she finally finished the kiss and stared up at him, he was suddenly not so sure and found himself breathing hard at the wonderful possibility.

He would make this dangerous trip, he would brave the elements, the winding river, the people he met on the way, and would come back.

But in the morning Hélène surprised Mickey by asking him *again* if she could purchase the mercantile.

"We cannot buy the mercantile, I don't understand this Hélène. I don't understand any of this. The whole reason I am going out is to earn us money--"

"We can use our winter savings for next year, I will make it work, I *swear* I will."

Mickey raked his hand through his unruly hair.

"No! We cannot. Did you...*think* to talk to me about this first? Or are you just waiting to do it after I leave?"

The color leaving her face told him he was right. "You are thinking about taking the money *I earned*, to buy a business without even *consulting* me? And by the way, if you use the winter savings, what exactly do *you* live on while I am gone?"

When he phrased it like that, it made Hélène wince because she knew if the tables were turned, she would be furious as well.

"You are going to be gone a lot—"

"Because I am out fishing and trading, for you Hélène, for *us*. And that money is for me to buy a new boat, a better boat. I don't want you to do this—" He silenced her protest with a look, but then relenting said, "not right *now* Hélène, I understand you want...you *need* security. I am not saying *never*, but not right now. Let us wait till we are better situated, then we can think about it." He had just enough money for the winter supplies, and to keep them fed. And he had dreams of clearing land, of building a proper house, and children.

Although the conversation ended, Hélène had her mind made up.

Hélène was never sure exactly when Mickey would be back. Some trips were only three weeks, most of them longer, and a month after he left, she arranged to purchase not the mercantile as she had wanted, but the tavern. The former owners got a commission from

Clément for land in somewhere called Alabama. Buying the tavern was such a fabulous opportunity, she could not pass it up.

Hélène did the meager inventory of the tavern, and haggled over what she would pay for it. With the reduced price and the winter savings she took ownership of the building and sparse contents. Clément helped her with a loan of sorts, and she felt guilty lying when Clément asked if Mickey was aware of what she was doing.

When she got into the tavern, and took a closer look, her heart sank, realizing it was in worse shape than she thought. She had to give free drinks to several soldiers in exchange for them repairing the roof. The first night she was working there late, a drunk sailor wandered in and scared her half to death, prompting her to have a better bolt on the door.

She whitewashed the inside, and cleaned the bar top till the grain in the wood was raised, and had to be sanded back down. With the last of the winter money, she ordered a window to put in the front and was shocked when the glass came in so quickly. She had Henri install the window and climbed the rickety ladder herself, and painted a sign over the front door that read in bold, black letters, HÉLÈNE'S.

A month after taking ownership, the men in the town nicknamed her "Hélène the horrible" because she could hold her own with the lot of them, as a result they respected her. But when a sailor new off a ship thought he could misbehave, she was not above letting them know that she was married to a man that had GAL tattooed on his shoulder.

And she was proud when she got to work each day. It was beyond her wildest dreams that as a discarded woman from France, she owned a business. It was not much money, but every day there was a tiny bit more in the till.

She kept detailed ledgers of all the transactions and made sure she was keeping enough money back to re-purchase what sold, while making her small payments to Clément.

It was exhilarating to be running this business, and each morning she awoke full of energy, and not even the annoying possum that took up residence under the porch could diminish her optimism.

In addition to selling tafia, she sold wine, demi and a local beer brewed from corn. She sold Maélle's wares there instead of at the Mercantile. They enjoyed each other's company during the day and took turns caring for Suzette. It was a situation that worked out wonderfully for both.

Hélène did still wonder sometimes when *La Nouvélle Orleans* would turn into a true town, for it was still a beleaguered place, full of swamps and canebrakes. The city if one could call it that, was rough and lawless. If the ill-behaving inhabitants were not bad enough, the weather was worse.

For half a year it rained, and it was damp, and chilly, turning everything into a sandy bog. Despite the best intentions of the residents, the brush and vines continued to encroach on the city, as if refusing to give up the land. The other half of the year it was so hot she sweated through her clothes daily and it felt as though the marrow in her bones was drying out.

There were signs of progress though, no matter how slow they were. Residences were popping up and plans for a church, and a market, were emerging. And the town even boasted more than one blacksmith in town. More people were hacking the canebrakes to get land, and more ships dropped off supplies, which was a welcomed relief. It was not the town the residents wanted yet, but it was growing.

Despite all the towns drawbacks, of insects, floods, stifling heat, and continued political upheaval, *La Nouvélle Orleans* was developing into a settled territory along the mighty Mississippi, and in the French quarter alone there were now over three hundred residents.

Five months after his departure, Hélène was startled to see Mickey standing in front of the tavern. He was leaning back, looking up he squinted as he read the sign above the window.

A cold panic started down her spine.

He looked different. She heard the rumors of what happened to men that frequented the winding, quiet bayous. How it would change a person to be alone for so long, see so many strange sights, have nothing to rely on but your wits for survival. And when he entered and stood in front her in those bright blue eyes of his she saw disappointment.

Hélène straightened her back. "Hello, Mickey I did not know when you would be back."

He nodded and glanced around the tavern, and seeing Maélle's clothing for sale, realized the two of them, despite the precariousness of the territory, were doing well.

"Mickey!" Maélle said coming out from behind the back room, she embraced him awkwardly because Suzette was in her arms. "I am so glad you are back. How was the trip?"

His eye's never left Hélène's face, "It was good. I've already traded most of it along the back bayous." He grinned when he touched Suzette's little hands, marveling at how soft they were.

The conversation stalled, and Maélle could feel the tension between Hélène and Mickey. Even though Hélène tried to hide it, Maélle knew Hélène missed Mickey, and was fonder of him than she let on.

"Isn't it wonderful what Hélène has done with the tavern? She has really turned it into a proper place, and in record time."

Nodding, Mickey walked a few steps, looking around. "I see that she has."

"I just come here during the day to help out and all." Maélle explained, adjusting Suzette.

Maélle glanced at Hélène, who's eyes were on the floor. Thinking they needed to talk alone, Maélle gathered up Suzette's things. "I've got to run along now. It is good to see you again."

It was a few moments before he spoke. "How did you pay for this Hélène?"

Her eyes were glued to the floor, her heart beating uncomfortably in her chest. It was several seconds before she spoke, as a cold sweat started at her temples.

"The winter money."

Closing his eyes, he sighed silently. A tired, deep sigh that came from the bottom of his soul. "The money that I *earned*?"

"*Oui.*"

"The money you took when I told you *no*, is that the money Hélène?"

She nodded and winced when he balled his fists at his sides. "Do you realize, you've made a *fool* out of me. I found out at the mercantile that my wife had taken over the tavern." He took a lot of ridicule from the men in town because he had married the 'ugly one.' If that was not bad enough, now he was the laughingstock because while he was gone, his shrew of a wife spent all his money.

"I had *other* plans for that money, and you *knew* that." He realized he would have to go out again immediately. He knew he could never explain to her how grueling the trips were, the courage it took to do what he did. Or how much he had looked forward to coming home to her.

"But Mickey, in time it will work, and if I did not do it, someone else would have and I am making it a success. I *swear* I am, as I promised you I would. I can show you the books. And as the territory is growing. The business will grow. It's not in the black yet, but it will be! I can make it a success," she gushed excitedly.

"*I* did this, and *I* did that, is that all you think of?

215

You're my *wife*! It was *our* money, or was it only *yours*?" The humiliation a red-hot poker in his brain.

He was in front of her, his hands gripping her shoulders so tightly she knew she would have bruises in the morning. "You have no idea what it is like out there on the river! I am out there on the bayous doing my best to provide for you." He thought about the thin gold band he had in his pocket, the ring he traded fish for from a Spanish settler who was starving. A fish she could eat, a gold ring she could *not*. "How will you take care of a house, our life if you are here working in a tavern?"

"We can live here Mickey, there is a perfectly acceptable loft above and even a back room."

"What about our children?"

Hélène tossed her head defiantly. "Maybe there won't be any children. I don't see how that can happen when you are gone all the time." She wasn't sure why she said it because she wanted to be a mother. And she had already promised herself that not only would her daughters receive the love that she never had, but they would also be educated and self-sufficient.

"What are you saying? I God damn *married* you, does that mean nothing to you?"

It did mean something to her, but she was rattled, "maybe I don't want to be married to *you* anymore." That stung, and she knew it. She also knew she had gone too far.

Grabbing her, he tried to kiss her.

Pulling back, she slapped him so hard his head snapped back. "Get out!"

His eyes burned down, "out of the tavern, that I *paid* for?"

"You'll never be anything more than a disgusting galley slave!"

In a flash he had her bent over the table, one hand on her back smashing her breasts and face against the table. Hauling up her skirts he kicked her feet apart. "You are *my wife*! Do you hear me? My *wife!*"

"Mickey *don't!*" squirming to be free, she fought like a wet cat. In a matter of minutes it was over. Trembling she adjusted her skirts, unable to believe what had just happened. She was fourteen again in an alley in Paris. She shivered with revulsion.

Panting he looked down at her, guilt and remorse etched on his face. "I'm sorry. I should not have done that—."

"No, you should not have." She stared at him unblinking, trying to let the pounding of her heart settle. "You will never touch me again. Wife or not, never again."

"Hélène, I am sorry." He dropped his face into his hands, knowing he had made a mess of things. "We can... get through this. I promise—"

"No, we cannot. Do you understand?"

He walked to the door then and looked back at her. "It is just not... *your* life Hélène, I had plans for that money for *us*."

She thrust her chin up rebelliously.

"Do you *enjoy*.... taunting me Hélène? Do you enjoy making a *fool* out of me?" He was going to add when *I love you but* was glad he did not when she interrupted.

"It's easy to do Mickey because you are nothing but a criminal, a brute. I hope I never see you again. I hope you never come back; I hope you drown."

He smirked, looking down, then pulled a small leather pouch from his pocket. He fingered the soft leather for a moment, tossed it carelessly on the table, and walked out.

When she was sure he was gone, she collapsed into the chair. Hyperventilating, realizing what she had done. She needed Mickey's income to make the payments. If that was not bad enough, she had been happy to see him. How had it all gone so horribly wrong?

Sniffing her tears back, absently she picked up the little pouch. It was fringed and had blue beads sewn on it. Dumping the pouch, a gold ring fell out. It spun on the table like a top, then wobbled and fell. Putting it on, she was surprised that it fit. It felt odd there at first, hitting against her other fingers. But it felt solid and real, like a circle that should be unbroken. She cried herself to sleep that night, wondering what would become of her.

Three months later Hélène finally acknowledged the reason she was feeling odd was because she was pregnant. Thinking back, she realized her monthly had been absent for an exceptionally long time, but in truth never paid much attention to the nuisance. Shocked, she examined herself in the mirror and to her bewilderment saw a pooch.

"But I can't be showing yet," she complained to

Maélle who was carefully cutting cloth on a long table. The sound of the scissors shearing the fabric competing with the night sounds of the summer evening.

"Maybe you are just getting fat," Maélle grinned. "I seem to recall you ate all the pastries Josianne brought over."

Hélène's eyes got huge, "*Mon Dieu!* Don't say such a thing." Into her mind tumbled the frightening ideas of giving birth and motherhood. "How will I know?"

Maélle shrugged, "how should I know. I just take care of babies; I don't have them. Let's ask Little Moon. She'd know better than any doctor would anyway," she paused a moment, then asked, "what about...Mickey?"

Hélène again placed her hand on her midsection, wondering what Mickey would think. "It's not like I can...reach him," she said, painfully remembering the last time she had seen him.

"I guess he'll be surprised then," Maélle said, knowing he had been gone an awfully long time, and wondered what was wrong between them.

# Twenty-Six

*Fall 1722*

In September, a devastating hurricane came ashore. The residents had weathered a few bad storms, but nothing like this snarling beast that threatened to devour everything in its path. The sky blackened to the point that it looked like twilight during the day, and wind kicked up with such force that those that had not witnessed the "evil winds" as the Indigenous people referred to them, were terrified. The fierce gale picked up trees and houses like they were toys, and then dropped them carelessly wherever. The wind moaned, shrieked, and howled relentlessly for fifteen hours.

Rain came then, and not a gentle, nourishing one, but one that came in blinding sheets. Pelting the houses, lashing sideways against the buildings. Seeping into the walls and through the roof, threatening to drown everything in its path. And if that was not enough, a surge of seawater came with the rain, drowning the coast, and reaching its watery fingers miles inward. When the storm finally died down, the next day dawned like it had never happened. Blue sky and bright sunshine fell upon the destruction like an spoiled child that had broken their own toys, and was now repentant.

Mobile was three-quarters damaged, as was the fledgling *La Nouvélle Orleans*, but later they would find out that Biloxi where they had first landed had been obliterated. Wiped clean from landscape as if it had never been there.

Terrified, Hélène holed up alone in the tavern, listening to the storm rage outside. She had not prayed much since coming to the territory. It had been such a strict requirement at the hospital, she resented praising God when her life was so miserable. But now on the strip of land along the coast where she found herself, she prayed fervently. As the hours dragged on, and the seawater came up to her ankles, and then her knees Hélène prayed. She prayed for the storm to stop, prayed that nothing would happen to the child she was carrying, and prayed that wherever Mickey was, he was safe.

She had been told that as the storm moved inland, it would follow the path of least resistance, which was the river. The hurricane's strength, although weakening, could still wreak havoc along its path. She imagined Mickey in his pirogue, the storm raging around him as the floodwaters rose. He would never see his child; she would never see him again.

Stopping at the edge of the city, Clément stepped out of the wagon, and after helping Josianne down, stared at the devastation that had been *La Nouvélle Orleans*.

Buildings had been flattened and puddles of stagnant water and debris was strewn everywhere. In total over thirty structures had been leveled.

Clément sighed and loosened his collar. It was still hot, and she worried about his health, and did not want him out in the heat too long.

"It's worse than I thought."

Josianne nodded in agreement, glad that their house, tucked away like it was in the woods, sustained little damage.

"We'll have to rebuild again." He said, poking at a rotting foundation board with his cane.

"Rebuild here, why that seems crazy! If a hurricane can come ashore once, it will do it again."

He stood then, still not looking at her but surveying the destruction with a determination she did not condone.

"Yes, here. Again."

Josianne had to swallow hard. She had been terrified during the storm. It was as if a watery howling monster had been unleashed on them. And she had been frightened for Celeste and Clara, and the three of them had huddled together for hours. "Why not, somewhere farther inland away from the sea?"

Clément shook his head. "We can't. As bad a spot as this seems, it was selected because the way the river bends, the safety of the harbor for the ships. It's higher ground here than other places." He glanced around the wreckage. "It is near the mouth of a great waterway. A waterway which one day will float all necessities and wares to the eastern seaboard. Through our port, wine, textiles, shoes, indigo and crops will travel." He breathed in deeply, swelling his chest. "And with that the coffers of the town will swell."

Sighing she looked out over the mess, having heard this speech before. She watched as the mosquitos were already making good the pools of trapped water. At night she had seen swarms of them so thick it was like a fog. Knowing she would never talk Governor Bienville, her husband and the other men that *argued non-stop* about where the capitol should be, out of placing the city there said, "then we better dig trenches and canals to deal with the water when it does come again, and it will." Shaking her head she realized the city would never survive without levees and wondered if these men really understood the need.

Maélle turned when Henri walked into the door. It was late, and she was half afraid something had happened to him.

"Are you hungry?" Immediately she went to him, but then, remembering herself, stepped back.

Henri noticed that she did this, and it both annoyed and angered him this odd practice of hers, because as far as he knew, he had done nothing to make her shy away. But he was tired and not in the mood to analyze his wife's silly behavior.

"Yes." He sat at the table and glanced over at Suzette asleep in her crib. A small smile curved his lips.

"Is it as bad as everyone says?"

"It's worse, and with the rebuilding we will have to do different things."

She placed the thin stew and flattened corn bread before him, and sitting folded her hands neatly in her lap. "Differently, how?"

He tore a piece of the bread apart and used it to sop up the thin gravy. "The wood here rots in a few years. In my estimation nothing is lasting more than five or at best ten years. We were putting the wood foundation on the ground, which in this place does not make sense. From now on we will have to build the foundations out of brick."

Maélle, nodded to let him know she was listening. This was when she loved him the most. The capable, smart carpenter who had been sent to help build the colony. She wondered if she could ever be worthy of him.

"Brick, we have brick here?"

"Yes, not enough of it yet, but we will. Clément has one brickworks near Biloxi, but we will need more. We could use stone, but I've not run into any stone within one hundred miles of this place. If that's not bad enough the only nails we have need to be imported."

"Will the brick foundation be enough?"

"No, but I've noticed that sometimes the Houmas cover their dwellings with a mixture of crushed oyster shells and mud, and it slows down the deterioration of the wood."

Her heart constricted, "You've been near the Indians?" She was frightened of them, although she knew without Little Moon telling them to plant the beans, squash, pumpkins and even sunflowers, they would never have made it through the first winter. Little Moon even told them about the maize that had not one, but *two* yields a year.

He stopped eating for a second, "Yes, they have lived here a long time and figured out some things that I surely have not. I'll take you there sometime, there are huge middens of oyster shells piled taller than me."

"Isn't that dangerous?"

"More dangerous for them, than for me." But he could see her uneasiness. "It's true I could anger one of them, not understanding their traditions, but seems to be they have *far* more reason to worry about me, than me about them, especially with everyone pouring in here."

His words soothed her some, but she was still frightened. There were constant skirmishes with all the different factions not getting along, and that her husband was openly visiting these differing tribes worried her. Just a few months ago indigenous tribes attacked a fort near Natchez, and there was fighting up and down the Mississippi. Many feared *La Nouvélle Orleans* would come under attack, and plans had been drawn up to protect the city, though luckily no such attack ever happened.

Finishing with his dinner he gently pushed the bowl away. "We did the roof lines wrong too. We made hipped and steeply pitched roofs, as if there was snow. Here we need a lower roof with *galeries* around the structures to ward off more sun and rain. Hopefully, with the brick foundations and plastering the structures with the crushed oyster shells it will make a difference." Henri did not want to tell her that the town was still struggling with negligent actions when it came to buildings.

There were settlers that flat out refused to build where they were told or dig the trenches and canals to alleviate the water. Neighbors were not above accosting one another when disputes arose over property lines. Henri knew of a man who had built where Perot and the other city planners had not allowed and ordered the building to be razed. When the poor man appealed to The West Indies company for indemnification, one of the city planners beat him with a stick and threw him in jail. A few days later when the man was released, he was near blind from the incident.

Later that night they crawled into bed. In the darkness Henri reached for her, although he noticed her reluctance. Hoping it was his imagination he went ahead and made love to his wife. But when it was over, he felt an emptiness when she turned away from him. In the quiet darkness he wondered what he was doing wrong and why she did not want him.

# Twenty-Seven

The rain that fell that year was heavier than anyone in the territory had ever seen. It caused massive floods and the colony was on the brink of starvation yet again.

Clément was beside himself with worry. The crops that did survive the relentless rain soon spoiled, the homes that were left continued to decay, rotting through. When the sun did at last come out, the land steamed from the semi-tropical heat.

Clément as well as Governor Bienville sent dozens of letters to the finance ministers in France pleading for help. But France, since the demise of John Law's schemes, was still in turmoil and had no interest that her countrymen were starving halfway around the world. Clément was so desperate he even commissioned a ship with his own money to bring supplies to the territory.

If the deluge of rain and famine were not enough to break the struggling colony a new danger arose. No one was safe from the sickness that ravaged the occupants.

Strange fevers took hold, abdominal pain, chills, nausea, and vomiting. In fact, so many people died that the brand-new hospital that had been built, intended for eighty occupants, was soon overrun.

When both Clara and Celeste came down with the illness Clément refused to transport them there because in a matter of days the only hospital was depleted of supplies. There were no sheets, towels, syringes, pots and spoons. The only people partially immune from the scourge of the disease were the African slaves. But the French and Indians of the territory succumbed to the disease in frightening record numbers.

Josianne had nursed the girls herself, and although she too came down with the fever, recovered in time to nurse Clément from the brink of death.

Amongst the dead were Marie Louise Letellier, one of the inhabitants of the *La Mutine*, who died just shy of her twenty-third birthday.

No one knew what caused it, and the Indians, Africans and others all had different names for the illness that sickened everyone. The disease claimed so many lives, graves could not be dug quickly enough. Which led Clément to grapple with a new problem of what to do with the dead. The water table was high, it made burying the dead impractical, because coffins would often emerge from the ground like gruesome phoenixes.

Clément commissioned that corpses be buried in the natural levee along the river. A decision that woke him up at night in a cold sweat, hoping the water in the soil did not uproot the dead from their slumber. Other than this levee, he had nowhere to put the dead.

It would be a full two years before the *Cimetière St-Piere* was built, where they could do some inground burials and they could enact a true policy for burying the deceased.

Mickey walked back through town a year after the hurricane, horrified at the damage that had been done. He'd braved some terrible storms and seen first-hand what the wrath of wind and water could do. He remembered how the sky turned black and the wind destroyed everything in its path. How defenseless he felt as the waves and rain juggled with his life, as the gates of a watery hell had been unleashed.

At the outskirts of *La Nouvélle Orleans*, he was amazed that clean-up was still underway. He made his way to where his little house should have been, and a painful hitch happened in his heart, it hurt him now that the little place he had brought his bride, was gone.

He could still see the remnants of buildings and piles of debris. Passing by the place he and Héléne had hidden from the storm he saw the tree was lying hideously on its side. The roots twisting furiously in the air, like an insect on its back struggling to right itself. The knowledge that Hélène had been in this storm alone, made his chest get tighter.

And yet the bright blue sky was cloudless, and warmth of the sun shone down on the beach as if nothing had ever happened.

"Mickey!" Clément called out. He was in a carriage with Josianne.

"*Monsieur* Heriot," Mickey said with a smile and taking the proffered hand, shook it vigorously.

"Mickey, you are back, we are so glad to see you. You've been gone so long I was worried something happened to you." Josianne smiled.

"Monster of a storm," Mickey said assessing the damage to the levee, "Is anything left of our *'Il de Orleans?*" Many still referred to the town as an island, a term Clément was not fond of.

"There is, but we will have to rebuild more than half the city. And as you can see, we are making progress."

"Is our greedy Regent going to fund it?" Mickey smirked. "Or whatever other greedy bastard is in power? They don't care about this colony. Because it is not turning a profit overnight, they abandon it."

Clément smiled wryly, "my guess is no we will not continue to be funded, but there are other ways."

Mickey nodded, but he disagreed with Clément who tended to see the world with rose colored glasses.

"Where were you? Did the storm hit you?" Josianne asked.

"I was way north. We got rain, and all the tributaries were swollen, but I managed to stay afloat."

It had been a hideous ordeal, the wind, the rain, he'd capsized once and thought for sure he would drown. How he had made it, he was not sure. And the snakes, he had encountered more venomous snakes fleeing from the storm than he ever had in his life. It had delayed him by weeks.

Clément smiled, "was it a successful trip?"

"Yes, I lost a lot but made up for it." It was a story he would tell, not wanting to talk about the nightmare it had been. "I see congratulations are in order." Mickey smiled, noticing Josianne's advanced pregnancy. He was envious suddenly.

"I just know it's a boy," Josianne beamed, at her much older husband, who cared only that his beautiful wife live through childbirth.

"Did you get sick? A terrible fever took hold of all of us." Clément asked.

Mickey knew this fever. Although he lived, whatever sickness it was, still plagued him from time to time.

"No, luckily, I did not. I spent some miserable weeks in the rain though."

"Does Hélène know you are back?" Josianne interrupted leaning near him.

"Not yet, did she come down with the fever?"

"No."

"Is she at the tavern?"

"I would imagine," Josianne said, wondering if she should tell him what happened, but decided to let him find out for himself.

Mickey walked to the tavern that although it had been damaged, was somehow still standing. He could see that the roof had been partially torn off, because a repair had been done.

He pushed the door open.

It was warm inside and cozy. Somehow the brick fireplace had withstood the storm, and inside burned a small fire. It was dim inside and he glanced around for any sign of Hélène.

"Can I get you a drink?" A pretty woman asked, a baby in her arms.

"No, not right now. I am Mickey Clavier and I have come looking for my wife Hélène."

A smile broke over her face. "Yes, she's here. I'll go fetch her for you."

Mickey stood looking at the structure, seeing salt watermarks, the tell-tale sign of how high the storm surge had been. It was amazing the place had survived.

He was surprised to see the woman and Hélène return, both holding babies.

Hélène's eyes were large in her face. She was still too thin, and yet her breasts were fuller. When it was clear she was not going to acknowledge him, he said, "Hélène."

Her eyes met his. When he moved to embrace her, she moved back avoiding the embrace.

He looked more like a bear than a man. A man nevertheless that had been living along the muddy unpredictable shores of the Mississippi for a year. A man who had assaulted her, a man that had the gall to be looking at her with a mixture of hope and caution.

"I am Elisabeth Vallet," the girl said when Hélène was silent. "I am married to the blacksmith, Marcus."

"I see more pretty girls have come into the territory in my absence," Mickey winked.

Despite his ragged appearance Hélène watched Elisabeth blush under Mickey's compliment, and jealousy lit up her insides. Elisabeth shook his outstretched hand while still holding a baby. It aggravated Hélène that the newest batch of women that arrived in the territory had it easier than she did. In February of 1721, *La Bailene* arrived. These women were also from *La Salpêtrière*, but they had not come in chains. And the single men of the village rowed out in little boats wanting to get a glimpse of the new girls coming into the territory. They were dubbed the "casket girls" because all of them came to the new land with a small wooden chest of belongings provided to them by The West Indies Company. Hélène remembered that she had come with *nothing*.

But what most annoyed Hélène about Elisabeth was although she was very pretty, she had the sense of a child and was all the time saying silly things. The fact that Marcus, had married her, only proved to Hélène that men *only* cared for beauty.

"You are the *voyaguer* I have heard about? Have you brought us bear oil and other things from far away?"

"*Our Mademoiselle*, I have."

He waited for someone to explain why they were both holding babies, and when no one did asked Elisabeth, "Are these your children?"

"Oh no, *monsieur*," Elisabeth laughed, "These are *yours!*" Moving to place a child in his arms.

Dumbstruck, Mickey stared at Hélène.

"*Mine*?" He was overcome with love, joy, and happiness. But then the awful thought occurred to him, that perhaps Héléne despised her children the way she despised him.

"What, what are they?"

"You are holding Genevieve. I have Jean Michel," Hélène said looking down at her son, still wondering why she had named him after his father.

"A girl!" Mickey said, surprising Hélène how naturally he cradled the baby. "When did this happen?"

"I realized I was pregnant... after you left."

"Shall I get him some *demi*?" Elisabeth asked interrupting, going behind the bar. Hélène wished Elisabeth would go home.

"*Demi* Hélène? You know it's illegal to brew?"

Hélène looked at him definitely, "I have to make a living."

Mickey nodded and took the offered drink from Elisabeth, then smirked, "What else are you doing, watering down the brandy as well?"

When her eyes flashed up at him, he knew he had hit a nerve. He wondered if she knew how dangerous it was to be in a business selling contraband, "I guess we are both criminals now."

Hélène bristled at the remark and repositioned the child on her hip.

"You work every day here?" Mickey asked Hélène, but it was the clueless Elisabeth that answered.

"*Oui!* And she has a knack for it. She can keep the patrons in line." Elisabeth smiled, "If they misbehave, she tells them she is married to a man with GAL on his shoulder."

"Oh, I see, you use my money to make a living and my reputation to keep you safe," Mickey smirked.

"What?" Elisabeth asked when her eyes flitted from Mickey to Héléne.

"You can run along Elisabeth; I'll take it from here."

When Héléne closed the door behind Elisabeth she awkwardly turned to Mickey.

"I haven't got much to offer you in the way of a meal." She began, half hoping he would leave.

Mickey was pleased she was offering even that. "I'm not very hungry, whatever you have is fine."

They sat and ate a humorless dinner, but Mickey barely noticed as he watched in amazement at how adept Hélène was with not one, but *two* babies. He watched her nurse, noticing how carefully she made sure to be as covered as she could. He wondered what to say to her, wondered if an apology could make up for what he had done.

"Are you staying the night?" She asked.

Mickey could not tell if she wanted him to say yes or no, and merely nodded.

He meekly followed her into the bedroom in the back. When she got the children down in their matching cradles she undressed and laid down on the bed. Not knowing what to do, Mickey joined her there. Although the mattress was thin, it was more luxury than he had felt in a year. Looking up at the ceiling he could not see the sky, and a panic came over him. It had been so long since he'd slept inside, he had trouble reconciling it.

"Where did you get the cradles?"

"Henri made them, but I didn't have enough money, so Josianne paid for them."

It embarrassed him that people had to pitch in to help Hélène.

"They are fine children," he said at last.

It was a few moments before Hélène replied. "They are a handful. If one is not spitting up on me, the other one is."

"Did you...have a hard time?" He knew nothing about women giving birth and could only imagine the difficulty caused by a dual labor.

"Actually no, although I don't have much to compare it by. Genevieve came first, and not too long afterwards Jean Michel. And I was still nursing them when the sickness came. Neither one got it though."

Mickey nodded in the darkness. Would a mere apology be enough? He swallowed hard. Boldly he found her hand, and feeling the gold ring around her finger, was surprised and encouraged. Perhaps there was hope for them. "I am sorry I have been gone so long. I had no idea you would be—"

She pulled her hand away, "Hand to mouth, starving? Pregnant by a force with no husband in sight?"

"I didn't know Hélène—" Annoyance edging into his voice, thinking there would have been enough money if she had not purchased the tavern, but decided to let that go for now. "And I certainly had no way of knowing a hurricane would down our house. If I had—"

"You would have, what? Done a better job figuring out the money you left me, have gotten me a proper house, let me sleep alone?"

"This is what a marriage is Hélène. It's not like you did not know this could happen."

"*Marriage*? Is that what you call what you did to me last time?"

"I am sorry Hélène; I am sorry from the depth of my black soul. I was wrong and brutal. And I apologize."

"*Oui*, and it's all happened to *me*. Your life will be the same. You will go off in your pirogue like nothing has happened. You haven't been sick for months, growing so big you can't see your own feet. You don't have to worry about dying trying to give birth, nurse the children, diaper them, be scared you will not be able to feed them."

"Are you saying this is *my* fault Hélène?"

"*Oui*, and it's not fair. I am starting to make a name for myself at the tavern. And it's hard to have children and no husband."

He angrily grabbed her chin in the darkness turning her face to him. "You *have* a husband. You realize these are *our* children? Not a *this*, not a *nuisance*, but children, made from you and me."

"I know that!" Hélène hissed, not wanting to awaken the babies. "But I do not want to live in fear of not having enough to eat, or not knowing if you are going to come back. I don't want to have this happen ever again."

"Ever *again*, are you saying what I think you are Hélène?"

"I didn't come all this way and endure all this heartache to fail and starve."

"And those are your only two choices? Be the patron of a tavern, or be a mother who starves? You're my *wife* Hélène, do you think I have no consideration for you?"

"Like the *consideration* you showed when you—" she

stopped then because she saw she was breaking him and wondered why she wanted to hurt him.

He sighed quietly, "I didn't know we were going to have a child. If I had, I would have come back sooner."

"You mean that *I* was going to have a child. *My* child."

Mickey squinted at her, "Don't you mean *our* children?"

"You left me alone, pregnant with no support, and not enough money."

He exploded from where he had been laying, "Well, you *did* have enough money Hélène, but you spent the winter savings on the tavern." But then guilt made him lower his head. "I am sorry, to the depths of my soul. I am sorry about what I did." He shook his head in the darkness, knowing he had spent countless hours thinking about her. "Can you... forgive me?"

He waited for some absolution, some forgiveness. And when it did not come, he broke the silence.

"I think, you *want* to hate me, is that it? Every man in your life has been wretched to you, and despite the good things I have done, you only remember the bad. The mistakes. Do you want me to go Hélène? Do you want me to go and not come back?" He reached for her hand again, feeling the smooth circle of gold ring around her finger, wondering if it meant something to her, since she wore it.

Her heart pounded. She still needed the money he brought in and as much as she did not like to admit it, she wanted Mickey. But she wanted *more* apologies, *more* contrition. But the more he apologized the angrier and more contrary she became.

She pulled her hand away.

He got up and dressed silently in the darkness. It was absurd, where could he go? When he had his hand on the doorknob she sat up, alarmed.

"What are you doing?"

"I don't know what to say to you, but one thing is for sure. You'll never have to worry about getting pregnant again, at least not by *me*."

An anger spread up her chest, humiliated at his insinuation that she would seek affection outside the marital bed.

"But they are still my children, and I will be their father, as much as you don't like it Hélène."

The anger spread to her face and made it hot. "I don't need you, and I will raise them *without you*!"

"Legally we are married, and they are mine as well as yours. Do whatever you want, take lovers, divorce me, I don't care anymore. But they are part mine. And I will claim them."

The door was shut behind him, and Hélène, shaking with rage, put her face into her hands. She sobbed. Deep sobs that came from the memory and humiliation of being a young, defenseless girl in Paris.

## Twenty-Eight

J osianne gave birth to a boy, and Clément was beside himself with joy. He loved his daughters and would do anything for them, but the fact that he had been virile enough to get this young woman pregnant with a son, was more happiness than he thought his heart could stand.

The second day after giving birth Josianne was up on her feet, recovering more than seemed decent for a woman. But Clément already knew his wife was not just *any* woman, and his affection for her grew.

He was accustomed to a woman being distant after giving birth, after all men were customarily kept away. But in the privacy of their home Josianne ignored the social conventions, and welcomed him into the nursery, even letting him watch her nurse, which he found aroused him furiously. Once when Clément was in the nursery, little Joseph spouted a fountain of urine during a diaper change, making his parents double over in laughter.

Three months after giving birth Jacques Perot paid Josianne a visit. After all the hurricane had partially downed the city. Nonplused, Clément, Governor Bienville and even Josianne were determined to create it again.

"*Madame* Heriot," Jacques Perot said, formally taking Josianne's hand, bringing it to his lips. "I have amended plans to show you for the city." He kept his eyes on her pretty face, liking the color of her eyes, although he was having trouble not staring at her engorged breasts, and had the lewd desire to watch her nurse her child. Her waist, he noticed, was back to its trim size. He ached to put his hands around it.

"I would love to see them," Josianne said and carefully arranged her skirt as she sat across from him at the table.

He rolled out the plans.

Josianne studied the large drawing that was amazingly color coded. She was proud she could read *Plan de La Ville de La NOUVELLE ORLEANS*, after her lessons with Celeste. Josianne had become more comfortable reading a map. She knew how to consult the legend and understood things were drawn in scale. She always thought that the crooked coastline looked innocuous on the map, but now knew how treacherous it was. How dangerously close the proposed new town was to the coast, and how incredibly winding and curving the Mississippi river was, especially with the numerous inlets. She wondered how Mickey ever found his way navigating the small streams that snaked out from the river.

And the river's name changed from map to map.

When La Salle and the other French explorers first arrived, they named the river *Fleuve Saint Louis*, but the native Ojibwa name *Mississippi* prevailed. Looking at the rendering, Josianne was amused that Perot had artfully placed trees and quaint dwellings to make it more attractive.

"Did you make the streets wider than Paris, with no dark winding alleys to traverse? I will not have my daughters accosted by thugs because of poor street planning."

"*Madame,* I assure you, the streets are plenty wide."

Her eyes lifted from the paper, disliking the humor she detected in his voice. "*Oui,* for the inhabitants *now,* but the city will grow, and when it does the streets will be too narrow. It is wise to think ahead. Why not widen the streets now before there are structures, afterwards it will be impossible."

It was annoying to him that she thought of things that he should have. Nodding, he made a note in his book. Thinking she was too pretty to have such a grasp on city planning and architecture. She had already changed several plans he had made on the house Clément had commissioned. When he incorporated her ideas, to his chagrin, realized they made sense.

She noticed structures such as officers' quarters were marked with letters, whereas private residences were left unmarked. It made no sense to her. She saw the cemetery, *Cimetiere St-Pierre* and near it a cathedral to be built, already named *St. Louis,* which would luckily be built of *brisques entre porteaux* to make it more hurricane-proof and retard deterioration.

The map was done in a grid-like fashion, with no

winding streets at all. "Why are there no curves or interest to the streets? They are all straight with rectangles as lots."

"*Madame* it is a checkerboard planning template and is a tried-and-true technique. Why even the Romans used this method." He smiled although he was irritated, "It is for expediency and efficiency. As you can see there are provisions for worship, markets, workshops, it is all cohesive within a fixed grid. The older towns as I am sure you are aware, the thoroughfare came from the belfry, connecting in concentric roads, thus circling the town. This way the streets here all converge into a central place."

Josianne's eyebrows rose, "Why do they need to all come together? Seems to me that lacks privacy." Josianne thought it excellent for being watched.

"In a way it is I suppose. But it is a geometry that eliminates urban crevices so to speak where the more *undesirables* tend to congregate." Perot smiled again, "The checkerboard simply provides a more perfect hierarchy. This way *Madame*, neighborhoods can be separated by class. *Les grands* such as you and *Monsieur* Heriot will reside on the higher ground, *les petites* will go to the rear of town."

"So, we are designing a city so that friends of mine like Maélle Genest, and Héléne Clavier or *les petites* as you say, have to travel along those roads, and look up to the grand houses and be reminded everyday of where they do *not* belong?"

Perot cleared his throat. He forgot at times how lowly

her start in life had been. But before he could answer she asked another question.

"Why do you have the blacksmith shop on the outskirts of town?"

"For fear of fire *madame*."

She nodded because it was sensible. "What is this... *Vieux Carré*?"

"Ahh the French quarter, an area that will be quintessentially like France." He was obviously proud of his homeland, and she wondered if he would be so enamored of it if he had been forced to leave the country of his birth in chains.

"I see you have taken the liberty of already naming some of these streets?"

Perot sighed quietly, they had already had one strained discussion about this, and he was not looking forward to another. "But—"

"I see *Bourbon* Street, *Orléans*, *Conti*, you even have a *Rue de Toulouse*. Interesting that here in the new colony a man that came of his own free will, uses names of the ruling families that forcefully deported scores of women like *me*."

"*Madame* Heriot, I meant *no* disrespect—"

Josianne interrupted him, "How much brick are we using?"

"We are using enough brick," he sighed impatiently, then realizing who he was arguing with pressed his lips together.

Josianne sat back in the chair waiting for the slight to pass. "You already know that the foundations of the houses are to be made of brick, but I think the first stories should be as well."

Perot scoffed and threw his pen on the paper, making a tiny ink blot. "That is preposterous, it will cost way too much and slow down the construction. The brick works could not keep up."

"And it takes *days* to cut down a giant cypress tree, *days* to cut the trunk into manageable sizes, and *days* to hone the boards for suitable building products. Even though things grow here quickly, I imagine it will take *years* for that tree to grow back."

"*Madame* if I did not know better, I would think you are trying to build a city of brick to line your husbands' pockets." The minute the words came out of his mouth he regretted them.

Josianne sighed and clasped her hands together, "No, it is not to make more money. Have you ever seen what a fire does to a town made of wood? It is an inferno. The flames leap from roof-to-roof devouring everything in their path. And dare I remind you what the evil winds and other storms have done to the city? It all but leveled it. Perhaps if it had been made of brick more would have remained intact. My husband and I want to make this a modern city, not a city modeled off the mistakes, like the roofs, and the wood foundations." She had already had conversations about this with Henri, and they were in total agreement, and knew Perot would have to acquiesce.

His face flushed with embarrassment, he coughed nervously, "With all due respect *madame,* it is monstrously over budget and with all that has happened since the hurricane—"

"Then build it in half timber and half brick. We can satisfy both our needs."

Despite that she was a married woman, and a mother, he could not help but imagine how she might satisfy *his* needs. He was twenty-three, a young man in the territory with a bright future, commissioned by France to build a city. It was a shame that a gorgeous woman was married to such an old man.

He made more notes and calculated the totals. True, it would cost more, but it did seem as if the benefits would outweigh the costs in time. "It is a good idea, but too costly I am afraid, I will have to consult with your husband."

She ignored him, when Clément got home that night, she would tell him how difficult *monsieur* Perot was being. "And the trenches and ditches, how are them coming?"

"I do not know why you insist on these. It only takes up space, time, and money to accomplish."

"*Monsieur* Perot, you were here were you not, during the last storm?" It was still with her. The terror, the feeling of complete helplessness, and hoped it would be *years* before another storm battered the land like that. "It is necessary, and it will be done."

He stood then, staring at her, "You are a remarkable young woman *madame* Heriot."

Uncomfortable with the turn the conversation had taken, she rose, signaling the end of their appointment.

He was all the time interjecting her looks or youth into the meetings, and she did not like it.

Yet Josianne was not immune to his charms. He was an attractive man with black hair and dark smoldering eyes. She doubted he coughed for fifteen minutes every morning or needed a sweater in the afternoons.

"Thank you, *Monsieur Perot*. I appreciate you taking into consideration me and my husband's opinion." She nodded expecting him to leave. An uneasiness came over her when instead of rolling up the plans, he walked towards her, moving around the table so it was no longer a barrier between them.

"You are a remarkable woman, and a *very*...beautiful one."

Josianne's smile disappeared; it had been a long time since she experienced a compliment that felt so unclean.

He reached out to touch her face, and she reared back preventing it. An empty, cold feeling took up residence in her stomach. Nothing had changed. She was Josianne Daudessot again, fourteen and defenseless from the old lecherous master of the house, and then his equally despicable son. She had lived in a convent prison for three years, been transported in chains to a wild land that had no mercy. But then, it occurred to her that things *had* changed, and not because she was the wife of a wealthy, powerful man, but because *she* had.

"Yes, a woman who is married to *Monsieur* Heriot, whom you report to, and a woman who is telling you to pick up your city plans and go." Josianne's eyes met his.

Jacques Perot had the audacity to laugh. Despite her

composure a faint blush started from Josianne's lace trimmed bodice all the way to her cheeks. She enjoyed collaborating with him. Enjoyed the exchanging of ideas, and thought he respected her dedication to re-building the city. Her admiration for him vanished.

He was rolling up the large parchment, "You want this as much as I do, even more than I do. It's a shame to save all your... *charms* for one so old. Give it time *Madame*. I am patient."

Josianne felt the burn of embarrassment in the cheeks. It was for a wild, unconceivable moment, tempting. She knew the upper classes turned their eyes away from romantic dalliances, but she could not shake the feeling that it was simply wrong. Besides, she was fond of Clément. He had been good to her and she suspected his feelings for her were deep. If she were to traverse this road, it would cause him egregious harm. The impertinence that *Monsieur* Perot was inviting her to an affair was an affront, if she ever did decide to stray it would be on *her* terms, *not* his.

"And when you are ready...I will be waiting."

"And what will you be *waiting* for *Monsieur* Perot?" Clément asked at the doorway. He saw his wife and Perot standing three feet apart, as if they were fencers, sizing each other up. Clément had the sinking feeling as he looked at his wife's strained face, that he was interrupting her, rather than rescuing her.

Josianne swallowed hard, feeling the red burn in her cheeks. "*Monsieur* Perot was leaving. We discussed plans for the city."

Clément had never seen Josianne flustered like this, and he sighed, fearing he knew the reason. He chastised himself, what a *fool* he had been. Not because he had married her, but because he had fallen in love with her. It was natural for her to want to be in the company of a young man, which was why at first, he spurned her advances. But their relationship was satisfying, and he was so enamored of her.

When things were good with business, he hurried home to tell her about it, and when they were not, he still hurried home because she had a sympathetic, sensible ear. In a flash he could see his whole world falling apart.

What would happen to his daughters? They were so taken with Josianne. Because by all rights, what should have been an uncomfortable situation with a new wife, not much older than his daughters, was working out better than he ever dreamed. But his daughters he knew, would eventually notice the change in he and Josianne's relationship. They would feel the coolness from their stepmother and disappointment from their father. And his son, what would become of him? Clément could sadly see it all crashing down around him in slow motion.

"Good day, *Monsieur* Heriot. Good day *Madame*." Perot gave a short, uncomfortable bow and left.

"Clément—" She breathed taking two steps towards him and one step back. She was wringing her hands, "it is not what you think."

He smiled down at her, "he did not accept the suggestion of half brick half-timber housing well I take it?" He moved to the small chest upon which stood the brandy and poured himself an uncustomary afternoon drink. She noticed that his hand shook as he did so.

He turned to face her. "Let me guess, he thinks I am trying to make a fortune rather than build a city that can withstand a fire, or rots in this climate, or a hurricane from that unforgiving sea?"

Her heart felt uncomfortably large in her chest, "Yes actually, he thinks it is a good idea, but it will be more costly. In the end I think I did persuade him to build half with brick."

When she paused, he noticed the rise and fall of her breasts against the delicate outline of lace, and fully understood why Perot was infatuated with her. "But that's not what I wanted to talk to you about."

Clément sighed and turning, looked out the window, wanting to discuss the matter before she could. Wanted to control how it played out, confront the inevitable. Wanted to lessen the pain it would inflict upon him. He lifted the crystal glass to his lips and swallowing, turned to face her. Kindness softening his sagging features.

"Josianne...I understand you are young, and beautiful. I know that I am... much older, and that you might enjoy the company of someone closer to your own age from time to time." He paused and she realized he knew what was being discussed earlier, and it shamed her.

"Clément, my love—"

He put a gentle hand up silencing her. "And no matter what happens, I will always be here for you. I want you to know, nothing you have *done*, or will ever *do*, will change that."

He looked down and ran his finger across the

brocade weave on the chair. "I will do nothing about it, provided of course, you are discreet." His eyes met hers, "And I mean that Josianne." He thought of the treacherous world he had brought his daughters to, the world that had taken Monique from him. The rumors he endured in town about his beautiful wife, the jokes made at his expense. He had ignored them, hoping it was not true. "I will never leave any of you alone in this unforgiving land. Never."

"Clément, I—" tears choked her words. It was not a romantic love. In literature, there were no dashing knights whose knees cracked when they walked or had bowel complaints. But their lovemaking was genuine and she knew he tried to please her. It was true he did not make a fire burn in her heart, and even if Perot could set her heart on fire, she wondered if it would be worth it. It was not that she was opposed to being swept off her feet, the captain had done that, and she remembered how painful that ended. She realized that other things were simply more important, and she was not willing to jeopardize the security, and companionship she had with Clément, for potential passion with Perot. "I wanted to tell you; I love you Clément."

He turned to her, his surprise sincere. His mouth suddenly dry. "Do you Josianne, really?"

She nodded, a hint of tears in her eyes. "Yes."

It dawned on him that she was not having an affair, and the realization reached a place deep into his heart, an even deeper place than his fair Monique had ever reached.

He came to her and kissed her tenderly on the forehead, holding his lips against her head as he whispered, "Other than my children, you are the most wonderful thing that has ever happened to me Josianne, thank you." He gazed lovingly at her.

She silently let out the breath she had been holding and smiled.

# Twenty-Nine

*Fall of 1725*

"Maman, when can I see Genevieve and Jean Michel?" Six-year-old Suzette asked. She had done her chores of gathering the eggs, searching under leaves and other places as instructed, and was proud she had not dropped one. Even though Genevieve and Jean Michel were still too young to play games correctly and follow the rules, she enjoyed mothering them. She also played with Pierre and Little Moons daughter, Kettle, whose baptized name was Marie Jeannette. The rumor in town was, because the first word Marie Jeannette could say correctly was *kettle*, it stuck as a nickname.

Suzette looked at her mother sewing. She was *always* sewing. But Suzette liked it, because with the scraps of cloth she sometimes got a new apron, or better yet a new dress.

Maélle looked at Suzette and smiled. A halo of gold curls framed her cap and touched her shoulders. The child looked so much like Suzanne that sometimes Maélle's heart would stall. It was as if Suzanne were a child again, and Maélle could raise her and ensure that no harm came to her.

"Not today my pet." Maélle answered.

Suzette pouted her red lips. "Maybe tomorrow I can see them?" Her sapphire eyes looking hopefully at her mother, "or could we go to the market?"

The market was a busy place. There were times that the sellers barely had their *pirogues* unloaded before the residents of *La Nouvélle Orleans* came clamoring for their wares. Without the grain from Illinois, the bear oil from the Arkansas and vegetables and chickens from the upper Mississippi the residents of *La Nouvélle Orleans* could not have survived.

"We'll see."

"Will Papa be late again tonight?"

Maélle sighed and dropped her sewing in her lap.

Henri was overseeing scores of men for the rebuilding, and often came home exhausted but with stories about the progress the city was making. He and Clément had more work than they could manage, and Maélle was proud of the contribution he was making.

Before Maélle could answer her daughter, Suzette piped up with another question. so startling Maélle that she pricked her finger returning to her stitching. "When will I have a sister and brother?"

"I don't know," Maélle smiled, recovering from her shock. "And maybe it's not such a good idea anyway.

You'd have to share all your toys, your food, your dresses."

"Uncle Mickey is always gone and yet Aunt Hélène has *two* babies. Papa is always here, why don't I get a sibling?" Suzette asked stumbling on the word. Her distress evaporating when her father walked in the door. "Papa!"

Leaning down Henri hoisted her into his arms and kissed her cheek noisily. Her father doted on her, and as a result Suzette was a confident, happy child that never heard her parents argue, or any harsh words spoken to her.

"Papa. why don't I have a sibling?"

"A *what*?" He laughed.

"A *sibling*. She's asking about a sibling." Maélle pronounced.

"Suzette, you don't even know what it is, why would you want one?" His grin was infectious but despite his mirth, Suzette's face clouded.

"I do too! Jean Michel and Genevieve have them and I want one. Can you get me one Papa?"

"Suzette, please set the table."

It annoyed Henri that Maélle abruptly interrupted the banter. He enjoyed his daughter and did not understand why Maélle was often dismissive.

Suzette sighed with frustration when her father put her down, but did as she was told.

Henri turned to Maélle, still smiling, wanting to continue the talk about "sibings," but Maélle would not look at him.

. . .

Later that night when Suzette was happily asleep, Henri neared Maélle and pulled her into his arms. "Siblings. Where in the world did she learn that word?" He laughed, disappointed when she squirmed out of his embrace, as she often did. If that was not enough, she sat in a chair away from him.

Henri crossed the room and knelt where she sat, and touched her face. "Is there something...wrong Maélle?"

If it was possible Maélle's back got straighter, her heart hammering at his touch. The same hand that had caressed Suzanne in the past. "No, why do you ask?"

He could not count the number of times she spurned his advances, the kisses not returned, the affection one sided and stilted. Although he occasionally still made love to her, he knew she could not wait for it to be over.

Sighing, he decided to change the subject. "I have plans for a new house in the *Vieux Carré,* would you like to see it?" He wanted to build a better house than they had now. One with proper glass windows, a new brick fireplace, and place for Maélle to sew. He wanted to give his wife and daughter a residence on a fashionable street near her friends Josianne and Hélène.

"Is it something Suzanne would have liked?"

He stared at her incredulously. "I don't know if Suzanne would have liked it or not. What I am asking is if *you* would like it."

Maélle had to swallow hard. "I suppose Henri, whatever you think." But when she tried to get up, he barred her way. She hated the way he was looking at her with a mixture of confusion and sadness.

"What's happened to you? Do you...no longer wish... to be my wife?" He thought back to the voyage, how he had often found her looking at him, how he thought he had read the signals correctly.

"Why would you say *that*! What are you talking about?"

He reached for her, and she moved from the embrace. He dropped his hands to his side, not knowing what to do. "That right there, you moving away from me. You...wanted me once, or at least I thought you did. Have your feelings changed? Do you regret marrying me?"

She was staring at the floor and did not answer.

"Have I not ... *provided* well enough for you?" He looked around the house. He would not be so cruel as to say it, but knew it was worlds better than she had at *La Salpêtrière.*

"Everything is fine." She closed her eyes willing the tears away.

"Really?"

"Yes."

He neared her and when he tried to lift her chin, she angrily moved her face out of his reach. "Why can't I touch you?"

Embarrassment coursed through her, "You have touched me."

"Do you...enjoy me?"

"Henri please—"

"I'm serious. Do you.... not want to be my wife anymore?"

Humiliation and fear slammed into her, "Of course I do! I could not bear to be away from Suzette!" It was a terror inconceivable to her.

"Oh, I see. You want my daughter, but not me."

"That's ridiculous."

"Really, asking why you don't want me is ridiculous?" He was angry.

"Your Suzanne's husband." She whispered.

"*What?*"

But before she could repeat, he dropped his hands and turning away sat at the table. It was a few uncomfortable minutes before he faced her again. "We have been living together for five years as husband and wife, are you telling me that all this time—"

"I'm sorry Henri, please don't be angry with me."

"I don't want you to be *sorry* Maélle, I want you to be my *wife*. And I am not angry with you, I am... confused."

Wiping the annoying tears off her cheeks, quietly Maélle joined him at the table.

"I know how much you loved Suzanne. And we were both distraught when she died, I know you married me because you needed someone to take care of Suzette."

He looked at her and a smirk played on his lips. "I married Suzanne because it was the right thing to do. And I married you because, yes, I did need someone to take care of Suzette. I had other women to choose from, but I *picked* you." He was hoping this would be the end of it, and reached for her hand, but Maélle pulled away.

Something in his words struck her as odd, "What do

you mean marrying Suzanne was the right thing to do? Because she was pregnant?"

Henri nodded, "Yes, she was young, and I worried about her."

Anger seized up in Maélle, "A young girl that *you* took advantage of."

"Ahh," Henri said sitting back in the chair, casually folding his arms in front. "Now we are finally getting to the crux of the matter. I imagine this will be hard for you to hear, but I did *not* come to her, it was Suzanne who came to *me*."

His words shocked Maélle, who had convinced herself of the terrible injustice done to Suzanne.

"But you are the *adult*. You should have known better."

"That's true," Henri nodded. "I am not necessarily *proud* of my actions, but there you have it. Suzanne was the one who came to me, I woke up with her kissing me. I found out later that she went to others as well. I like to believe Suzette is my child, but we will never know. And I have also decided that I do not care."

"*Others*?" Maélle cried in shock, "Why would you say something so awful about Suzanne?"

Henri shook his head, "This, *this* is why I knew I could not tell you any of this. You loved Suzanne, and you cannot fathom she was not innocent, that she was not the angelic little sister you wanted her to be."

Maélle calmed her breathing, taking in the tale.

"Did you love her?" Maélle asked.

It was a moment before Henri could answer, "I

didn't really... *know* her that well. She was pretty, and then she told me she was pregnant." He shrugged, "What else was I to do? I mean the child *could* be mine." He shifted uncomfortably in the chair, "In truth I was more interested in you, but you and Suzanne were always together. And when Suzanne died, I was terribly sorry. But then...well...I was able to marry...the one I wanted." His eyes met hers.

"I don't know what to say to you."

He smiled and reached for her hand, "How about... Henri, I love you. You are the most handsome man the colony has ever seen." He had to lower his head to see Maélle's eyes. "And that tonight I will make love with you because you are *my* husband, *not Suzanne's.*"

Although she nodded, he worried she harbored the notion he still belonged to Suzanne.

Hélène finally finished with the tavern work for the day, fed and bathed the children, and put them to bed. As she washed their cups and plates and set them to dry on the cupboard, she heard the night sounds of birds. Despite the cooler air felt the humidity curl around her like an animal.

Once in bed, she rolled over on her side. In the darkness she could make out the old lantern with the cracked glass shade. It was a miracle it was not destroyed by the hurricane and was the only thing from the house she shared with Mickey that survived. New ones had long ago come into the Mercantile and she had almost purchased one.

It had been over a year since she had seen Mickey, and in quiet moments she wondered where he was. Her anger with him had faded, but she feared it would never be right between them. Not that she needed to worry about her *marriage* because it seemed as though it was over. She heard twice that he came back into town. He did not stop to see her nor the children he had professed to care for so much. But he saw Josianne and gave her money for his children. Hélène did not want to take it, but in the end, had. The tavern was barely surviving, and she needed the capital for inventory, food and clothes for Genevieve and Jean Michel, both of whom grew so much she wondered if Mickey would even recognize them if he did see them again.

She missed him though, missed the sound of his laugh after a particularly bawdy joke, the sleepy way he made love to her in the mornings. The simpleness of him. When she walked the lonely beach she was often reminded of the afternoon of the storm, and wanted to re-live it. Of course, all of this she kept intensely private. When someone asked about her husband she was curt. Making sure they knew he was an ex-galley slave that had run off on her. Even though she knew she had made him go.

It was curious, the only one that questioned the odd none-marriage was little Suzette, who annoyingly still remembered "Uncle Mickey" and wanted him to come back. She found out that Mickey had twice sought out Suzette and had a trinket for her. Jealous, Hélène wondered why he did not want to see his own children, but realized it was *her* that he did not wish to see, rather than the twins.

In quiet moments Hélène fantasized sometimes that he would come back, only this time they would embrace each other.

# Thirty

B y 1726 *La Nouvélle Orleans* was emerging from its swamp-like beginnings. Although for many years it was referred to as *'Ile d'Orleans'* because it was surrounded by water. City blocks were dubbed *iles,* and even early sidewalks were called *banquettes.* Because the majority of the population lived along the river, the city put in several bridges for the residents to cross when the water got deep. But it was changing because there were now bakeries, smithies and stores sprinkled about the area.

As Maélle walked up to Josianne's new house on *Chartres* Street, she marveled at the lovely three storied house.

It was made of brick and did not have primitive bulrushes for a roof, but black shingles that were edged in shiny tile. There were *balcons* jutting out from the upper windows and graced by ornate iron railings, which had taken the blacksmith Marcus weeks to make. The windows were slim and the ones on the first and second floor had glass panes, which gleamed against the brick, and proudly Maélle made gathered cotton curtains. But on the very top floor *pastille* still covered the windows. It was not that the cost of glass was too dear for Clément, but rather, he simply could not get them yet.

The street was rumored to be the most fashionable in *La Nouvélle Orleans* because it ran behind *La Nouvélle Orleans'* central square, the largest public space of the *Place d'Ames.* It was a place where those with money showed off their finery if they possessed it. And Maélle knew why Josianne had selected the lot, it was after all one of the best in the town.

"*Maman* it is so pretty," seven-year-old Suzette exclaimed.

"It is," Maélle agreed, knocking on the heavy door. It was six paneled and three inches thick. She was surprised when it was Josianne herself who answered the door and not the maid Marie Madeliene, who spoke haltingly now, which was an improvement.

"Oh, my favorite little girl!" Josianne gushed down to Suzette, who loved her *Tante* Josianne as much as she loved her *Tante* Hélène. "And you too Maélle!" they kissed cheeks, and Josianne led them into the house.

There was a center entryway with several doors leading off. One Maélle knew was Clément's study, then a parlor, a dining room, and behind that a hallway that led to the detached kitchen.

The staircase was wide enough to accommodate two people side by side and had a gentle curve that led to the upstairs.

"*Maman*, look!" Suzette pointed to the eight-armed

crystal chandelier, which threw a kaleidoscope of color around the hallway. Suzette's eyes were huge as she looked at the dangling prisms, "Are those diamonds?"

Laughing, Josianne cupped Suzette's chin, "No, my sweet but for you I will get some diamonds."

"Oh, *mon Dieu,* what use could we have for diamonds in this world." Maélle groaned, thinking about the accounting she had to do for the business she ran with the textiles. It was proving to be as lucrative as her sewing, and she enjoyed the notion that she too was a businesswoman like her friends.

"Perhaps not for you Maélle, but for my sweet Suzette, nothing will be too good."

Hearing company in the hallway Clara and Celeste hurried down the stairs.

Celeste was already as tall as Maélle, and yet her thin body seemed reluctant to mature. Her dark hair was center parted, and she smiled when she saw them. "Hello *Madame* Genest."

"It's wonderful to see you Celeste, and you too Clara. You both have grown so much."

Clara's onyx eyes were shiny. "*Maman* says we are growing into proper young ladies." She nodded her head as if saying it, made it so. She turned to Suzette. "Come up to my room, I have a butterfly to show you."

Suzette looked up questioningly at her mother, who sent her off with a gentle shove.

"Let's have our tea in the parlor." Josianne waited for Celeste to come with them, and was annoyed when the young girl held back, as usual picking at her short nails "I'd like you to join us, Celeste." Josianne was trying to teach Celeste to be social, which was contrary to her solitary personality.

"I was reading, and if you don't mind *Maman*, I would like to finish my book." Her eyes were downcast. Celeste had no interest in things a girl her age normally would, and Josianne could not put her finger on why.

"All right, finish your book. But then come back down before they leave, and you can say goodbye."

Celeste nodded and ran up the steps two at a time, causing a flash of underskirt to hit the spindles.

Maélle followed Josianne into the room and was surprised that there was only two upholstered chairs and a small oval table between them. She knew the dining room was furnished with an enormous table that sat twelve as well as matching chairs. Maélle understood why. Things were still difficult to get in the territory, and if Clément Heriot could not procure items for his home for his wife, *no one* would be able to.

"I hope it's still warm," Josianne said, lifting the cozy from the porcelain kettle. Maélle noticed a chip out of the lid. She was amazed it made it in such good condition with the distance any fine goods had to travel.

Josianne poured two cups and delicately picked up the saucer and sipped. "How are you Maélle?"

Swallowing the tea before she was ready, Maélle sputtered, "I'm fine, why do you ask?"

Josianne shook her head slowly, wondering if Maélle had heard the rumors around town. The French countryside was full of superstitions and beliefs. And unfortunately, those beliefs had been brought with the settlers, and at times, edged out reason and fact. In addition to that, living in this wild territory with dark woods, gave some to entertain more fanciful thoughts than was prudent.

If the French superstitions were not enough, Indian, and African ones were also mixed in which led to some interesting stories. Just yesterday Josianne heard an African woman ranting about putting a hex on a cheating husband, although Josianne did not believe in curses, she crossed herself because the woman's lamentations were so powerful.

Josianne shook her hands as if to make light, "It's nothing."

"Go ahead and tell me Josianne, what are the rumors about this time? That I am a spinster, even though I am married?" Maélle put her saucer back on the table.

Josianne's face got noticeably whiter. "No. Worse than that, I'm afraid."

Could she tell Maélle that some thought she had willed the death of Suzanne to have her child and husband? Snakebites were uncommon, and that Suzanne died that way only increased the rumors. And if that was not enough, it was obvious that Henri had married Maélle to have someone in his home, and that she was madly in love with him. It made Josianne irritated when she heard these grumblings, and she tamped down the talk whenever it flared.

"No reason I suppose," Josianne replied taking another sip of tea. She tried a different tactic. "How is Henri?"

Maélle sighed, but the pause before the answer let

Josianne know things were not all right. "I don't know what to do."

"About what?"

Maélle was uneasy. This was embarrassing talk. "He's a good man, He's a good father and he loves Suzette, of that I have no doubt." She wrung her hands for a moment, appreciating that Josianne was giving her time. "I know he loved Suzanne, and I think he still loves her."

"He may. But that does not mean he cannot care for you as well," Josianne offered.

Maélle picked up the tea and took a drink. It was surprisingly delicate and refreshing. "I know he does not love me, which is only harder because—" but she could not finish. It was too hard to admit the obvious out loud.

"He seems very devoted to you."

"He is devoted to his daughter, and to making a success of himself." She paused a moment; unsure she should burden her friend. "There is something I have not told you. I *feel* Suzanne, and not as a memory but as if she is still here. The first time it happened Suzette was just a baby and kept giggling at something on the wall, and when I turned there was nothing there. I know it sounds crazy, but I wonder if Suzette, sees her mother's ghost or spirit. And I know she means no harm but still—"

"You'd prefer she go and leave her husband alone and let the woman caring for her child be a mother."

Maélle blushed profusely with relief. She could not bring herself to think such a thing, let alone say it aloud, and here Josianne had done it for her.

"You make it seem like it's-it's all right for me to feel this way. "

Josianne put her hand on top of Maélle's. "That's because it is. We all loved Suzanne, you the most. And you did everything you could for her. You have taken her flesh and blood into your own heart. You are a wonderful mother to Suzette. But Suzanne is gone now, and Henri should be glad to have you around."

"Oh, I think he appreciates me, it's just that—"

"Does he make love to you?"

Maélle flushed purple. She wondered if she would ever get used to Josianne's bluntness. She looked down then trying to stop the tears from blurring her vision.

Josianne studied the painted flowers on the teacup, and asked, "did you...ask him to stop?"

"No."

Josianne's brows furrowed. "I it just doesn't.... happen anymore?"

Maélle could not answer.

"Do you...approach him?"

Maélle's shocked eyes met Josianne's practical ones. "I couldn't."

Josianne placed the cup back on the saucer, "why can you *not?*"

A hundred unpleasant thoughts crashed around in Maélle's brain. Half the settlers were lucky to just be surviving. Living in the wild place with hurricanes and famines, it seemed ridiculous to worry about romantic feelings "I feel like a...*fool* even worrying about any of *this-*"

Josianne interrupted her, "So you are saying if you

are poor, you have lesser feelings than someone rich? I understand life is harsh and not always fair. But *formerly* poor women such as us, have every *right* to love and happiness."

"I know but I have more important things to concern myself with, my business and keeping house and my sewing. Just to survive life is such a struggle."

"But *love* is what makes it all worthwhile! Otherwise, what would be the point? Maélle it is all right that you love him."

"But I don't think he loves me. And sometimes, I think he wishes I were Suzanne."

Josianne thought for a moment, then steadied her teacup on her knee. "He may have loved Suzanne, but she is gone. It is your *fear* that he wants Suzanne. You are the reason you are feeling so unloved. Have you talked to him about any of this?"

"Of course not," Maélle said, feeling the heat of the blood in her face. "I could not ask him any of these things." Painfully remembering when she and Henri had hashed it all out. She knew Henri thought it was solved, but for her it was not.

"Are you enthusiastic about the lovemaking? Could that be a reason he has stopped reaching for you?"

"I cannot believe you are *asking* me these things!"

"What's wrong with talking about it?" When Maélle did not respond, Josianne knew the answer. "I make love to Clément as often as he can. I do not love him in a... *romantic* way, but I do love him. You are in a different situation than I am. You are married to a healthy young man that you love, you should be entwined with Henri every night."

"Perhaps, I would be if I thought he was thinking about me and not Suzanne."

Josianne sighed, "Yes, he loved Suzanne, but unfortunately, she died. Henri did not die with her. He wants to live, enjoy his work, his children, his wife if you will let him."

Maélle stood up not wanting to discuss it anymore.

At once Josianne was afraid perhaps that she would make things worse. "Maélle, please just talk to him. I'm afraid you are making all these things up in your head."

"I'm not pretty like Suzanne."

Josianne nodded as if admitting the truth, "But again he chose you, he could have married other brides. I don't think you understand."

"I understand that I was convenient."

"Ahh, I see. You are going to continue to feel sorry for yourself no matter what anyone says."

Maélle's eyes flashed with anger, "your life is so easy Josianne!"

Josianne nodded, "oh, is it? I did not know we were competing for tragedy. I married a much older man with two daughters. They gossip about me in town too by the way, but I do not let it bother me. No one in the colony here knows our histories, we are isolated from France, and we can...make up our own past. We have a unique opportunity here in this new world to make something of ourselves. But no, you would like to wallow in self-pity because at first Henri was turned by a pretty head, then married you because you were willing. And what is wrong with any of that? The rest is up to you whether to make it a success or not. Why Suzanne could not line up more than three stiches, and you, *you* are a fabulous seamstress and a businesswoman as well!"

Maélle's eyes filled with tears, "I loved Suzanne, I feel guilty for taking her place."

"Is there no *end* to your excuses? She is dead, she no longer cares what Henri does! You are still alive, live or do not live. It is totally up to you."

Although by the time Suzette and Maélle left they wished each other well, Josianne hoped she had gotten through to Maélle, that her life was of her *own* making, not the other way around.

# Thirty-One

When Clément shocked Josianne by inviting Captain de Martonne to dinner, she wondered if her face betrayed the terror she felt.

She heard that the captain had been in town a few times in the last years, and she had successfully avoided him. But the day she accompanied Clément on a business outing, she ran into the captain.

She was gazing out at the sea while Clément went into an office to speak with a merchant about supplies. The supplies either came too infrequently or were ruined along the way.

The afternoon was brisk, and she turned to the ocean, letting the wind blow with its full force on her face, stealing her breath away. She felt her hair loosen from its chignon, and shaking her head, did not care. The sky was a brilliant blue and she breathed in deeply.

The ocean was violent, churning and frothing into

colors of violet, and gray. She loved its power, its unabashed force.

"Josianne."

Recognizing the voice, she turned slowly.

"Or should I say *Madame* Heriot."

She realized he knew of her marriage, and wondered how he felt about it.

He was standing close, and he seemed even taller than he had before, or perhaps it was because as Clément's ailments mounted, he hunched over.

The captain's eyes had always been intensely blue, but there were lines around them now. He was tanned and lean, and when he brought her hand to his lips, she noticed how rough not only his hand was, but his lips as well.

"Captain," she said, hoping he would not notice the fall and rise of her chest, or sense the pounding of her heart. Sooner than polite, she pulled her hand away.

Sensing she did not want him to touch her, he looked at the workmen, the sawdust and disarray. "I see you have re-built the city again. It makes me wonder if we will *ever* get this city off the ground. It might be a better idea to find a new spot, or better yet, abandon the idea altogether."

Even though she had once said the same thing, Clément's determination and hope for the city had rubbed off on her. "Just because things are not easy does not mean they are not worth pursuing."

He turned back to her with a smile, his eyes drifting unabashedly all over her.

She was ever so grateful for a bodice that was neatly buttoned up to her throat.

"I suppose you are right." He stared at her. It was as if he wanted to ask her something, and yet was unsure if he should. "And how are your friends, the women who came over with you?"

"You mean the women you transported in chains and left on *'lle de massacre'* to starve? We are all still here, alive and prospering. Hélène, the tall one, owns the tavern. No doubt you have seen her there, she is married and has two children now."

The captain nodded, rubbing his chin.

"And Maélle is a seamstress and is also married with a child. She runs a textile business, and without her none of us would have cloth." She did not want to tell him about Suzanne, it was a private and she wanted to keep it that way.

"And you *Madame*, you married *Monsieur* Heriot." His eyes so like the sea, were burning a hole into her soul. "Do you have children?"

"Yes, I have two stepdaughters and a son." She saw the annoying nod again and wanted to get away from him. She had made her peace with him; he was part of a past that was painful. He stirred up feelings she had worked hard to squelch, and did not want them resurrected.

She turned to leave, but he reached out and stopped her. "How are you, Josianne?"

The way he said her name, caused her already pounding heart to nearly stall. Why was he here? Her life was uncomplicated, and she was content. She had pushed the ache for the captain deep into her soul because she never wanted to feel the pain again. Glancing towards the office, she saw Clément coming down the steps, and felt a swell of relief.

"Captain, I am so glad to see you! How are you, my boy?"

She watched as they greeted each other, wanting nothing more than to escape. Although she was proud, she had moved on with her life, she needed no reminder of her broken heart.

"It is wonderful to see you again," the captain said, shaking Clément's hands.

"How long are you in town?"

"A few days." The captain looked again at Josianne and if he was not mistaken, she looked relieved that he was leaving soon.

"Please, be our guest for dinner, won't you? Night after next? I'd like to show you the brickworks I've started and plans for new levees for the city."

"I couldn't possibly put you out like that—"

But Clément interrupted him, "we won't take no for an answer, you simply must join us."

There was a short pause before the captain smiled at his friend. "I would be delighted then."

Again, the captain looked at her. In the years since they parted, he often wondered if his memory made her more beautiful. Now as he looked at her as a married woman who had given birth, she was even more alluring than as a young girl. Her eyes, confoundingly he could still not decide their color, her hair still lustrous, and her lips that he still remembered kissing, were ripe. As an adult she exuded a confidence that he found arousing. "It is impressive what you two have accomplished."

The three of them said their goodbye's, and as the captain watched her walk away, could not help but think he had made the biggest mistake of his life, ironically, she felt as though she avoided the biggest one of hers.

The day before the captain was to come to dinner, Josianne was uncharacteristically curt with her African cook, Alisa. Although Alisa knew Josianne took an interest in what was served, entertaining Clément's business associates like she did, Alisa had never seen Josianne so cranky.

"*Madame* Josianne, you cannot keep changing your mind for this dinner." It was unusual for Alisa to raise her voice to her mistress, but she was older than Josianne and at times could not help it.

"Why can't I?" Josianne huffed, putting her hands on her hips. Having been a lady's maid herself, she was never quite sure how to react to slaves, and it was alien to her to give them orders.

Despite the respect they had for each other, they did not always get along. Even though Josianne was the mistress of the house, she was not above going to Alisa for advice on everything from child rearing to folk remedies. And Alisa, who had come to the territory as a child, enjoyed an affection for Josianne that she concealed. And Josianne worked hard to keep the secret of their closeness unknown, because even as the social codes and morals were still forming in *La Nouvélle Orleans,* certain customs remained.

"I need this dinner to be--" Josianne stalled.

"Be what, a *disaster*? Because that's what you are going to have on your hands if you don't stop changing the menu." She sat down on the only stool in the detached kitchen, folding her arms against her chest.

"Well then, you think of something to have." Exasperated Josianne leaned against the kitchen table waiting for Alisa to come to her rescue.

"How 'bout some salted pork in white gravy with roasted squash?"

"No, it has to be special."

"Who's coming? Somebody who thinks we's in the land o' plenty? Have you seen what Miss Celeste's garden produced last year? Have you seen what's at the market? We've got some squash, and no sweet potatoes to be had."

"All right fine!" Josianne shrieked moving from her place in the kitchen, "Just make it lovely, all right? And I will make a pecan pie. I assume we still have pecans." She remembered the girls collecting gobs of pecans during the fall.

Surprised by her outburst Alisa eyed her suspiciously. "Ya kin, if ya can git some flour. We got eggs. And I could make a blueberry pie if I had them, but we won't have none of them again till summer. Who all's coming that got you so riled up?"

Josianne felt herself flushing, "No one important. I just want to-to make Clément proud of me."

Alisa put her hands beneath her chin, "Uh huh, he

always proud of you. You goin' to tell me what's goin' on?"

"Nothing's going on, please just do as I ask." But Josianne feared eventually Alisa would figure it out.

When the night of the dinner came Josianne's hands were trembling as she put on her gold earrings. Clara, who liked to help her stepmother while she put on her pretty things, noticed she was nervous. And poor Marie Madeliene was staring at Josianne like she had lost her mind.

"Is something wrong *Maman*? You are jumping like a frog in a skillet!"

"For *heaven's sake,* Clara! Where in the world did you hear such a thing?" Despite it not being the ladylike decorum, she was trying to instill, Josianne laughed.

"Robert says it," Clara reported.

Josianne closed her eyes as she sat at her dressing table. "Honey, I have asked you more than once, do not go down there and talk to him. It's just not proper." Josianne did not totally trust Alisa's son Robert, and Clara was much too trusting.

Marie Madeliene was carefully hanging the silk robe Josianne had taken off while she dressed. Although Marie Madeliene talked now, she did not seem to enjoy it. She grunted and knowingly met Josianne's eyes.

"But *Maman,* you are in the kitchen all the time with Alisa, and I hear you two laughing like hens."

Josianne turned and looked at her stepdaughter. She

was fifteen now and maturing even faster than her older sister Celeste.

"What is it with all the *animal* references Clara?" They dissolved in giggles.

Clément heard the commotion and stood at the entrance of the bedroom. "What's going on in here?" He asked, but he never tired of hearing Josianne's loud, unladylike laugh. He had never known a woman who enjoyed a belly laugh the way his young wife did. And that his daughter was laughing too, was a bonus.

"Nothing Papa," Clara said composing herself.

Josianne was dressed in an emerald gown, which showed off her ample chest to perfection. It had a deep square neckline, and needed no other embellishments, because it had been expertly tailored by Maélle. Josianne's hair was piled on the back of her head. Her dark hair with the burnished red highlights had a natural wave to it. It was fashionable to curl hair with hot iron and wax, but Josianne's hair was too thick and had a mind of its own. After many frustrating failures with curling, Josianne decided she would make her own unique look the fashion.

And her eyes, those glorious not green not brown, eyes. In his entire life Clément had only met one other person with eyes that color. And the lashes that swept over them, thick and black, were enough to send his pulse hammering.

"You look radiant my dear."

Josianne's reflection smiled at him as she sat at the dressing table.

"Which?" Marie Madeliene asked awkwardly holding

two necklaces. One, an oval filigreed locket, the other a delicate gold cross.

"Do you have a preference Clément?" Josianne asked turning on the stool to face him. It still shocked him sometimes that the gorgeous creature before him was his wife. And that she was good to him was a blessing he could scarcely fathom.

"The cross."

He watched then as the necklace was placed around her neck. As the cross laid delicately against her bare breast, he smirked thinking he would indeed need divine intervention to keep her from straying. He knew so far, she was faithful, and it endeared her to him even more because he knew she had the opportunity and had not acted upon it.

From the time the captain walked in the door Josianne was a mess. She talked too much at dinner, interrupting the captain to hurl barbs at him, especially when he criticized the colony. Normally, a teetotaler she had two glasses of tafia, and nearly died from embarrassment when she belched at the dinner table. She was looking forward to retiring early when Clément suggested they all go in the parlor. Still with only two chairs, the captain unapologetically pulled in a dining room chair and placed it too close, she thought, to hers.

Clément poured each of them a small snifter of brandy and she tried to focus on what they were saying but in truth, wanted nothing more than to disappear.

There were so many bad things going on. The Natchez Indians had been fighting with the French military and taken over Fort Maurepas and sadly Josianne could understand why.

The two cultures collided violently. It was sadly obvious to her that only one would survive intact. The only native person she really knew was Little Moon, and she did not know her well. What she did know of Little Moon's situation did not sit well with Josianne, who had the feeling that Pierre had coerced her into marriage. It had been bad enough to be abused Josianne thought, by another tribe that had enslaved her. Josianne could not imagine a bigger culture shock than what Little Moon went through being thrust into this new world with the French and others that still flooded the territory.

Because Little Moon's French was so limited, she and Josianne tried to understand each other with gestures and expressions. And what Josianne regretted the most was that she was not able to adequately thank Little Moon for helping them keep Suzette alive during those first days. Without Little Moons help, Josianne was sure they would have lost the baby. And although Josianne wanted to comfort Little Moon if she could, knew so little of her culture and upbringing, Josianne felt like a fool when she tried.

And there were so many different cultures, the Chickasaws had slaving raids against the Choctaws and fought with the Natchez. Treaties were enacted, then broken hours later. In addition to all the chaos they all spoke different dialects and claimed different parts of the colony as their own. And although she understood why they felt this way, the ships that braved the coast were testament to the changes that no one would be able to stop.

It was not just the unhappiness and threat of war from the Indigenous tribes, but *La Nouvélle Orleans* was constantly threatened by the river, the weather, disease, famine. It was a never-ending worry.

"Captain de Martonne, how is the sailing?" Clément asked and crossed his leg over his knee. It was an effeminate pose, and sitting next to the masculine figure the captain cut, Josianne felt sorry for her older husband.

Sipping the brandy, Captain de Martonne sighed before answering, "It is profitable some trips, less so on others." Leaning forward to place the snifter of brandy on the table, he brushed against Josianne's bare arm.

"I can understand that" Clément said nodding, "crossing the Atlantic in the winter must be very difficult."

Josianne turned and stared at her husband, surprised he was so cavalierly talking about a crossing, like the one his *own* wife had done years earlier. It was not difficult, it was *hideous.*

"And I sometimes wonder why I keep bringing people here," the captain said under his breath. "Ten years in and still struggling." He sighed and looked down. She noticed the lines around his eyes, wondering if they were from years in the sun or worry. And although she tried not to, felt a burst of compassion for him.

"Why, you keep bringing them to populate the settlement, to make a New France." Clément said with a smile.

The captain's smile was brief, "My work with the

West Indies *Compagnie du Senegal* is no longer transporting settlers from France. Instead, I am now in the business of bringing slaves from the African coast here. What troubles me is that I fear I am bringing them to the Louisiana coast to starve, if they don't die en route that is."

It was a practice rampant by greedy men seeking a fortune by rounding up slaves from the Barbery coast and Senegal in Africa and sometimes the captain, a self-made man, could not fathom how he had gotten mixed up in it.

"Iberville and Bienville and the rest of the brothers have made a mess of things." Captain de Martonne knew of Iberville's Canadian father, Charles Le Moyne. Le Moyne was an ambitious man and handed down an insatiable ambition to his twelve sons. Le Moyne was also in the habit of handing out titles to his sons, reminding them every moment of their existence that they should set their sights on becoming part of the gentry or ruling elite.

"What makes you say that?" Clément asked.

"The brothers started out as naval men. In fact d'Iberville gained notoriety in places like Hudson's Bay. But all his maritime adventures were marked by acquiring land, and increasing his *own* wealth, and as always, a brother or two was along to reap the monetary rewards."

Clément visibly bristled, and Josianne did not know why. "Is there something wrong with that, Captain? Being a naval officer yourself I would think you would understand."

"The problem is that for a military campaign to be successful, the "colonizers" are required to put up money, expecting a hefty return on their investment, becoming *seigneuries*. It's a practice most Frenchman would like to see *end*, the titles, and the ruling elite. And Iberville and his brothers stick together no matter what. They always did what was best for themselves financially and to the devil with the rest of us. And besides Bienville had other reasons for wanting the city here. He already had large land grants, it had everything to do with self-interest, rather than it being a superior site."

"Are you suggesting family is not important?"

It was clear that even though the captain was outwardly calm, inside he was agitated.

"I am sure family is important, although because of my career, I have none." He thought fleetingly of his four older sisters, knowing that two had died in childbirth, the other two from a pox disease. Although he tried not to, he glanced longingly at Josianne, thinking of what might have been, before turning his attention back to Clément. "The problem is that Iberville and his family had so much financially at stake, favors owed to them by the crown, so many titles and lands given to them, they made decisions purely with their own *pockets* in mind. They were given land grants, and wanted the capitol to be built here, in this swampy, mosquito laden, God forsaken place. Simply their nepotism and greed put *La Nouvélle Orleans* here on this site, despite there being better places for a settlement."

He was thinking of Baton Rouge, which had been an alternate site at one time, and shipping wise made more sense. There was a bend in the river called *Bayou Manchac*, which made it far easier for a ship to navigate. And Captain de Martonne knew he could never make men like Clément understand that trying to bring a large ship near the coastline was a nightmare. For the petulant river was constantly changing. In fact, none of the early planned sites for the city were on the treacherous Mississippi River that refused to stay within its banks. The site for the capital had changed several times. Oceans Springs Mississippi had been an early site and after 1701, Mobile Alabama, then in 1717 to Biloxi where in De Martonne's opinion it should have stayed.

The captain thought about mentioning how Bienville with his sheer bravado at only nineteen had duped a British captain into turning around twelve miles south of the *Vieux Carré* or what would become the French Quarter. Bienville told the British captain he was on a different river, *not* the Mississippi and that all the land had been already claimed by France. Bienville bluffed the captain who had a heavily armored ship into thinking there were reinforcements nearby and ordered the captain to leave.

The horseshoe bend in the river became humorously dubbed 'The English turn' and prevented for another sixty years another foreign power from controlling the lower Mississippi territory. Although Captain de Martonne was not fond of Bienville, it was a tale humorously told by Frenchmen for decades.

"But Governor Bienville commissioned a ship, and it made it up the river with its cargo."

The captain shook his head. "Yes, it was successful,

*once* but it was a circus act, a trick. It's a grueling route. And I can tell you from experience it is incredibly difficult to enter the Mississippi River pass from the sea, it is impossible to find the entrance. The Choctaws even have a word for it *manchac* which means rear entrance. Even *they* had trouble finding the entrance."

He glanced longingly at Josianne, thinking that if he had been able to get her to the mainland and not that wretched island, their lives might have been different.

"Surely, it is not that difficult captain."

"I assure you; it is. Rumor is the Spanish fleets from Vera Cruz en route to Havana have passed up the entrance *hundreds* of times. In their defense, it is usually mired in fog, and the silt the river brings forms cones of mud in the ocean, which if you don't know any better look like petrified trees or jagged rocks. And they ooze a dark blue sludge and even erupt. It's no wonder they stayed as far from the shore as they could." He could tell Clément was not convinced. "The river has a crowfoot entrance, which is forever silting up, and changing. It's a nightmare. And all this is the easy part. During low tide, I would have to anchor the ship 150 meters from the mouth of the river, then when they can, ascend the river which takes *weeks*. And there is *constant* tacking from shore to shore." The captain sighed with frustration, "And to add to the difficulty, it is near impossible to assess the waters depth, all the while dodging submerged logs, and sandbars that seem to appear overnight."

"Well, fine captain, the Mississippi is not suitable for cargo ships to go up the river. But you must admit the land grants are beneficial to all of us."

Not willing to argue with his host, the captain shrugged.

It occurred to Josianne that Clément too had been one of those land grant recipients, and that he too had profited by having the town placed on his land. She glanced at her husband thinking back to how loftily he had painted the new territory, how it had been scouted out as a practical place to build a town, despite the swamp, encroaching river, the need for levies. In the span of a sigh, her affection for him waned. He had lied to her. Not a major thing. She knew scores of women who had little interest or knowledge of their husbands' business dealings. Why did it matter that he told her half-truths?

But it did.

"Captain you must admit, for the colony to flourish we should have more settlers, more workers."

The captain reached for his glass, and again was so close to Josianne that she held her breath.

"*Workers*?" the captain said with a wry smile. "Are you referring to slaves?"

"Well, not exactly. And besides these people are protected by a code."

"I assume you are referring to the old *Saint-Domingue* code. Adapted into the *Code Noire.*"

"It's beneficial to the workers."

"That's true it was designed to be," Captain de Martonne said, knowing Clément had never seen a slave ship. Had no idea the slaves were packed in like spoons in a drawer, had no idea the horrors of the trade.

"Why there are over fifty articles in the *Code Noire* of 1724 regulating the statutes of slaves and free blacks, and the code of the Caribbean spells out the relationship between masters and slaves. It expressly prohibits the separation of husbands and wives, children under the age of fourteen from their mother, and slaves that are freed by their masters are encouraged and allowed to become naturalized French citizens."

The captain had heard countless men like Clément tout these things about slaving, and realized none of them had any idea what they were talking about. "It sounds good in theory, but do you believe these things *actually happen*?" The captain stared at Clément.

"Of course, I do not know specifically, but the code encourages the owners to take care of the slaves when they are ill, to house, clothe and feed them. It even goes so far as to give Sunday as a day of rest, as dictated by the Catholic religion."

"And none of these slaves' owners ever... *violate* these edicts? Never bend the rules. We all know they do because no one ever enforces them. And do you know who rounds up the slaves? Other Africans in the area trying to get rid of the undesirables in their own culture." It proved how cruel it all was, and how easily the oppressor could become the oppressed.

Josianne suddenly thought of Alisa, whom Clément did provide for, but deep in her heart she wondered how magnanimous he was really. Alisa worked all day, in a house that was not her own, and never would be. Her children, born into slavery had no way out. For a moment Josianne turned the tables and tried to imagine if her life was like Alisa's with no choices, no hope. The thought was chilling.

"Slaving is a bad business. And I have participated in it. And I am not proud of myself." The captain looked at the floor.

Josianne turned and looked at the captain. Could feel the internal struggle he had, and felt her affection for him stir, and then chastised herself for caring about him.

"Well, the colony will prosper eventually," Clément said.

The captain sighed, "It could, especially if the men running it would not try to wring every bit of profit out of it overnight. If they sent supplies as promised and let the city get on her feet. But they expected overnight returns on their investments, then turned their backs on the colony when it was not producing like it should." It seemed more personal to the captain than it should be, and she wondered if he cared more for the city than he professed to.

# Thirty-Two

Hélène wiped the sweat from her brow and glanced out to the street. The window she had put in, her pride and joy, was dirt-streaked from the recent spring downpour. Although she ran a tavern, it was important to her that it be respectable and tidy.

"Maélle, I'm going to clean the window."

It took a while to gather the bucket, water, cloth, and ladder for the task. By the time she was up on the ladder, she was drenched with perspiration.

Even though she was tall, she had trouble reaching the top corners of the window, a fact that annoyed her. Struggling on tiptoe, she stretched.

"Hélène, get down, please," Henri said, shielding his eyes as he saw her precariously on the ladder. He always thought it was apt that the street the tavern was on was called *Bourbon* Street.

"I can do it Henri."

" I am taller than you are. Get off that ladder. Please."

Dropping the wet cloth down to him, she climbed down and glared at him. "I don't need your help."

"Sure, you do, you just can't admit it." He scurried up the ladder and washed the corners she could not reach and, to further annoy her, re-did what she had washed. "Was that so hard, Hélène, letting a man help you?"

"I could have done it; I was doing it."

"But not as well as I did!" Henri laughed, "Maélle in there?"

"Yes, of course. Come on in." Hélène started towards the steps, expecting him to follow her.

"I just came to tell you I saw Mickey. He's in town." He pulled out a wad of money from his pocket. "Asked me to give this to you."

Hélène hesitated. She always needed money, but she both hated and liked that it came from Mickey. She hated that he would not see his children and liked that he still wanted to provide for them.

Henri saw her wavering. He heard all about their troubles from Maélle and did not want to be involved. "Just take it Hélène. It's for Genevieve and Jean Michel."

Begrudgingly, she took it and folded her hands against her chest. Why did it hurt? Why did she care?

She sat down on the front step and looked out over the town. There was a proper church now whose spire pierced the blue sky, and there was even a clockmaker in the city who sold jewelry. Her children so far were healthy and happy. She had good friends, and the tavern was busier all the time. She was content—content until something reminded her of Mickey and the life she had thrown away with both hands.

# Thirty-Three

⸙

The summer that followed was the hottest Josianne ever experienced. The air was humid, thick, and still. No one rushed anywhere; it was too hot to hurry. The summer vegetables burnt up where they grew despite regular watering. The air that blew did nothing to cool, and even the nights stayed hot and muggy. The river slowed so much it looked to be still, and the thick brown sludge teemed with insects.

When they thought the incessant heat could not get any worse, another sickness crawled out of the shadows.

It started innocuously enough, with a headache and a slight fever, but soon there was nausea, vomiting, and yellowing of the skin and eyes. Josianne had already nursed her family a few years ago from a similar illness, the one that sadly claimed the life of Marie Madeleine. But this new fever was worse.

Some got over it in a few days; others who lingered within its grasp got sicker, and when they vomited, it was black. Josianne's household was worried about her husband and son because the young and the old succumbed to the fever in record numbers.

It was a particularly hot, stagnant afternoon as Josianne sat in the airless bedroom, nursing Clément, whose fever was so high he was delirious and saying nonsensical things. Dust motes rose from the floor, and Josianne had already sweated through her bodice and had taken it off because of the heat. Even though the thick curtains were drawn, the heat baked the house. Even when she opened the windows to let air circulate, it was stiflingly hot. She shuddered, remembering Bible verses that described the relentless heat of hell.

She leaned down with a damp cloth to wipe Clément's face, trying everything she knew to reduce the fever. She wished she could get him into a tub of water but alone, could not manage it.

"Adele, where are you?" Clément asked, his face a sallow sickening shade. He had aged years in a few days, and it hurt Josianne's heart to see him this way.

"Adele was your younger sister back in France. I am your wife, Josianne," she said gently for at least the twentieth time. She wrung out the cloth again, her back aching from bending over so much.

"Adele, you must keep to your studies. No one wants to marry a girl who is unread. As your elder, I will see to it that you are knowledgeable and make a good match."

Josianne smiled, "I will read, dear brother."

He quieted for a second, but then his feverish eyes popped back open with alarm. "Where is Monique? She should not be out too long in the sun."

Josianne was trying to scrub the vomit from his

nightshirt when he grabbed her wrist, surprising her that in his weakened state, he could hurt her. "Where is my *wife?*" His eyes were fierce in his feverish face.

"I am your wife Clément, I am Josianne."

He stared at her in disbelief, then tossed her hand away from him. "That's ridiculous. Where is Monique? I have not seen her in so long."

"She'll be here tomorrow," Josianne fibbed, but it made him quiet, and for that, she would do anything. She had explained to him countless times already that Adele and Monique were both dead, but the sickness sent his mind back, and his fevered consciousness could not remember the present.

He vomited then. Strings of saliva and blood-tinged bile went all over the front of him and the bed sheets as well.

Josianne felt tears prick her eyes. She had just put clean sheets on the bed and a clean nightshirt on Clément that morning. Now, the bed was soiled again, and she had no one to help her. Although Josianne was strong, she had an awful time lifting and cleaning Clément. And it was nearly impossible to remake the bed alone.

After all, Alisa had her hands full caring for not only her daughter Elise but also Celeste and Joseph.

For a week, Josianne had been locked in a never-ending nightmare of cleaning up the vomit and feces. And when he slept, she gathered wood and water to scrub the linens, hanging them to dry, only to put them back on the bed. She was an uncomplaining caregiver, but as the days dragged on, her hope for his recovery dwindled. No one knew what to do to stop the spread or ease the pain.

Later that day, Josianne was again placing a wet cloth on Clément's forehead when she heard a loud knock on the door. No one was out in the city; it had come to a standstill with anyone not sick nursing those who were. No shops were open, and the hum of insects in the hot air was sometimes the only sounds of life.

Another insistent knock echoed through the house. Worried that it might be Maélle or Héléne, Josianne hurried down the stairs to answer it.

It took two hands to pull open the heavy door, and she saw Captain de Martonne standing there.

"I hear your family is sick."

A wave of relief swept over her. A few years ago, when Clara, Celeste, and Clément had come down with a different sickness, Josianne had dutifully nursed them through it. But this fever was worse, and Josianne was afraid.

She gasped once and fell into his outstretched arms, her face crushed against the coarse wool of his captain's uniform. He smelled faintly of the sea.

He pulled back and brushed the sweat-dampened hair from her face. He kissed her sweetly on the mouth and, cupping her face with his rough hands, asked, "where is your son?"

"He is with Alisa. Thank God, so far, he has only had a touch of fever, and it has broken, and he is better."

"And the girls?" He followed her into the house.

Tears fell unchecked down her face, "We lost Clara first, then Celeste got it, but she is recovering. Clara was only fourteen." More tears fell from her eyes. "And little Genevieve, we lost her too." Josianne sobbed.

"Is Clément upstairs?"

She nodded.

"Go back and help Alisa. I will tend to Clément."

She grabbed him, "But you're not sick. I can't let you endanger yourself!" Tears were blinding her vision, "I don't want you to get sick."

"I've already had the yellow jack and survived."

She glanced at him longingly and wondered why she did not get it, wondered what miraculous invisible properties spared her from the illness.

Moving away from her, he said, "take care of your son."

When Captain de Martonne entered the room, he had seen enough cases of yellow fever to know Clément Heriot was not going to survive. His skin and eyes were already yellowed, he was shaking uncontrollably with chills, and when he vomited, it was black.

Regardless, the captain got him into a tub of water, bathing him to cool his fever. Josianne was not able to lift Clément into the tub and wept when she saw how tenderly the captain ministered to his friend. The captain held him as he vomited and talked to him when he was lucid. Two days later, Clément Heriot died in the arms of his friend Captain de Martonne, who openly wept at his passing.

At her husband's short funeral, Josianne was unable to conjure up any more tears. She had already cried so much for little Genevieve, Clara, and Elise, who, despite Alisa's best efforts, also succumbed to the fever. Josianne was beyond relieved that somehow her little son had survived. She kissed and hugged him so much that Joseph fought her whenever she tried to kiss him.

Captain de Martonne walked into the quiet house behind Josianne and the rest of her family after the funeral.

"I'm gonna make a light supper," Alisa announced, although she knew no one was hungry. She had to do something. Her daughter was buried, and her owner was dead. Even though she was close to Josianne, no one ever knew what another person would do. She ushered her remaining two children, Deidre and Robert, out of the parlor. "I'll leave it in the kitchen ifn ya'll wants it." She took Joseph with her, who was excited, knowing Alisa would give him a piece of hard molasses.

Without anyone asking, the captain poured a snifter of brandy for both he and Josianne.

"What about me?" Celeste, seventeen, asked.

Shrugging, the captain poured her a drink as well. They sat in the parlor, sipping their drinks, as the heat baked the house. The sun was pouring in the windows, and the captain quietly got up and drew the curtains.

Josianne could hear the late afternoon drone of the cicada. They listened to the birds, especially noisy, as they made their flight back to their nests for the night. For one of the first times in her life, she was at a loss for what to do.

Ironically, it was Celeste who broke the silence. "What will you do now, *maman*?"

Josianne looked at her stepdaughter, who still was uninterested in fashion, dancing, or anything feminine. She was a curiosity Josianne did not understand.

"I-I don't know exactly."

Celeste looked at her still-young and incredibly beautiful stepmother. She always wondered what attracted Josianne to her father. But, then again, Celeste did not care. Josianne had been good to her and Clara, and Celeste knew her father had been happy with his *femme trophee.* That was all that mattered.

Celeste put the brandy to her lips and took a sip. She noticed how the captain, as well as the idiot Jacques Perot, looked at her stepmother and figured it was only a matter of time before Josianne married again. She was too beautiful, too alive, to be alone. She was not bitter like her stepmother's friend Hélène Clavier. The town joked how the mighty Mickey Clavier paid for his wife's upkeep, but got nothing in return.

What Celeste wanted to know was what would happen to her. She wondered if her father's fortune went to his wife, or to her, or both. Sadly, Clara was dead, so she felt she had less claim on her father's wealth. And it was not that she wanted to see her stepmother banished or even disinherited. What Celeste wanted more than anything was for nothing in *her* life to change. She wanted her solitude, her books, and most of all, her privacy.

"I suppose I will have to see an *avocate* to see what you father left us, or what we have or do not have."

This alarmed Celeste; she was not aware that her father might have any financial difficulties.

"I can make the inquiries for you tomorrow if you like?" The captain asked softly.

Josianne smiled at him, "thank you, but I can do it." It was not a chore she was looking forward to but knew its importance.

Sighing, Celeste finished the brandy. It was good, and she wished she could ask for more.

She got up and kissed her stepmother goodnight. She wondered if Josianne would marry the captain, and hoped Josianne did.

When she was gone, the captain refilled their drinks.

"It was good of you to-to take care of my husband the way you did." Josianne stuttered.

The captain shrugged. "He was my friend. I wanted to ease his pain if I could, but I don't think I did in the end really."

She eyed him, noting his height, broad shoulders, and quiet confidence. She had always thought he was attractive. Even as he aged, he retained his appeal. "And you said...you've had the yellow jack before?"

He nodded, "More than once. I've seen countless deaths from it. It's odd, for some, like the Africans, seem to have some sort of...*immunity* to it. Others like me get it and recover; others perish in as little as six days."

"Where did you see countless die of it?"

"The islands of Barbados, then later in the Yucatan Peninsula, the Mayan people called it *xekik,* which translates to blood vomit. In Barbados, on the sugar plantations, it spread lightning fast. I always wondered if it had something to do with the rainwater trapped in the huge broken pots. You could see wiggling maggots in the stagnant water, and before long, every other man would be sick. Or maybe it had something to do with cooking all that sugar cane. It attracted all kinds of flying pests."

"I suppose you have seen a great many things in your travels."

He smiled at her, thinking that although he had seen hundreds of beautiful women, it was her face that still possessed him. "I have. It's been a good life."

"How soon before you leave again?" She finished the brandy. She could not remember the last time she had eaten, and the alcohol was going straight to her head. She felt woozy and weak.

"Soon, but it will be my last voyage."

Josianne stared at him, waiting for the words to make sense. "Why? You are a ship's captain, and sailing is your passion."

"At one time, it was."

They stared at each other.

"I let you go once. I have regretted that day...for *years*. I don't plan to make the same mistake again."

Josianne stood up, dizzy, trying to comprehend what he was saying, but at the same time, too shaky to care. "I'm going to bed. My apologies for not seeing you out."

He hung his head and reluctantly put the glass on the table. "Good night, Josianne."

When she heard the door close behind him, she climbed the stairs and got into bed fully clothed and sobbed. She sobbed for Clément, Clara, Elise, Genevieve, and all the others who were lost.

# Thirty-Four

O n the day of Clément's funeral, something shifted inside Maélle. She realized she was living in a ridiculous world where she got to play the part of injured party. And she had played the part so long it became a habit. But with the jarring reality of the deaths of her friends and especially five-year-old Genevieve, she had an epiphany. She could continue to pine away and use her hurt to push Henri away, or she could take off the heavy mantle of victimhood and *live*.

"Henri," Maélle said as he walked in the door the next night.

The September evening was still hot, and she longed for a time when she would need a shawl.

Henri's face was haggard. To say the sickness that had thrown off the summer building was a *gruesome* under-statement. He had lost two of the best foremen, as well as countless laborers, to the fever. Maélle had not seen him weep since Suzanne's death, but he had the day he had come home, relating to her the deaths of his friends.

"Where is Suzette?" he asked, pulling his boots off.

"She is with Hélène."

Henri understood. Hélène had always been close to Suzette, but with the loss of Genevieve, Hélène wanted Suzette more than she usually did. Maélle did not mind and would do anything to ease her friend's pain. Suzette always enjoyed Jean Michael's company and that of Kettle, so the situation worked out as well as it could.

They ate quietly. Maélle would ask questions, and Henri would answer. To the outside world, theirs was a companionable relationship. They had been living like brother and sister for so long that Maélle was not sure how to ignite the passion again.

When Henri sat down at last by the hearth, Maélle joined him.

"I'm not exactly sure how to say this, but I've changed my mind about something."

Henri, who had in recent years taken to smoking a pipe, fiddled with it, waiting for her to continue. "And what have you changed your mind about?"

He was still handsome, and she wondered if he found his solace elsewhere. There were women available with and without morals, and he was a red-blooded man. If his needs were not being met at home, they must be being met somewhere. But if Henri had taken a lover, Josianne would have known about it and would have told her.

"Maélle?"

"I was just thinking that, with so many of our friends having lost someone they loved with this horrible fever..."

He sighed and looked away. Maélle knew he was thinking of his friends Antoine and Girard and all the others. "It was a trying time, that's for sure. But we survived, and thank God Suzette did too."

She was quiet again, not sure how to broach the subject. "Yes, a very trying time. I just feel so lucky to have you and Suzette."

"Suzette is a blessing." He re-lit the pipe. Maélle admired how much he loved his daughter. He was not above playing silly games with her and swinging her in the air until she sometimes got sick. The daughter that may or may not have been his.

Suddenly, unsure of herself, Maélle looked down. Perhaps it was too late. Things, once lost, are lost for good, and trying to breathe life back into them is futile. But she shored up her resolve. "You are a blessing to me, too."

"Am I now?" he joked, sucking on the pipe to keep it lit.

"Yes, you are. And I am...lucky to have you as my husband."

He was surprised when, nearing him she knelt in front of him. "I see now that I have been very...*wrong*. Silly really. I let my love—" She wavered, summoning the courage to continue, "Of Suzanne, get in the way of loving you. And you tried to make me see that. I wanted you to know that I am...over it. This recent sickness made me realize that life is so short. So bittersweet, so fragile. I don't want to waste any more time...and if you still would like to have me as your wife. I am ready and," her eyes drifted up to his, "and willing."

She hoped he would gather her in his arms, expected some reaction. When nothing happened, embarrassed, she tried to move from the kneeling position, but he stopped her.

"Are you...telling me what I think you are?" he asked, afraid to hope.

She nodded, too mortified to have to repeat it all.

"You...love me?"

Again, the nod.

"Really, you have a rather *odd* way of showing it."

"I'm sorry. I know now I was wrong. Terribly wrong. And I have...wasted so much time."

Henri put the pipe down, "what are you asking me for?"

"Well, to start perhaps... more children. Siblings for Suzette?"

Henri laughed, remembering the night.

With her heart pounding, Maélle leaned up and kissed Henri. She kissed him with a passion she had finally unleashed. She knew he was just a man who had been turned by a pretty face. A man that when faced with a dilemma, did the right thing. A man who, when his world was turned upside down, had chosen a mate of which he was fond—a man who tried to love her.

He pulled back, breathing heavily, "Are you sure, are you sure about this Maélle?"

"Yes." She stood. With shaking hands she undressed until she had nothing on but her thin shift.

With wide eyes, stripped off his clothes and met her in the bed.

"If you don't love me, it's all right," she said, getting comfortable underneath him.

"Who says I don't love you?"

"You... love me?"

He laughed, "Do you think I would still be here if I did not? I can't explain it. I just hoped someday-you would *want* me."

She burst out, " I want to have children, *your* children."

Henri laughed again, kissing her upturned face, but felt the need to bring her down to reality. "Every love-making does not produce a child."

"I know; I mean, I understand," she said, placing her hand against his bare chest. "Then make love to me until I'm pregnant."

He grinned, "*That* I can do."

When the hot weather subsided a month later, the killing fever abated. One third of the population had perished. Pierre Godfrey died, and Little Moon, lost without her husband, moved in with her daughter Kettle to the tavern with Hélène. Hélène was trying to help Little Moon through her loss. But Héléne had already sunk into a stark, unreachable silence when Genevieve had died. It was as if Héléne's soul had been buried when Genevieve breathed her last. And Hélène, already bitter about what fate had dealt her, became more aloof than ever.

# Thirty-Five

J osianne heard Deidre greet someone at the door and idly wondered who it was. It was late for a visitor. She knew the other fashionable women in town would not dare to call on her at this hour, unannounced, and besides, everyone was still reeling from the fever, and societal norms had not yet been resurrected. As much as Josianne did not adhere to their "rules," she put up with them for the sake of Celeste and Joseph. Josianne had even finally cracked the façade of Etiennette, and although they were not quite friends, Josianne was glad she had bridged the gap with the influential woman, and the two of them joined forces to help the community.

"Josianne," the captain said.

Josianne looked up and had to swallow hard. A few days after Clément's funeral, she heard he was gone. Since his voyages could be many months at a time, she was surprised to see him back in only three months.

"Captain," she said, standing up. She had on a plain

blue dress and had simply pulled her hair back in two combs. Nervously, she brushed loose strands from her face, stupidly wondering why she cared.

"Please, call me Philipe. It is about time, don't you think?"

"All right." She paused, then asked, "where have you been?"

"Back to France. I have resigned my commission. I plan to make *La Nouvélle Orleans* my home."

"How delightful for you."

He looked her up and down, smiling at what he saw. "You look well."

"Thank you." She hoped he did not notice she was shaking.

"How is Celeste?"

"She is coping." Josianne was amazed that Celeste could stay in her room all day reading, although sometimes she went for walks. Celeste preferred the company of cats, so there were always cats milling around the back door, begging for the scraps she fed them.

"And Joseph?"

A smile blossomed across her face at the mention of her little boy. "He is fine."

"I see you are working through the papers."

Sighing, Josianne sat back down. "Yes, I have found out some good things and some *not-so-good* things about my dear husband's business."

Philipe sat across from her at the dining room table.

"This house is paid for. The brickworks are not. There is precious little money in the bank and a few bills I am not sure how I am going to pay. The two properties he leased out are barely breaking even. If I pay the workers at the brickworks, I barely have enough to sustain the household. I cannot sell the leased land because there is a clause in the contract that says it cannot be sold for another ten years. And besides that, I don't know *anyone* that would buy it."

"How do you know how much money you need?"

Josianne shuffled papers, looking for the ones she had done the calculations on. "I have done some math. I asked Alisa how much it takes to feed us all per month; I multiplied it by twelve, then factored in wood for heating the house, upkeep of the horses and carriage, and oil for lanterns. I mean, there are more expenses than just food. I also did the math for what it takes to run the business, and I realized everything you earn is not *profit*. The running of the business eats into it and must be taken out first, such as materials and labor."

He nodded, impressed and amused by her no-nonsense approach as she rifled through the papers on the table.

"What are they cultivating on the land?" Philipe asked.

"Tobacco, on the part of the fields, and at a loss, I might add. I don't know why Clément did that. We talked about it years ago that the climate was not suited for tobacco. It's too hot here and wet. It's a stupidly needy plant. When it rains here, it's either too much or not enough." She shook her head, "And it must be sowed in open fields, with worms picked off the crops, then cut and dried in sheds. If all of that is not bad enough, it rots on the way to wherever it is shipped." Her brow was wrinkled as she studied the papers, "And he planted indigo on the other. I didn't know what it was for but Héléne told me it's leaves are fermented then the liquid parched and set in blocks. It whitens clothes apparently." She went back to her calculation. "Even though it is useful, it is not as profitable as it should be."

"What would you like to plant?" He shifted in the chair. This was *not* what he had come there to talk about, but he sensed he needed to take it slower than he wanted or risk losing her a second time.

"I honestly don't know, and I don't know if I'll have enough money to make a large change. Because I have found out, changing what is cultivated is *also* costly."

Throwing caution to the wind, he said, "you could always marry me and use my money."

"That's all fine and well, but I must provide for Celeste and leave a legacy for Joseph. I want him to at least inherit the brickworks. His father would have wanted that." She eyed him suspiciously, then realizing what he said, asked, "since when do you have any money?"

He laughed. "I've been a ship's captain a long time, with no one and nowhere to spend my fortune. How about...I help you with this new venture. We get it off the ground, making provisions for your stepdaughter and son. If we marry and join forces we should be able to provide for them amply."

It was so long before she answered he wondered if she had heard him.

"That has to be the most *unromantic* proposal I have ever heard, captain."

"I was not aware that wooing was required, and please... call me Philipe."

She put the papers down, "I am sorry, but I do not understand what you are doing?"

"I have resigned my commission. I have lots of money and no one to spend it on. I want to marry you."

"You've had a change of heart," she said, thinking back to the horrendous voyage. "If I remember correctly, you told me you were not interested in marriage." It was still there, the burn of being rejected by him.

"I did. I have changed my mind."

"Well, perhaps so have I."

For the first time, Philipe was afraid. Perhaps she would not be so easily enticed. Perhaps she would not have him.

"I will figure it out myself. I have friends who will help me." She knew Hélène would be an ally, and so would Maélle and Henri if she needed them. It would not be easy, of that she was sure, but she was not going to fail.

"That's it? That's all you have to say?" he snipped, growing angry. "I ask you to marry me, and you say you've changed your *mind*?"

"Do you remember that voyage? I know you have been on many, but the one *I* was on. You *used* me. I was... young and vulnerable. You made me think—" She closed her eyes at the bitter memory. The embraces, the kissing, the way she had felt about him and wanted him to feel about her. "Then you left me on that *island*! Do you have *any idea* what that was like?"

"Actually, no, I did not. Please, believe me, Josianne.

If I had known, I would *never* have left you there." He stood up and neared her.

She jolted from her seat in anger, remembering the wind, the cold, the desolation, and the God-awful hunger. "Really, and I am supposed to...just take your *word* for it?"

"All I knew was that it was a barrier island, I had orders to take you and the other women there, then unload my cargo. I knew *nothing* about that island." She was unmoved by his explanation. "Most of the maps didn't even *show* those islands, and I had to protect my ship and my crew—"

"At the expense of defenseless women that were chained together—"

"Your chains were off by then," he interrupted.

"Yes. They were. *Thank you so much, captain.* Thank you for finally removing the chains from us." The sarcasm dripped from her words.

Sighing, Philipe hung his head in frustration. "What can I do? What can I do, Josianne, to prove to you...how sorry I am for what you had to endure?" His eyes met hers.

Josianne's heart was pounding. She was not sure why she was behaving like this. She thought she was over that horrible memory; she thought she had reconciled herself to it. But having him so glibly talk about it resurrected feelings she did not know how to deal with. Was it because of Clément's death she was acting this way? Was it finding things out about her husband's business dealings that were not favorable? Was it the worry that she might not be able to provide for her household? Was it the illness that stole the innocent, young and old alike?

She had wanted the captain once, wanted him desperately. But she was too confused to trust her feelings. "Please go. I don't want to talk to you anymore." Her head was pounding; she felt a queasiness in her stomach.

"No, I won't leave you. Josianne, I want to marry you. I have *always wanted* you. I've not been with a woman since I saw you."

Amused, she laughed, "Do you really expect me to believe that? A handsome French captain without a woman in every port?"

"It's true. I could never get you out of my mind. When you married Clément, I was... *devastated*. I stayed away for *years* because I could not bear to see you. But then I saw you that day at the wharf, it all came back to me. I was a fool, an *idiotic fool*, to let you marry that old man. I know you did not love him and only did it for security. I can offer you that now, as well as my deepest and most sincere affection."

He leaned down and, pulling her up on her tiptoes, kissed her. He Kissed her with the passion in his heart, the passion in his soul, as well as all the plans for the future.

Pulling away, he was horrified to see her eyes boring a hole into his face. "I think you had better go."

"Josianne, *please*!" There was a sheen of tears in his eyes.

"I will figure it all out. I will cultivate the land and make a profit. I will increase the production at the brickworks, I will pay the bills, I will take care of those that depend on me." Adding to the list of those who depended on her were also Alisa, Deidre, and Robert, to say nothing of the men who worked for her. Since Clément's death, Josianne often woke up in a cold sweat with so many depending on her.

He dropped his hands from her in disbelief. "I can't believe you are...throwing it all away. I *love* you, Josianne. Does that mean nothing to you?"

"Honestly, I don't know. If you had offered me any hope, I would have waited for you. I nearly risked my whole *future* with you that night." She shook her head at the memory of wanting so desperately to make love to him. "I don't think, as a man, you can understand what a risk you were asking me to take. If I had gotten off that ship pregnant and unmarried, can you even *imagine* what would have become of me? No, you cannot. Because for you, it would be just another conquest."

He well remembered the night. The passion, the ardor, how he had lusted for her. He also realized she had never come to him again.

"None of that is true, Josianne. Besides, it hasn't all changed. You love me. *I love you.* We can make a future together. Take care of Celeste and Joseph, and have *more* children." He was astounded that she was going to let it all go. "Josianne, I am in *love* with you. Please, don't make me go. Don't break my heart."

Her eyes flashed up at him. How dare he speak of a broken heart when hers had been shredded long ago. "It is only fitting, don't you think," she said, her beautiful eyes staring at him, "for me to break your heart as you broke mine?"

# Thirty-Six

*Spring 1731*

"Josianne, I am pregnant again," Maélle gushed, her hand against her still-flat middle. Her son Denis had been born six months ago, and she was elated to be once again expecting.

"Oh, my heavens, I am so happy for you." They hugged as they sat in the parlor.

"And how are things with the brickworks?"

"Better, much better. I have a brick mason who shows up to work and does as I ask him. I think we may be profitable by fall." Josianne had learned a lot about brick making, more than she ever wanted to know! But she needed to understand what the men told her, understand what supplies were needed, when, and why. Early on, she learned that they were made with a mixture of clay, sand, and water, and there needed to be a dependable kiln to fire them, as well as wood for the kiln and a place to stack them and on and on and on.

"Yes, and most of this I have learned the hard way. Did you know that bricks too near the heat in the kiln will be scorched, and those that are stacked too far away will not cure correctly? It is more complicated than I ever imagined."

"That's amazing, Josianne. I never thought of you as a businesswoman. You have really done well."

Josianne laughed, "Nor did I ever *want* to be a businesswoman. I still would rather look at patterns for dresses than add up columns of numbers at the end of the day. But it calms me to know that money is coming in. Money, such an ugly yet necessary thing to worry about."

"Neither did I," Maélle laughed.

"Without you trading with the textile men in France, we would all be naked!"

They both laughed.

"And I hear Philipe is still helping with the land?"

"Yes, he would not take no for an answer. I am relieved to have his help, though, and some days he takes Joseph with him." Amused, Josianne thought about how Philipe carried five-year-old Joseph on his shoulders. "Thank God he was here to help me."

Josianne had no idea how Philipe had done it all. Realizing he did not know the intricacies of rice cultivation himself, he engaged the help of the Senegalese workers who knew how to plant the rice, dike the marshes, and flush the fields. He and the other men had even figured out an irrigation system from the Mississippi. With the creation of earthen dikes, they could control the amount of water needed for the fields. It was, she thought, nothing short of ingenious.

"Yes, I saw him last week, and he told me all about it," Maélle grinned. But she liked Philipe and wanted Josianne to marry him. "Are you...still engaged to him? How long has it been now, *two years*? Are you ever going to marry that poor man?" Maélle knew he had a small place in town, and rumors were that he stayed nights there, *not* with Josianne.

"Oh, if I must, I suppose," Josianne laughed.

It was a unique arrangement. Philipe started working her land without asking her. The first time she caught him there, they got into a bitter argument. But she had to admit he knew more about cultivation than she cared to learn. And instead of sharing in the profits, he purchased fifty arpents of land adjacent to hers. Making him the third largest landowner in the area, even clearing some of it himself. In exchange for his help, he made her promise to someday marry him. Luckily for her, he had not said *when*.

"Are you not worried he might get...tired of waiting?" Maélle asked curiously.

"Oh, I make love to him. He's not waiting for *that* if that's what you are referring to."

"Oh my God, Josianne, you are *terrible!*" Maélle laughed, "he loves you; he doesn't just want that."

Josianne's eyebrows rose humorously, "says the woman who is already pregnant again in six months."

They were both laughing so hard they did not see Philipe come in. He was dirty from working, although he had stopped and washed his hands and face. He stood in the doorway for a few moments, enjoying the sound of their laughter.

"Oh, Philipe!" Maélle said, jumping to her feet. "Good afternoon, how are you?"

Maélle wondered again why Josianne would not marry him. He was tall, good-looking, and a hard worker. "Is Joseph in the kitchen? I'd like to say hello to him."

"He is. Alisa is giving him some dinner."

Maélle disappeared to see Joseph.

"It's all done. All under cultivation." He was proud of himself. He had worked hard to get the land to produce, and it was working. This landowning and cultivation were all new to him. But he read incessantly, he asked questions, and he listened to the Senegalese men. He tried, he failed, he tried again. He attacked this new venture with a vigor that impressed even Josianne. And if that was not enough, he had made a few improvements at the brickworks as well. And because he had been a ship's captain, he was good at giving orders but also being fair. Because of that, he was able to effortlessly command and receive the respect of those who worked for him.

"That's wonderful."

He came to her then and, leaning down, kissed her. It was a long, intimate kiss, one they both enjoyed.

"I'll bathe and then join you for dinner?" Normally, she allowed that, but he still had to ask.

Nodding, she watched him head to the kitchen.

Later that night when everyone was in bed, quietly, Philipe opened the door to her bedroom. She was on her side with her back to the door. He had a lantern with him, and she heard him set it on the table. Then, she felt the mattress sag as he crawled into bed with her.

They began to kiss, but she stopped him before it went further.

"Why do you stay?" she asked in the dim light of the room.

He grinned, lightly touching her cheek. "Because this is the only place I want to be."

"I've tried to chase you away, you know."

His hand smoothed out her eyebrows, and he bent and kissed her parted mouth. "I know you have."

"Why don't you go?"

He laughed, "Because I don't want to, and *you* don't want me to either."

Josianne sighed and untied the ribbon to her shift, offering him easier access to her breasts. Their love-making was passionate and satisfying. Philipe was a generous, patient lover and explored every inch of her. It was hard for her to remember being with Clément. The two experiences were *worlds* apart, she was glad she did not know then what she was missing. "I guess I will marry you then."

"Oh, wonderful," he said, kissing her breast. "How soon can I make you my wife in the eyes of the law?"

She shrugged, "Next... month sometime?"

He shook his head, "Tomorrow."

# Thirty-Seven

Spring 1744
Twenty-Five years since arriving in the colony.

L ittle Moon's daughter Marie Jeannette, *or Kettle* as she was called, grew into a beauty. She had her father's blue eyes but also her mother's Indian features, and Jean Michel could not stay away from her. A month after Suzette was married, Kettle and Jean Michel were going to be married at the St. Louis Cathedral.

They had all lived in the same household since Pierre died during the fever years. Hélène still remembered the day she realized Jean Michel was fond of Kettle.

They were twelve and fourteen, and Helene could not keep the two of them apart. They did their chores together, fished together, gathered fruit in the summer and nuts in the fall, and gathered the wood in the winter.

Kettle was a wonderful mix of reverence and spirituality for the natural world, coupled with the practicality she inherited from her father. Jean Michel was in awe of the older girl who spoke to her mother in her language and then could answer him in fluent French.

Hélène was relieved that Kettle felt the same way; she was not sure what would have happened to her lovesick son if she had not. Since Little Moon had died eight years ago, Héléne was both a mother and father to Kettle.

At Kettle and Jean Michaels' wedding, it was the first time Hélène had seen Mickey, except from a distance, in years. When she should have been listening to the mass uniting her son in marriage, she found herself staring at the man who was still her husband since neither of them had ever *demander le divorce.*

He was older but had not lost his muscle tone, as sometimes older men did. His face was more lined, and she realized that, more than any person she had ever known, he had lived his life outdoors.

Across the expanse of the church, he nodded politely to her. She nodded back and dropped her eyes to the floor. She smirked, seeing that Josianne and Philipe paid to have the front pew at their disposal, a custom Héléne always thought ridiculous. After all, did the Lord really care where one sat in the church or what one was wearing? But Josianne always strived for the most luxurious life, and Héléne was glad that she had it.

The church never meant a lot to Héléne, and she thought it shameful the way they incorporated the *calumet* into mass, trying to induce the native people to convert to Catholicism.

. . .

When the mass was over, Hélène embraced her new daughter-in-law and smiled at Maélle, Henri, and their ever-growing brood of children. In the last ten years, Maélle and Henri had eight more children. Henri had built a two-story house on Royal Street, just two streets over from Josianne's, and the three of them remained good friends.

Josianne and Philipe had five children in addition to Joseph. Joseph, because he was the oldest, ruled the roost with his siblings, who adored him and fought to be the subject of his attention.

Hélène felt the painful prick of tears in her eyes with how happy she was for Josianne—finally married to a man who could keep up with her. Although Philipe was devoted to her, they butted heads often, and unlike Clément, Philipe would stand his ground with his opinionated wife.

Together, they were a force, and *La Nouvélle Orleans* was a better city because of them. Josianne got involved with the women of the town, hosting events to help those in need, even helping at the charity hospital on Rampart Street. Bienville founded it before he left for France in 1743. Regardless of the good intentions, the charitable hospital had issues with funding, and Josianne was more than willing to donate her time as well as cash.

Philipe never stopped trying to improve the lives of the Senegalese and Congo men who worked for him. They were not *engagés* but sharecroppers and part owners. They helped Philipe design the complicated drainage necessary for rice cultivation. The cultivation of rice later proved to ease the chronic food shortage in the colony. Although it cut immensely into his and Josianne's profits, Philipe felt forever guilty about his part in the slave trade and thought it was a debt he owed and one he wanted to pay.

Although his contemporaries teased Philipe for his generosity, he was in the habit of silencing them by saying: *"I am a rich man. I have more than I need. I have Josianne."*

And he never entirely relinquished sailing; unbeknownst to Josianne, when he retired from his commission in France, he purchased a ship. From Louisiana, he sent wood to France, and from the French islands of the Caribbean, he brought back not only the maligned and misunderstood tomato seeds but also a precious and profitable commodity, *sugar.* And that he named the ship *La Beauté Josianne* which made Josianne snort with laughter when she saw it anchored in the harbor.

Josianne insisted they all come back to her house for a celebration after the ceremony, and the large house was filled with talking, laughter, and merry-making.

Alisa made an enormous pot of gumbo. She had worked hard on the roux of sassafras and pig fat, making sure it was cooked until it became a golden brown. When it thickened enough, she added corn, okra, and white pieces of fresh catfish. She'd even put in tomatoes from plants she had grown from the seeds Philipe brought back. But because some still thought the lumpy vegetable was poisonous, she said nothing.

"Alisa, please come join us," Josianne asked, coaxing her into the parlor. Alisa was proud of the meal she had made and enjoyed the commotion and mayhem that was her mistress's house. She could barely remember being worried about what would happen to her and her children when Clément died.

Because Alisa had never known any other life, she stayed working for them. She was glad Josianne taught her daughter Deidra to read and write. Although her son Robert had gotten into trouble, and run away, her daughter married one of the men on Philipe and Josianne's farm. Deidre and her husband owned land, owned a house, and had already given Alisa four grandsons. Deidre wanted her mother to come live with them, but Alisa, content with her living arrangements, declined. Laughingly telling her daughter she liked to "visit" her rambunctious grandsons, *not* live with them.

Halfway through the evening, Hélène was busy cutting pieces of *croquembouche* for the guests. The wedding revelers were so numerous that she was forced to use not only all the dessert plates but also saucers.

"Hello, Hélène," Mickey said suddenly at her side.

Startled, she had to swallow. "Hello, Mickey."

He watched his son and new bride laugh as they held their glasses of champagne. He did not know how Héléne managed such an extravagance.

He looked back at her, "you look well."

She knew she did not. The only time in her life she had any breasts at all was when she had breastfed the twins. She was so flat that Maélle always lined the front of her bodice with silk ruffles. If her scrawny figure was not enough, the birthmark had darkened with age, and her hair was graying.

She realized he was trying to be kind and said, "Thank you."

"You did a good job with Jean Michel. He's an honorable young man."

Jean Michel was a bricklayer for the brickworks Josianne and Philipe owned. Jean Michel appreciated that they employed him and, seeing it as a bit of preferential treatment, worked hard to become a skilled craftsman. Priding himself for knowing where and when to use which brick depending on how they had been cured. He liked to oversee the men who forced the clay through the wood molds, which gave the bricks their texture, size, and shape—knowing that the type of clay and temperature gave the bricks their color and hardness. And he was a master at how he laid the courses.

"Yes, I suppose I did." Although she promised herself there would be no bickering, she could not help herself. "It would have been nice if he had a father that saw him more frequently. He might have enjoyed your company and influence."

Mickey sighed quietly, he had expected this. "I don't know how you managed it so well all those years ago. When Genevieve died, it just..." He did not finish, but she sensed he was going to say, 'broke me.' It was a shame, she thought, that they never consoled each other.

After a few more minutes of awkward silence, he said, "I suppose I will be going then. Goodbye."

It occurred to her that this was the end. With their son now married and Genevieve buried, there would be no reason for them to see each other ever again. Although they had been living apart for twenty years now, she felt her heart rate quicken at the thought of no longer having any connection to him. She tried to think of something to say to stop him but couldn't.

Josianne and Hélène stayed up hours after the rest had left. Re-telling stories of their life at *La Salpêtrière,* their life when they came to the territory and tales of child-rearing.

"Josianne, you have had a glass of wine in your hand the entire night," Philipe teased. But he adored his wife, tipsy, sober, any way, as long as he was with her.

"I don't drink it; I carry it around, then pour it back in when our guests leave. I learned this trick when I hosted parties for Clément. I had to be *looking* like I was having a good time, but keep my wits about me. This is the first actual drink I've had." Lifting her glass to demonstrate, she took a small sip.

Philipe, amused, continued to fill their wine glasses as they talked. He teased them that if they were not careful, they would have hangovers in the morning. Three-year-old Yvette, awakened by the laughter, toddled into the room.

"What are you doing, my *mon petite fille?* Philipe asked and reached out to hoist his daughter on to his lap. He placed three kisses on her fat cheek.

"*Maman* you and *Tante Hélène* are too noisy!"

Josianne and Hélène laughed harder, and Yvette slipped off her father's lap and climbed up into her mother's instead. Josianne stroked her daughter's long brown hair and pressed her lips to her daughter's temple. "Ahh it is past your bedtime, but you can stay down here with *Tante Hélène* and I if you are quiet. Will you be?"

Yvette's brown eyes got huge; she nodded and placed her thumb in her mouth.

"Stop that, Yvette, only babies do that," Josianne admonished, pulling Yvette's hand away.

Before long, Yvette's eyes closed, and Josianne and Hélène continued their talking, more quietly now.

At midnight, Philipe announced he was going to bed. He picked up the sleeping Yvette from her mother's lap and carried her to bed.

Josianne changed out of her dress and had nothing on but her shift. She was wrapped up in a quilt on the overstuffed sofa. Hélène had loosened her bodice, removed her boots, and propped her feet up on the table.

The conversation had been light and jovial, Héléne finally admitting to Josianne that she had been part of the infamous 'sedition' at the prison. That *Madame* Pacletain had exaggerated everything about the incident, and that Héléne had been inches away from being able to escape.

"I always knew you had been part of it," Josianne said, taking a sip. "What I regret is not helping you."

Héléne laughed, "Truly, it was not much of a plot, and Madame Pacletain made it far more glamorous than it was. I just hope it was not what got all of us sent here." Héléne finally admitted what she had been burdened with for so many years.

"Don't be ridiculous. All the trouble France was in, the idiot Scotsman's treachery, the bankruptcy. We were all just caught in the wrong place at the wrong time."

Héléne laughed, "or the *right* place and the *right* time!"

"Touché," Josianne said, and leaning near her friend, clinked glasses.

But sometime during the second bottle, the wine became a truth serum for Hélène. Josianne listened in horror to the ugly tale Hélène told of the long-ago night when Mickey assaulted her. Listening to the ghastly story, Josianne wondered if anyone really knew anyone at all. She had always liked Mickey and never dreamed he would be capable of something like that.

"I understand why you live apart from him," Josianne said.

Hélène smiled grimly, wondering if she would ever be able to adequately describe the relationship. "I miss him though. No one understood me as he did. No one cared for me like he did." She thought back to the good times with Mickey and how many good times she knew she had missed. She picked up her wine glass and just held it. "And it is not that I am condoning what he did, but it is more... *complicated*. We were always rough in our lovemaking; we liked it that way. And he was so happy to see me when he got back that time, he'd even brought me a wedding ring. And he asked me *not* to spend the money, the money he had earned, and of course...I did it *anyway*." She swallowed the last of the red wine.

"But he had no right to stop you, forbid you."

Hélène put her hand up to stop her friend's defense, "he did not really forbid me; I mean, he tried, but of course, I fought him. He told me we would consider it later. He was not really saying no. And I did it anyway. I fought him about really...*everything*. Again, I am not condoning what he did, but I think he felt it was his last resort to exert any control over me."

"You needn't explain his horrible actions."

"But that's just the thing. This is precisely why I *never* told anyone. Anyone who hears this story immediately paints Mickey as a...monster, a beast. And he is not. He was good to me. And he loved his children and wanted more, and I told him he would never touch me again." She still could not talk about Genevieve and was not sure that she ever would. Mickey did not hear about her death till months later. Hélène noticed that someone was putting flowers on her grave once and figured it was Mickey. He also gave her the same amount of money he had when he had been supporting two children; the amount never decreased.

"Still, it is inexcusable what he did."

Hélène shrugged, "It was also inexcusable what I did to him as well. I have said...*terrible* things to him before and after the assault. I really think part of my hatred of him was that I could not really believe that he wanted me. That he was vulnerable when he was with me. He put his heart and hand out to me, and I refused to take it. Refused to be unguarded. And unfortunately, I have had *many* years to muse back on what happened. And besides, I am the only one who gets to decide if he is a heinous beast or not, not what the world and society think. We both made mistakes and paid dearly for them."

Josianne was quiet, wondering how all this turmoil could have been going on all these years with her friend and that she knew none of it. She was sorry she was not a better friend. "I mean, other than today, do you ever see him?"

"Occasionally, from a distance. But he turns and goes the other way. I know he avoids me."

"He has never taken a lover."

"Well, I did, and it made it no better," Hélène scoffed, remembering the young man who had, at one time, shared her bed. There was nothing wrong with him, but she soon tired of him. It annoyed her when he wept when she broke it off. She knew he was weeping more from the loss of her monetary support, than from the loss of her affection.

"I am...so sorry Hélène. I am sorry that you have lived with this silent pain all these years." Josianne, sobered by the tale, reached out and touched her friend's hand. "I wish you had told me; I would have tried to help."

Hélène shrugged, "There was nothing you could do. And in a way, it saved me."

"Saved you from what?"

"I didn't have to...open up to him. Be vulnerable; be dependent on him. Wait for him to come home, wonder if he would someday leave me, not want me anymore."

"So...you cared for a man and then pushed him away, so you'd never have to suffer the pain if he...*left* you?"

"I know, it's ridiculous. I am crazy. Maybe all those days at *La Salpêtrière* damaged what was left of my mind."

They both laughed.

"Well then, *all* of us were damaged. Suzanne seducing poor Henri, me throwing myself at Philipe, then marrying an old man, Maélle, afraid of a ghost, and you, I always thought *you* were the sensible one."

Hélène nodded, "Fooled you, didn't I?" She looked out the window to the street. Her business was thriving, and for that, she felt some pride.

Hélène ended up sleeping on the couch in Josianne's parlor and woke stiff in the morning. Wiping dried drool off her cheek, tiptoed out of the house, wanting to be gone before Philipe came down and teased her.

The morning was beautiful, and stepping outside, Helene had to squint at the brightness of the sky. She picked her way along the rutted street to the tiny house Mickey lived in. It was behind Jaques Perot's formidable brick structure. Perot, always the business-man, had built it to rent out. She remembered Josianne telling her how Perot had pursued her after Clément died, almost as vehemently as Philipe did. Perot, Hélène found out, had been difficult to deal with after Clément died. He had challenged the ownership of some of Clément's assets. It was as if he was trying to win Josianne by making her dependent on him. Hélène smiled smugly, knowing Perot had grossly underesti-mated the beautiful widow. Hélène remembered doing the laundry for him, and that his shirt collars had been particularly grimy.

Hélène knocked on Mickey's door.

He answered immediately, and she smiled, realizing that as a one-time fisherman, he was always up early. Without waiting for an invitation, Hélène walked inside and helped herself to a cup of coffee from the pot hanging at the hearth.

Silently she refilled his cup, and since he was in the only chair in the room, she sat on the edge of the bed.

"Good morning," he said, a grin on his lips.

"You knew I would come by," Hélène smirked.

Mickey laughed, settling back in the chair, "I actually didn't."

Hélène eyed him over the tin coffee cup. She disliked the tin cups, feeling they transferred the taste to the coffee. From now on, they would have porcelain cups.

"I have something to tell you that I probably should have told you a long time ago."

"You're a secret heiress?"

"No, Mickey, this is serious."

He waited for her to continue.

"When I was fourteen, I was late coming home, and a man cornered me in the alley. He stunk like wine and piss, and I remember there was dirt under his nails and that they were sharp as they dug into my arm. He hit me once across the face and told me if I made a sound, he knew where I lived and would come for me again. He had me up against the stone wall, with my face jammed against it. I remember my skirt being on my shoulders and how, when he rutted me, my teeth scraped the wall. When it was over, and I was limping home, I felt his seed running down my thigh. Only then did I cry. I've never told anyone this before."

It came back to him then what he had done. That day, his life had careened off course. "I am so *sorry,* Hélène..." He rubbed his face with his hand. "No wonder you have...*hated* me all these years." He wished he had known.

"Thank you."

They sat for a few minutes; Hélène heard the low, soothing coo of the mourning doves. They were such timid creatures, and she always thought it was a soulful sound. A moment later, she heard the happy, piercing tweet of the cardinals, and it occurred to her that one bird sounded sad while the other was happy. She wondered if, like birds, people could be sad or happy, depending on how they chose to view the world.

"I think we should live at the tavern. I've got my business to attend, and the back rooms are perfectly suitable to live in. There is a decent hearth for cooking, and I had the roof repaired two years ago."

He was staring into the dying fire in the hearth. She noticed the gray swirling through his unruly hair and beard. She remembered that even at their wedding, his hair was unwilling to obey a hairbrush.

"Are you sure you want me back?"

When she saw his eyes brightened with tears, she knew she could not trust her voice and merely nodded again.

"You've taken lovers?" He asked, jealous at the thought.

"I did, only one. But that was years ago, and I have no interest in taking another."

Outside, she heard a Carolina wren and remembered when Genevieve was little, she used to sing *"Teakettle, Teakettle, Teakettle,"* mimicking their cry. It was a bittersweet memory.

"And you? Did you ever take a woman?"

He shook his head. At first, she didn't believe it was

334

possible, but there was no deception in his demeanor, and she realized he had no reason to lie.

Uncomfortable, suddenly, she got up. "I guess I should get home and get the chores done."

She walked to the door, opening it, waiting for him to say something.

Putting his cup down, he met her at the door, closing it.

His eyes met hers. "Come here," he gathered her in his arms with a gentleness that was a balm to her soul. He held her head against his chest. She could feel him breathing against her, slow and steady, with a calm that she craved.

Even though she was tall, she had always had to look up at Mickey.

He was smoothing back her hair. "Your hair is a mess. Where did you sleep last night?"

"At Josianne's. I drank too much after the wedding and spent the night on their couch. My back is sore."

He smiled. "If you were a *Biloxi* woman you would not be seen out in public like this." He stroked her tresses to get them in order.

"I guess the *Biloxi* women care more about their hair than I do."

He laughed, "they do, but whatever you do is fine with me."

It was amazing to her all the things he learned, how fascinating he was. "Do you need to give Jaques notice?"

He shook his head, "no written agreement."

She opened the door again, "I'll expect you sometime in the afternoon then."

Everyone was shocked when Hélène Clavier began living with her husband again. He was still going out on trips in his *pirogue*, but because he had saved much of his income over the years (not spending it on wine and women, as Hélène convinced herself he had), they had enough with his savings and the income of the tavern to live.

During one of their long talks when he first moved in with her, she told him stories about their children. She enjoyed his laughter at their antics, both happy and sad to hear them, knowing all he had missed. And they clung together when they remembered Genevieve. This time, when Hélène cried for their daughter, Mickey held her until she was out of sobs.

"How did you learn English?" Hélène asked. They had finished dinner, and she had locked up for the night. Tired, Mickey lay down on top of the quilt, and eagerly, she joined him, pulling his arm up so that it was around her.

"I don't think I speak it that well."

She leaned up on her elbow, "say something to me in English."

"Like what?"

"I don't know anything."

He blew out a breath and then said, in English, "Hélène Clavier, you are the best thing that ever happened to me."

"What did you say?" She asked, marveling at how well he spoke.

"Héléne Clavier you are a skinny wench who annoys me."

She poked him in the ribs, "what did you really say?"

"Nothing."

"And how many Indian dialects can you speak?" Laying against him, she had her chin on his chest.

"Three to four. Again, I am not fluent, but I can get my point across and understand what they are telling me." He stroked her hair, "I've traded with them all— Indigenous, English, and Spaniards. There is a large German settlement about thirty miles north of here, *les Allemands*. I will take you some time. And luckily, since all of them fought at one time or another, I remained neutral enough to avoid being cheated, robbed, or murdered."

She raised her head, "is it really as dangerous as that?"

He shrugged, "I have been worried *more* than once."

"Honestly, I had no idea what you did was that hard."

He smiled at her, "it has afforded me a living, and now I can reap the benefits." He kissed her temple.

"Who were the hardest to deal with?"

"They were all hard in different ways. One of the things that really pissed me off was the traders that would smoke the *calumet* with the Indigenous people, then give them rum. Those poor people never had any alcohol, and it ruins them. They can't manage it. I remember a Choctaw leader telling me that drink was like a 'great sea coming from Mobile surrounding his people.' These traders would ply the native people with alcohol, taking their deerskins and other staples as payment. I ran into these scoundrels and was wary whenever I had to deal with them."

She shook her head, thinking it was indeed despicable behavior. "Is it odd being inside? I cannot imagine sleeping outside like you have for so many years."

"I got used to it," he grinned, playing with the gold ring again around her finger. I even got so I could tell when it was going to rain. I woke up some mornings with frost on my eyebrows and beard, other mornings drenched in sweat."

"So, running into lots of different people, what was the next hardest thing?"

"Negotiating that river. I thought I knew a lot when I started, but I had a lot to learn. I got so I knew exactly what bend to take and what tributaries were safest. And there is not just *one* current in the river. The currents compete and are even at different speeds."

"I don't understand."

He loved that she was interested. "So many other rivers and streams feed the river, it crashes against the land, sometimes shearing an entire bank off, when the water slows down, it deposits new soil in another place making in fact, a new shoreline. It is all the time tearing down and rebuilding. Landmarks that I depended on could be gone in months. And the Indigenous people knew this and were all the time pulling up stakes and moving villages."

"You must have made some...friends along the routes."

"I did. I had some. But it's a hard, unpredictable life.

Sometimes they just disappeared, and I never knew if they moved on or died."

He wrapped his arms tighter around her.

"Was it a good life?" She asked, hoping it was. Her heart was so connected to him now that she could not bear the thought that he had been unhappy.

"There were things I liked, but what I wanted most was a...home base, somewhere to be safe and wanted."

Hélène kissed him then, a kiss that told him their hearts and souls were connected and that, at last, he was *home*.

But being a voyageur had been Mickey's life for many years, and he was not ready to give it up. When the morning came for him to leave for what she hoped was his last trip, she pulled him back into bed.

"*Mon Dieu* woman, you have drained me of my seed!" He laughed. But he loved that she wanted him, loved their new life, loved her.

"A voyageur and ex-galley slave turning *down sex*? Your reputation will be ruined when this gets out."

When they finally got out of bed a half-hour later, lustily she kissed him goodbye.

She had no idea she would never see him again.

In the years that followed Hélène heard varying accounts of what happened to her husband. Some say he drowned in the Mississippi during a storm; others said he had been attacked and killed by *Alibamu* or the *Creeks*. Others say he met another *voyageur* and simply headed north. But she knew the last guess was not true because Mickey would have come back if he could. For the first few years, she held her breath when suddenly someone showed up at the door and was constantly disappointed because it was never, and never would be, Mickey.

Two years after his disappearance, Hélène took the pearl Mickey had given her to the jeweler in town. He drilled a small hole through which he slipped a delicate silver chain. It had yellowed slightly over the years to a beautiful shade of cream. The jeweler told her it was one of the largest pearls he had ever seen. Hélène wore it for the rest of her life.

# Thirty-Eight

*1756*
*Thirty-seven years since coming to the territory.*

The colony they had started in 1718 had been knocked down by greed, deception, hurricanes, famine, and disease. Yet, among the marshes along the unquiet waters of the Mississippi River, the town clung to life and then finally, flourished.

Hélène hurried along the street. She was late. It was drizzling, and she pulled the shawl tighter around her shoulders, grateful for its warmth. Kettle had made it, and she could crochet the most intricate, tight designs. The shawl was not only warm, it was a work of art.

Reaching the shiny black door at Josianne's house, she didn't bother knocking and simply walked in, calling, "Josianne, I'm here. I'm sorry I'm late."

"You are dripping all over the floor, Hélène," Maélle admonished, taking off her apron, she dabbed at the black and white marble floor.

"Oh, I'm sorry."

"It's fine. Don't worry about it." Josianne smiled, "I have not seen you for a month. What have you been doing with yourself?" Josianne asked as she poured three small glasses of port, a monthly treat they indulged in.

"I'm doing all right." Héléne settled in the chair, glancing around the room.

Philipe had surrendered the pocketbook to Josianne, and the house was luxuriously furnished. There was gold and white striped wallpaper on the walls in the parlor, ornately carved teakwood furniture, and an abundance of mirrors and crystal. Josianne had always been glamorous, and her taste was as well. As it was now, Josianne was sitting on a pale pink couch rather than a sensible brocade one.

Josianne was dressed in a purple and white muslin dress with taffeta inserts. Her figure was still trim despite giving Philipe three sons and two daughters. They were a happy couple who did not hide their affection from anyone.

"Did you see the new Spanish flag by the courthouse? It seems France has finally had enough of us," Héléne said with a smirk, wondering what this new world power wanted with their swampy town. The city of *La Nouvélle Orleans* had a diverse population, slave as well as free—a city where multiple languages could be heard.

Josianne nodded, "Yes, I hope it does not spell trouble for any of us."

Maélle shrugged, "Henri is still busy building, so hopefully that won't change."

"And the Spaniards are Catholic and enjoy their

wine, which I have been supplying steadily," Héléne added with a grin.

"I still don't understand why France would give us up just when we are actually starting to be a respectable town," Maélle said, turning to look at her friends.

"Respectable?" Héléne sniggered, "We still have neighbors fighting in the streets and hogs running wild. It's no wonder they finally got rid of us." Some followed the laws, as well as those who had rampant disregard for them. Those that prospered and those that failed in spectacular fashion. Those that came against their will and those that decided to throw the dice and come. Although Héléne knew all of them were nervous about what this regime change might mean, she was prepared to meet it head-on. Afterall, it was not the first time *La Nouvélle Orleans* would be turned over to a foreign power, and although none of them knew it, not the last.

"I sort of agree with you." Josianne balanced her wine glass against her knee, "It's like France tried taking a swamp and turning it to a little France. Why when the last war has ended, they seemed happy to get us off their hands. But what they seemed to forget was that it took men like Henri who wanted to make changes for France, and men like Mickey who France had incarcerated, and women like us that were *abandoned* by France."

In the coming years, the Spanish would soon find out that the people of *La Nouvélle Orleans* refused to be tamed, refused to be pigeonholed into anyone's ideas of a city, no matter who's flag they were under. Not surprisingly by 1801, the Spaniards too threw their hands up in the air, and the land was ceded back to a reluctant

Napolean, who then, under pressure from The United States and the threat of another war with Great Britain, sold the entire Louisiana territory to Jefferson in 1803.

"How is Celeste?" Hélène asked, changing the subject.

Josianne nodded. "She is happy in her new little place."

Maélle and Hélène glanced at each other and then back at Josianne.

"Oh, I know what the town says about Celeste, that she prefers the company of women over men," Josianne said.

"Is it true?" Maélle asked.

Josianne shrugged because she did not care. She loved her stepdaughter no matter what. "I am not sure; it may be. But what Celeste wants more than anything is her books, her cats, and her *privacy*."

All three of them laughed. "And why should she not have them?" Hélène remarked, "she works hard doing the accounts for you and Philipe. She is a kind girl."

"I totally agree, which is why I tamp down the rumors when they surface. And we are still close, and I will defend her *forever*." Josianne saw Celeste weekly, and although they talked of many things, children and finding a husband were simply omitted from their discussions. Even her son Joseph, a successful *avocat* in town defended his stepsister with a passion that proved that even *diluted* blood was a bond not to be trifled with.

"And how is Jean Michael?" Josianne asked.

"He's well, and Kettle is pregnant again," Hélène laughed. She already had four grandsons and was hoping for a granddaughter. Either way she was thrilled her son was happy and healthy. It made the loss of Genevieve and Mickey less acute.

"So is Suzette." Maélle laughed.

"For heaven's sake, Maélle! After eight children of your own, and you with a four-year-old still at home, you are going to be a grandmother again."

"I know; I guess I'll never stop sewing baby things." Maélle rolled her eyes.

"Is she still running the bakery?" Josianne asked. She remembered the day Suzette had come to her against her parents' wishes and asked for a loan to start the bakery. Without a second thought, Josianne loaned her the money, and to no one's surprise, it was a resounding success.

"*Oui,* she's a worker, that girl."

Suzette looked just like Suzanne: blond, blue-eyed, angelic. Although she inherited her good looks from her mother, she inherited her drive and work ethic from Maélle. Suzette was as passionate about baking as Maélle was about clothes. "I still see Suzanne in that girl."

"Well, of course," Hélène smiled.

"I know, but its more than that. I still feel Suzanne's soul, if you will. And instead of being frightening, her presence in comforting. She is watching over us," Maélle admitted.

Josianne finished her port and daringly poured her friends another. "Well, Suzanne has done a good job then."

"How do you mean?" Hélène asked, curling up in the

overstuffed chair. She was comfortable with her friends, who were more like family.

"Maélle was meant to be with Henri," Josianne said, looking at her friend.

Maélle blushed at the truth of the words. "Thank you."

"And you, against all odds, Hélène, found a man that *genuinely* loved you. He loved you when you had nothing before you were a successful business owner. And if he had not died, no doubt he would still be with you. He was not perfect, but he loved you."

Hélène felt tears prick her eyes. It was cathartic to hear Josianne speak kindly about Mickey. Hélène had long ago forgiven Mickey, but did not know if Josianne could, and that Josianne had, made a lump form in Hélène's throat.

"And me, Josianne Daudessot. I made a match for money, which surprisingly was not without affection. The second match I made for love." She looked at both of her friends. "The three of us, transported in chains, then left on an island to starve, we have all done quite well."

Laughingly, they leaned together in a circle to clink glasses. "I am excited to see what our children and grand-children accomplish." Maélle said with a smile. All of them wondering what hardships and triumphs were in store for their descendants.

Phillipp walked in. He warmly greeted Hélène and Maélle and robustly kissed Josianne. He poured himself a glass and, noticing the jovial mood, asked, "what are we toasting today, *madams*?"

Hélène and Maélle were often at his house, usually

with a brood of grandchildren following. The doorbell rang frequently with deliveries and neighbors stopping by, and he *loved* it. He loved the liveliness, the fullness of his life. It was like his love and admiration for Josianne, bursting, happy, *rapturous*.

"We are toasting each other, actually, and our children," Josianne said with a smile, looking up at the man she adored.

"Then I commend you all. *Madame's*, as you know, as a ship's captain, I have been around the world. I have seen many things, and *never*... in all my travels have I *ever* met women as formidable, determined, and as kind as the three of you. I am a lucky man to know all of you. And if your children are *half* the women you are, the world... will be a better place because of it."

# About the Author

Barbara Sontheimer has a B.A. from a little college in the bootheel of Missouri and spent 15 years researching and writing her first novel, *Victor's Blessing*, while raising three children. One of her greatest hopes for all her books is that someone turns out the light a bit too late on a work night or (like she did) occasionally hid from her kids in the laundry room to finish a chapter. Barbara is married and lives in Lake Ozark, Missouri, or wherever her husband parks the RV. She is currently at work on her third novel.

*www://sontheimerwrites.com*